A TRIAL BY ERROR

THE FRINGE CYCLE

BOOK ONE

A TRIAL BY ERROR

THE FRINGE CYCLE
BOOK ONE

SUSAN ESCHBACH

FLEET PRESS

an imprint of
OGHMA CREATIVE MEDIA

OGHMA
CREATIVE MEDIA

Fleet Press
An imprint of Oghma Creative Media, Inc.
2401 Beth Lane, Bentonville, Arkansas 72712

Copyright © 2018 by Susan Eschbach

We are a strong supporter of copyright. Copyright represents creativity, diversity, and free speech, and provides the very foundation from which culture is built. We appreciate you buying the authorized edition of this book and for complying with applicable copyright laws by not reproducing, scanning, or distributing any part of it in any form without permission. Thank you for supporting our writers and allowing us to continue publishing their books.

Library of Congress Cataloging-in-Publication Data

Names: Eschbach, Susan, author.
Title: A Trial By Error/Susan Eschbach. | The Fringe Cycle #1
Description: First Edition. | Bentonville: Fleet, 2018.
Identifiers: LCCN: 2019937260 | ISBN: 978-1-63373-298-8 (hardcover) |
ISBN: 978-1-63373-299-5 (trade paperback) | ISBN: 978-1-63373-300-8 (eBook)
Subjects: BISAC: FICTION/Science Fiction/Space Opera |
FICTION/Science Fiction/Action & Adventure | FICTION/Science Fiction/General
LC record available at: https://lccn.loc.gov/2019937260

Fleet Press trade paperback edition March, 2018

Cover & Interior Design by Casey W. Cowan
Editing by George "Clay" Mitchell & Gordon Bonnet

This book is a work of historical fiction. Apart from the well-known actual people, events, and locales that figure in the narrative, all names, characters, places, and incidents are the product of the author's imagination or are used fictitiously. Any resemblance to current events or locales, or to living persons, is entirely coincidental.

*To my loving and supportive husband Carl,
and to my sons Ben and Matt, my inspirations.*

ACKNOWLEDGMENTS

Thanks to my friends in the Mid South Writers Group: Barbara Warren, Linda Sartin, Prix Gautney, Matt Eschbach, Sherri Akers, and Nita Waxelman, great writers all of them, without whom I would never have started this journey in the first place. And thanks to George Clay Mitchell and Gordon Bonnet, my editors, Casey Cowan, creative director and publisher, and all the staff at Oghma Creative Media, who made a dream a reality.

CONNECTED

RECIEVING....

CHAPTER
01

Freedom.

Dahvin Tave's heart quickened as he gazed at the starfield spread out across the forward viewport of his one-man freighter. Some people couldn't take the loneliness of solo interstellar flight. Having escaped brutal slavery three years earlier as he reached puberty, he reveled in it.

One blue gem shone brighter than the others, the blue-white star near Mira, his destination. The most important trading post on The Fringe of the Milky Way, it stood as the last outpost before The Great Rift, a planetless void separating one arm of the galaxy from the next. A prime hunting ground for pirates.

He entered Mira's approach vector into *Gilded Starlilly*'s computer. What a name for a ship. He'd inherited it from Marlon Tave, his adoptive father, the man who'd found him beaten, bloodied, and starving after his escape from the Pruzzians.

An alert pinged and a red light flashed on his control console. Another ship had appeared, tracking not far behind him. It might have just dropped out of warp, as he had seconds before. Or it could have been lying in stealth mode with all its systems shut down, waiting for prey.

He pulled up a holodisplay of the region. An asteroid belt lay an hour's flight forward and below. The ghost of Marlon's voice invaded his mind. *Run, you can beat them to the planet. No need to take a chance on fighting them.*

He ignored the voice. Time to have some fun. The normal approach path avoided the asteroids. He altered course toward them. Would they change course and follow him? He checked her identification—registry unknown. Yup, pirates. He pushed his engines to maximum. They wouldn't be able to catch him before he entered the field.

For the next hour he watched as the other ship struggled to catch him. They gained ground, but not enough. That must come as a surprise to them.

At the outer edge of the asteroid belt, he searched for a moderate-sized chunk of rock. There—that one. He steered *Starlilly* to its far side, landed, and shut down all systems, internal and external. She became an undetectable piece of cosmic debris.

The pirates would know where he'd entered the asteroid field, but once he moved behind the rock he'd landed on, they would have lost him. They'd know the game—a common pirate ploy. They probably figured coming after him was worth the risk. He carried a valuable cargo and his ship was smaller than theirs. They'd expect to have him outgunned.

He had another surprise for them. He'd spent every spare credit over the past year ramping up *Starlilly*'s defenses. Now he'd wait for them to take the bait. Bide his time. "Patience is a virtue," Marlon used to say. It just wasn't one of Dahvin's virtues.

Ah, a flicker of light in the darkness. Patience. Soon the prey would become the predator.

He waited for frustrating minutes as the pirate ship crept toward his position. He had the advantage. They doused their external lights. Flying blind in the debris-strewn darkness, they would have to rely on their computer to avoid a collision. A gutsy move. Dahvin couldn't suppress a touch of respect for his adversary.

His display tracked the energy signature as it glided past him. Time to move. He powered sublight engines, swung into position behind the pirates, and fired a simultaneous burst from all forward lasers. A reading on his console advised her proto shields still held. They must have added some upgrades themselves.

Laser fire burst from the rear of the pirate ship landing direct hits on *Starlilly*'s shields. With the element of surprise defeated, the battle became a simple slugging match. Dahvin fired another round of lasers. He needed those shields to come down before he fired the cannons. Still holding. Damnation, these guys were tough.

Another burst shot back at him and he had to turn his head from the brilliant flash across his viewscreen. With spots floating across his vision, he checked *Starlilly*'s status. One more blast would take out his shields.

"*Unknown assailant's shields have collapsed,*" reported the computer.

A flash in the exhaust cones of the pirate ship alerted him that they were powering up to make an escape. He'd become more trouble than his cargo was worth, and if he managed to land successful canon shots, there was a good chance they wouldn't survive the encounter.

His fingers moved to the firing button. Two shots aimed up their exhaust pipes would take out their sublight engines. They would be stranded here until rescue arrived, and Dahvin could make sure that "rescue" would be Miran authorities who had little desire to allow pirates to threaten their trading route.

His console pinged. Another ship! Where in damnation did they come from? Would they help him, or did the pirates have backup? A laser shot to his flank answered that question. He didn't have enough power left in his proto shields to fend them off. Flight was the better part of valor at the moment.

He had a decision to make. The idea of leaving the pirates to prey on another ship irritated him, but if he blew them up, their collaborators would be all the more motivated to take him out, even if they lost the cargo in the process. If he fled, he had a chance to outrun them.

That's what Marlon would have done. His species believed violence bred violence in a never-ending cycle. Marlon's approach had worked well for his mentor. Marlon had spent over twenty years flying cargo in *Starlilly* and had only lost one shipment to pirates—an unusually long and successful career for a small freighter. He'd fought when he had to, but avoided it whenever possible.

But he wasn't Marlon. He'd rather die fighting than be boarded or run.

He fired all three cannons up the tail of the first ship. To hell with letting them live. The ship exploded in a fiery burst, snuffed out by the vacuum of space. *Starlilly* rotated to face the second ship. He fired all forward laser banks and a spread of cannon fire as well, even though their shields hadn't yet failed.

The laser shots flared against their shields.

"*Warning—deflector shields depleted. Attacker's shields now at twenty percent.*"

Thanks, computer.

What happened next came as a surprise. The attacking ship disappeared.

"Computer—"

"*Attacking ship initiated warp.*"

For a stunned moment, Dahvin stared at the empty space where the second pirate ship had been. Surely they knew his shields were down. Why had they fled? Had he inflicted some damage with his first shot? After watching the destruction of the other ship, maybe they had decided he wasn't worth the risk. Or maybe, they'd be lying in wait again closer to the planet. In her current state, a surprise attack would destroy *Starlilly* with a single volley.

"Computer, forward one-quarter ken-per-second, vector one-eighty by sixty by twenty. Engage."

Starlilly shot up and out of the asteroid field as he fled for the safety of Mira. If he could reach their proximity beacons, planetary defenses would help protect him. Once clear of the rocks, he deployed the warp rings. A three-second jump would carry him closer to the planet. Pilots weren't supposed to use warp this close to a planetary system. If the matter-anti-matter chamber powering the warp rings became imbalanced and exploded, the resulting shock wave could take out one or more planets in the system. A little reckless, but he had his systems inspected on every landing. Overly cautious, but another precaution Marlon had taught him, and it would pay off in stardust today.

"Computer, activate warp, three-second interval."

"*Acknowledged.*"

Dahvin turned his head and closed his eyes. Even through closed lids the glare of the brilliant galactic glow visible during warp hurt his eyes. Normally, he'd drop a light shield over the forward viewscreen, but for such a short trip, he hadn't bothered.

When the brilliance faded, he looked back out the viewscreen. Mira lay as a dark red ball silhouetted against the blue dwarf sun.

A ping in his headset signaled a voice communication. "Gilded Starlilly, this is Mira Space Command, welcome to our space. We have you on approach vector minus ninety-eight by forty-five by eighteen."

"Thank you, Space Command. Vector verified. Please check for any unidentified ships in my vicinity. Their partners already attacked my ship near the asteroid field and I'm being pursued by a second pirate ship. Do you show them as well?"

"We do not show another ship in your vicinity. Perhaps they turned away when you reached our proximity beacon. That explains, perhaps, why you risked using warp just beyond our border. Do not do so again, or you will be banned from trading on Mira."

He smiled. So, he'd won, after all.

"Acknowledged, and my apologies. The battle with the first pirate ship took out my shields. I destroyed them, but I couldn't have survived a battle with the second. They hid in stealth mode until my defenses were compromised. I'm sorry to say, it was a most effective ploy by the pirates."

"We received reports of wreckage near the asteroid field a few days ago. You may have been the first ship to survive their strategy. Do you have any identifying information on their ships?"

"They turned off their identification beacon, but I will send you some video from the encounter. I hope you will be able to get a clear enough image to identify the ship and take action against it."

"Thank you for notifying us. As you know, we are not a space faring species, but we will share your information with all incoming ships. Proceed to landing on vector minus eighty by thirty-five by nineteen."

"Thank you, Space Command. Adjusting trajectory."

Dahvin sent the instructions to his computer.

He didn't hear any more about what happened to the second pirate ship. As he descended, a wispy cloud layer gave way to a view of mountains and desert plains. The spaceport gleamed in the distance.

His headset pinged. "Gilded Starlilly, *Spaceport Control. You may land on cargo-space twenty-five-A.*"

"Thank you, Spaceport Command. Initiating landing sequence."

Starlilly settled safely into her assigned spot. Mira didn't offer much in the way of entertainment. The locals didn't allow traders to go anywhere beyond the spaceport market. But he could spend a couple of days wandering the thousand or so merchant booths. He gazed out the viewport, looking forward to some ground time.

CONNECTED
RECIEVING....
CHAPTER 02

Dahvin stepped off his ship in the Miran spaceport and eyed the Alliance Enforcer ship sitting nearby. What in damnation were they doing here, way beyond their jurisdiction? A cold chill ran down his spine in spite of the blazing blue sun. The Alliance represented authority, control, regulation. All ways to curb his freedom. Never again would he submit to someone else's control.

Three crewmen came down the lowered foot-ramp of the Enforcer ship. One was a large, ugly brute—one of the Pruzzian slave masters? Dahvin's chest tightened, cutting off his breath. He closed his eyes, fighting to suppress the memory of himself in chains, bound hand and foot. He forced another look. The creature looked part ape, and part reptile, with a raised set of scales running from his brow over his head to the back of the skull. But this ape-lizard was not purely reptilian, like the Pruzzians. A genetic cousin? Though tall for a human, Dahvin was no match for this fellow.

He shuddered and shook his head to push the terrifying images from his mind, then crept around behind his own ship where he could observe undetected. The other two crew mates were smooth-skinned male humans like himself. The three stood talking at the bottom of the ramp. The taller human studied a square hand-held device and gestured toward the Miran marketplace that encircled the spaceport as they ambled toward the stalls. Dahvin slipped past his ship to keep them in view.

The Mirans were not spacefarers. They shunned technology and held to a primitive lifestyle, but they were avid traders—no holds barred. Here you could buy or sell anything that could be bought or sold. Anything. That made Mira the most important trading port on The Fringe where the number of planetary systems thinned out, giving way to the planetless void of the Great Rift. Supplies were critical out here.

His hand moved to the bulge of his sidearm beneath his long vest. In the heat of the blazing Miran sun, sweat tickled his back and he wished he could ditch the vest, but the weapon had to remain hidden. Mira was a peaceful planet and weapons were forbidden in the market. He had bribed the port master to look the other way.

The three Enforcers stopped at an electronics stall at the edge of the market. Perhaps they were just looking for parts and supplies, though that didn't explain why they were out here so far beyond their jurisdiction. They represented spacefaring planets in the interior of the galactic arm. Charged with policing the trade routes and controlling piracy for the planets in the interior of the galactic arm, the Enforcers made cargo runs safer for pilots and therefore cheaper for the traders. But Mira was not a member of the Alliance.

Dahvin took a deep breath. He couldn't think of any reason they would be after him—he hadn't done any pirating or carried illegal cargo… lately. Out here, pirates outnumbered legitimate cargo pilots. The line between pirate and pilot was pretty thin at times, and that suited him just fine.

Everything in the crowded plaza seemed normal. Thousands of voices created a constant ill-defined din. The pathways were crammed shoulder-to-shoulder with an eclectic mix of races representing the grand diversity of sentient life in the galaxy. Merchants' booths stretched in all directions from the spaceport for a thousand paces.

Dahvin wound his way through the crooked paths of stalls, haphazardly built out of bits of wooden planks, poles, and scraps of fabric. The merchants tended to trade just long enough to get whatever they needed that they couldn't grow or raise, then abandon their stalls to the next comer. They didn't put any effort into maintaining their stalls, patching them here and there as they threatened to collapse. He never found the same merchant twice when he landed here.

He drifted over to a nearby stand. The Mirans were a likable race, if odd-looking. The merchant stared up at him with small, solid black eyes set in the middle of his saucer-shaped head. When he spoke, the round mouth reminded Dahvin of a fish. The Miran stood on spindly legs and waved his spidery arms with enthusiastic salesmanship. Admittedly, he was no beauty in their eyes, either—tall, slender, beige-skinned, with a thick, dark head of hair. A merchant had once called him a green-eyed "illkin." It clearly had not been a compliment. Oh, no, wait, come to think of it, that was a port master he had bribed, just before he grabbed the offered credits. Dahvin snickered.

He'd stopped to admire some fabric with an intricate pattern of hand-woven colored threads, thinking it might be an enticing tidbit for some saucy young girl elsewhere in his travels, when he heard a racket behind him.

The ape-lizard shouted at him. At a distance, he couldn't make out the Enforcer's words, but his body language and that of his companions told him all he needed to know. The ape-lizard already had his weapon drawn, and the tall man had taken aim with some other sort of device.

He dove behind the nearest stall and wove an irregular path among the gaggle of merchants. He angled away from the Enforcers a few paces, then doubled back toward his ship. They caught sight of him through the crowd as he jumped between booths, and all three shouted at him to "stand to."

No way he was going to do that. They ran toward him, knocking off-worlders and Mirans off-balance in all directions. The general din turned into a clear expression of alarm in a hundred different languages. The Mirans uttered almost super-audible shrieks, and his own heart pounded in his ears. He pulled his hand laser from its holster and held it to his side, hidden under the vest.

He kicked a stack of poultry crates in the direction of the Enforcers. Some of the crates broke open and the startled fowl flew straight at the officers, squawking madly and showering them with a cloud of feathers. Ape-lizard fired his hand laser at the flock, frying one hapless creature in midair. It plummeted to the ground, still ablaze. The Miran merchant leaped from the safety of his stall and made the inane move of trying to grab his roasted bird, letting out a howl when he singed his fingers. The stink of burning feathers melded with the stench of adrenalin-juiced sweat glands from the panic-stricken traders.

The merchant in the next stall tried to run away from the oncoming Enforcers, but tripped over his booth's support pole and brought his entire structure crashing down on his own head. The booth fell in the Enforcers' path. Dahvin ducked behind a nearby cart, planning to let the officers bypass him so he could double back the other way. The three Enforcers marched over the rubble of destruction, dispassionate and relentless. Frightened traders fled past him, raising a cloud of pink dust that partially shielded him from view. Sweat drenched his clothing and blinded him. He wiped his dusty sleeve across his eyes. Still they came, now just a few paces away.

Crouching to Miran size, Dahvin zig-zagged three more times, keeping the running throngs of traders and shabby stalls between himself and his pursuers. He rounded one last corner and came face to face with a woman who brought him up short.

She seemed as surprised as he was, and for a moment they stood blinking at each other. Her eyes were like blue ice. Her hair, pulled back in a bun at the back of her head, reflected every color of flame, from white and blue to orange and deep red. But she was also an Enforcer, her weapon already half-raised.

Mesmerized, he remained rooted to the ground until he heard the buzzing hiss and felt the intense burn of a broadband laser sear into his back. The force of the shot knocked him forward. The woman fired, the heat from her weapon burning into his chest. Dahvin's finger closed on the trigger of his own weapon with a reflexive jerk, and his knees crumpled under him.

His discharging beam swung toward the woman, threatening to sever her head. In spite of her attack on him, he couldn't bear that, and in one last wrenching movement, he twisted his body so that his weapon narrowly missed his own neck.

Tess d'Tieri stood numb, frozen in place, staring at the motionless body of the man she had just shot. Closing her eyes, she put her palms to her forehead, the laser still in her hand, hot metal burning a reproach into her skin. For an instant, before the scene had exploded in front of her, she'd felt—what? A tingle of attraction flowing between herself and the young man? No, stronger than that—a jolt. What in pitfire had just happened?

Her crew mate Moag, who had shot first, kicked the motionless man over with his foot. Pink dust coated his fair face, but couldn't obscure his youth. He looked even younger than her twenty-one Alliance Standard years of age. She knelt beside him. With trembling fingers, she checked the side of his neck and his throat, finally finding a faint pulse just below his right ear.

"He's alive—barely. We've got to get him to the medbay. Moag, what have we done? We never should have fired." She brushed a lock of black hair from the young man's face. His eyes were closed, but she remembered them, bright green, wide with fear.

"He had his weapon drawn. We fired in defense. Within our rights." Moag's voice was devoid of emotion, as always. His reptilian Troglan frame towered above her as she knelt. He'd always intimidated her a little, even though they'd been on the same team for the past six tennights. Dirk Treiner, the landing team leader, knelt down and checked the pulse-point for himself.

"Yeah, we'd better get him on board as fast as possible. Defensive or not, it's better if he doesn't die on us."

Moag reached down, lifted the boy like a limp rag, and lumbered toward the ship in the dock.

Tess jumped to her feet, shaking with anger or shock, or maybe both. She wasn't sure. "Moag shot him in the back! How can you call that defensive? And I—I—" She didn't dare finish. She had fired on reflex, not intentionally. Not the way she was trained to react.

She started after Moag, but Treiner caught her arm.

"You haven't had much field experience yet, and you've never had to shoot a live target. The duty commander didn't expect an incident or he wouldn't have sent our team. It's unnerving, no matter the circumstances. You fired in self-defense. He had his weapon drawn. It was a legal fire. That's it. Period. Understand?"

Her mouth dropped open. She shook her head, but Treiner held up a warning finger.

"Like I said, it's always unnerving. If you let yourself, you'll spend the rest of your life questioning every move you made today. Accept it. Now move. We don't want to hold up the shuttle."

"Maybe I should! Maybe we all should."

"If we do, we cease to be able to do our jobs. It was legal. *Accept* it." She fell into step behind Treiner. Delan Krugg, the fourth team member who'd been with Treiner and Moag, followed a couple of paces behind her. Had he witnessed Moag and her fire on the suspect? She couldn't remember.

Tears stung her eyes, but she didn't dare let them see. Her feet moved on their own, one in front of the other, and she reached the shuttle without being able to recall what she had passed on the way.

Duga Rigi, the landing party's med tech who'd remained on board the shuttle, moved the man into a temporary stasis pod that would maintain life support for the half-hour it would take to reach the orbiting Enforcer ship. Treiner keyed up the onboard computer and entered an initial report of their encounter.

> Target number GHN 43, male, age estimated late teens by Alliance Standard measure, positive DNA identification. Target fired upon after raising a weapon in an offensive manner. Two contact points, front and back. Target alive at the time of boarding, being transported in stasis to ship. Enforcers present at the time of incident: C-2 Dirk Treiner, EN-2 Moag, EN-2 Tess d'Tieri, EN-1 Delan Krugg. On board the shuttle but not involved in the incident: ME-2 Duga Rigi.

The shooting replayed over and over in her mind. The shock in his eyes when Moag fired on him. Her own weapon discharging. And the boy's final moment. His discharging laser swung toward her head. He had looked directly into her eyes, then twisted his body as he fell. He'd almost cut off his own head. The entire event looped through her mind like a damaged data disk.

"Treiner, how did this all get started? I thought we were just here to find parts and supplies."

"I ran a broadband DNA scan, just like we always do. I got a ping that indicated the scanner had matched DNA to one of our warrants. I narrowed the scan until I got the target. Then I sent you and Rigi an alert since you were the only ones that weren't with me when it pinged. Standard procedure."

"But we're out of our jurisdiction on Mira. Why were you scanning?"

Treiner shrugged. "I always scan."

"The captain's going to have a major fit. We made a mess of the marketplace."

"He won't care. We got our man. That's our job. Besides, we didn't make a mess. It was all those idiot bystanders stampeding like crazed livestock."

Tess rolled her eyes. He was probably right. "What's he wanted for?"

Treiner keyed up a file on the ship's console. "Well, this should make you feel better. He's wanted for murder on Gehren."

"Murder!" She frowned and leaned back in her seat, trying to make the new information jive with what she had felt when she looked at him. They'd only had an instant, but there had been a connection between them.

"Treiner, did you see how he went down? His weapon was aimed at my head, but he deliberately twisted away to save me."

"Lucky muscle spasm," growled Moag.

"You shot him in the back! You didn't see his eyes. He turned away. He saved my life."

"You fired, he fired, you got lucky," said Moag. "Next time be more careful."

Treiner raised one eyebrow and nodded. "Don't let your imagination carry you away, Tess. He's a murderer. He could have killed you."

She folded her arms across her chest and glared out the viewport. There was no point trying to talk to these primitives.

CHAPTER 03

CONNECTED
RECIEVING....

Tess studied the indicator on the sensor display above the prisoner's regenerative bath-bed in the medbay. It floated in the lower range of the field, showing he was still unconscious. Not surprising, since it had not been a full Standard day-cycle since the shooting on Mira. The man's head rested on a cushion, with the rest of his body submerged in the healing blue gel. A thermal unit obscured his lower half, maintaining a constant temperature in the bed. The reading showed a high temperature, several degrees above normal for a human. Through the gel, where the lasers hadn't burned away the skin, she could detect lines crossing his chest and abdomen, paler than the surrounding tissue. They were random in spacing and length, not symmetrical, like a natural feature. Scar tissue? She watched as Dr. Martsa Bruin ran a hand-held diagnostic reader over him. "Martsa, did you find out his ID yet?"

"No." Dr. Bruin frowned at the readings on her instrument, and her soft, furry ears flicked back against her head. "It's very odd. We have the DNA tracer from Gehren, whose government has had an outstanding warrant for him for the past couple of years, but there's no identifying match in the database. He is a descendant of the progenitor race that seeded human DNA throughout the galaxy, but his DNA doesn't match any of the species known to the Alliance."

Tess leaned in closer. "That's really strange. It's been a long time since we've gotten word of a new sentient planet being discovered. He's not a native of Mira. He's adapted to space travel and had a modern weapon, so he can't be from a primitive world."

Dr. Bruin nodded, her long auburn hair spilling around her softly-rounded ears. "There are still a lot of unanswered questions about this young man."

Tess stroked an unruly lock of jet-black hair back from his face.

The doctor gave Tess a sideways glance, eyebrows raised. Her cheek whiskers twitched. "You seem to be taking a particular interest in him."

"Yeah, I know it's crazy, when he's supposed to be a criminal, but he seems so young."

"Well, looks can be deceiving, especially with an unknown species. I've done a deep cell scan on him. If my readings are accurate, he is young, perhaps in his late teens. Of course, his species may age slower or faster than average for humans, but there are environmental markers that give me an idea of…well, how many Alliance Standard years he's lived."

Tess laid her hands on the edge of the bed near the too-still form and studied the sleeping face. His features were fair, young, but etched with a certain aging, as though he'd seen trouble in his few years. And those marks.

"Martsa, what are those white marks across his chest and abdomen? They look like scars."

"That is exactly what they are. This young man's had a rough life. But why are you so interested? What's going on?" Dr. Bruin laid a brown short-furred hand over Tess's. In spite of her security training, her hands were smooth and milky-white compared to the doctor's.

She sighed and folded her arms. Her gaze moved to the far wall as though she might find answers there. But there were none. "He came running around the corner of one of the stalls in the Miran market. You know what that place looks like. It's so chaotic, booths just thrown together, and no straight path anywhere."

Dr. Bruin nodded. "I've been there a couple of times."

"This guy stopped just about ten paces from me. I could tell he'd been running, he was out of breath and sweating. Treiner had issued an alert, so I knew they had targeted somebody, but the whole market was in a panic and people were running every which way, so I didn't know he was the one they were chasing. We just stood there looking at each other and this—like—bolt of electricity shot between us. I felt it!"

Dr. Bruin chuckled, a series of soft, short, murring sounds. "I haven't heard a description like that since I was mid-kit myself." She shook her head. "You know the regulations about fraternization between Enforcers and prisoners. You don't want to go down that path."

"I get that. But what if this guy is special? We know so little about him—don't know his name, don't know his home planet, don't know his species. There's a lot more to his story." She inhaled deep and sighed, stroking the anonymous boy's face. "And what if there's something special there for me? If it's okay with you, I think I'll just sit here awhile."

Dr. Bruin shrugged and moved on to business on the other side of the medbay.

Tess pulled a chair over to the bedside and raised the seat to put her at eye level with the patient. As she watched, the indicators flickered upward on the wall-mounted readout.

—

When Dahvin opened his eyes he was in a state-of-the-art medical center. Medbays on spaceships tended to be very compact, with an advanced, ultra-sterile appearance and antiseptic smell. Hospitals on The Fringe planets were more spacious, but less technologically advanced.

Must be the Enforcer ship. It would have the best mobile medical facility in the galaxy, and its medical personnel had contributed to saving his life. But right now, they were his enemy.

He struggled to control his breathing and narrowed his eyes to just slits, hoping to look around without alerting anyone that he was conscious, until it dawned on him that the effort was futile, because with their equipment, even a slight change in breathing or heartbeat would be easily noticed.

Forgoing stealth, he turned his head to get a better view of the far side of the medbay and looked straight into the gaze of the fair creature who had put him there. She sat close beside his bed, putting her right at eye level, her expression one of concern and compassion. She stroked his face with her fingers as he focused his gaze on her. In spite of his stupor, her touch shot a tingle through his entire body. He shifted slightly, and realized he was submerged in some type of thick liquid.

"It's a miracle you aren't dead, you know," she said. "Are you in a lot of pain?"

Barely conscious at best, he couldn't speak. Not much pain, but drained of all energy. He managed a meager shake of his head, creating a minor wave in the gel. Beyond her, he could see another person from the back with shoulder-length auburn hair. He could spot two other beds besides his regen unit, but was too weak to try to twist around and get a solid view of the rest of the medbay.

Besides, for now, all he really wanted to do was gaze into those fire-and-ice blue eyes. She wore her hair pulled back and tied up at the back of her head, but he could see the range of its color. He couldn't help but wonder if her personality was as fiery as her looks. He managed the weakest smile, and she rewarded him with a wide grin.

Against his will, his eyes closed and he drifted off into a half sleep. Snippets of conversation drifted around him, but he couldn't move or respond to what he heard. Those who were speaking didn't seem to realize he could hear them.

"You'll have to let him sleep, Tess," said another female voice.

Ah, her name was Tess.

"It will be hours yet, perhaps another day-cycle or more, before I can allow him to gain full consciousness. As you said, it's a miracle he isn't dead. I don't know for certain yet that he will survive. Since he was lasered from both directions, even his internal organs were burned."

"He could have killed me. His weapon was pointed right at my head. And then, as he fell, even after Moag and I both shot him, he twisted to keep his ray from hitting me. Moag insists it was just a lucky muscle spasm, but I saw his eyes. I know it was deliberate. It doesn't seem like the act of the cold-blooded killer he's accused of being."

"Cold-blooded killer" were the last words Dahvin heard before total darkness overtook him, but the impact of those words was so severe that they were the first words that popped into his head the next time he regained consciousness.

—

The young man needed to sleep, and the mid-shift break would end soon. Tess headed to the ship's cafeteria, then changed her mind. Most of her teammates would be in The Bar instead. Though it didn't serve true alcohol, it offered several concoctions that mimicked home-world brews favored by the crew, which had earned the small recreation spot the seedy nickname. Her team preferred its more relaxed atmosphere. It did not serve a selection of salad greens, however. She'd have to settle for a protein snack instead. She needed some input for her incident report. Thus far, she'd written and deleted the first sentence five times.

The Bar was on the same level as the medbay and her duty station in the investigations unit. The ship was an elongated horizontal tube with four main levels. Level 1 held the command and control section, duty stations, medbay, two engineering sections, the cafeteria and the bar. The corridors on this level formed a rectangle, with the cafeteria in the center of the level. She turned left out of the medbay, then right across the connecting spoke that passed between the cafeteria and the duty stations. She could smell roasted meat mixed with the pungent-sweet scent of her favorite fruit as she passed the cafeteria.

It took a few seconds for her eyes to adjust to the reduced light level in The Bar. This close to the end of mid-shift break, a lot of people had cleared out. Tess looked around at the remaining diners. The only one of her teammates present was Krugg. She strode in and plopped beside him.

"Hiyo, how's it going?"

Krugg gave her a quick sideways glance, then downed the last glug of his fake ale. He had never been a very talkative fellow.

"Have you finished your incident report yet?"

"Yes." He didn't look up from his empty mug.

"I'm having a hard time with mine. I didn't get to see most of the incident, you know, just the final moments when we actually took the target down."

The words sounded strange in her ears. It was the way Enforcer crew generally discussed such events, if they discussed them at all. But it felt strange to refer to the young man in the medbay as a target. "Would you mind filling in some details? Do you know what happened at the beginning?"

Krugg raised a hand, cutting her off. "If you haven't filed your report we shouldn't be talking about it. There's nothing to talk about anyway. Just write what you saw and let it go at that."

Tess waved her hands in mock defense. "Hey, I didn't mean to cross any lines. This was the first time I've been involved in a shooting." She tried to soften her tone to a pleading note. "I could use some help."

"Not from me." Krugg got up and walked briskly out of the bar.

What was that all about? Even for Krugg his manner had been abrupt. Shootings were more difficult for species with strong emotional characters, including herself, but Krugg was an experienced Enforcer, a rank above her. Was he disturbed by the incident, because of the way it proceeded, or was she that far out of line for asking him for details?

No one but her own teammates would know of what happened on Mira, so there was no way talking to anyone outside of the team would help her fill in the blanks. Blanks—pitfire—a gaping hole, and she needed to know what happened. Had Moag fired without provocation, or had the suspect fired at Moag and Treiner before he rounded that fateful corner?

She hadn't noticed his laser being drawn when she first spotted him, and she just couldn't accept that he'd fired first.

At least, that wasn't what she wanted to believe.

She was so lost in thought she'd made it back to her duty post before she realized she'd forgotten to get something to eat. Oh well, she'd just have a bigger post-shift meal. Plopping into her seat at the data analysis console, she allowed the form-fitting "flexer" chair to mold itself to her shape. She picked up the holographic headset and activated the display. Three assignments waiting, a good enough excuse to put the incident report on hold for now. Plus it would get her mind off the boy. She'd have to quit calling him that. If he was old enough to be traveling the galaxy and getting into legal trouble, he was no boy.

CONNECTED
RECIEVING....
CHAPTER 04

After a prolonged period of drifting in and out of consciousness, Dahvin came to and felt stronger, but the pain was more intense. He had no way of knowing how much time passed in between periods of wakefulness. He sometimes heard fragments of conversations, but couldn't remember them the next time. He thought he'd seen Tess hovering over him once or twice, although he couldn't tell if her image was real or a dream. Several times he had struggled to ask a question. Why was he accused of murder? But he had drifted in and out without being able to speak.

More alert and with the words "cold-blooded killer" still ringing in his mind, he tried to move and discovered that his hands and feet were bound. Frantic, he struggled to free himself, sending ripples running through the healing gel. Pain racked his body, making it impossible to break free.

His involuntary moan brought the doctor to his side. Older than Tess and striking in appearance, her face was covered with short tan fur, and she had a cute little pink nose. Dark auburn hair cascaded around short rounded ears and fell to her shoulders in gentle waves. Her black Alliance jumpsuit bore a medical insignia.

When the doctor reached out to touch his shoulder, he saw that her hands and arms were covered with the same soft, tawny fuzz. Gold eyes with vertical pupils shone with compassion. Her gentle touch and warm expression calmed him somewhat. "Why am I here?" He couldn't manage more than a whisper.

"We found you on Mira." The doctor brushed a remnant of gel from her uniform and laid her hand on his forehead. "Our patrol had an arrest warrant for someone matching your genetic imprint."

"For what?" Though he'd already heard, maybe he was wrong.

"You are accused of murder on the planet Gehren."

Too weak and in too much pain to mount a detailed defense, he could only shake his head, hoping that would suffice for the moment as a protest of innocence.

"By the way, my name is Dr. Bruin, Martsa Bruin. What's yours?"

"You shot me and you don't know who I am?" His voice sounded strange in his ears, raspy and distant.

"We had a genetic match for a warrant from Gehren, but you're not listed in the Alliance database."

"I'm not an Alliance citizen."

"You need to rest. I don't want to drag this out at the moment, but I would prefer to address you by your name, rather than some ID number created by our computer."

He debated the wisdom of revealing his true name. Would it be safer to give them an alias? When they learned his identity through other channels, would it make them more inclined to believe he was guilty of the trumped up murder? As fatigue overtook him and his logical processes failed, he had an overwhelming need to be known and cared for by his real name.

"Dahvin Tave," he whispered. "You can call me Dahv."

Dr. Bruin laid her hand on his forehead, a gentle touch brushing over his eyes just enough to cause him to close them.

"Rest now, Dahv. We'll talk later."

—

Tess stood outside the captain's office. She knew why she'd been summoned.

It had been two full days since the incident on Mira, and she hadn't yet filed her report. Not that she hadn't tried. She'd written and revised it a dozen times or more, and deleted it each time. She firmly believed Moag had fired without provocation, but reporting that might get him demoted. She knew she had fired on reflex, not with intent, but if she admitted it she would at the very least be referred for additional training, and maybe lose rank. Treiner would sweep all the challenges away and let the "target" take all the blame. But she was waging war with her own conscience.

She straightened a stray wisp of blue hair, tugged at her uniform, and took one final deep breath. Then she pressed the buzzer.

"Enter."

The door slid open and she took two steps forward and stood with her feet a tenth-pace apart, hands clasped behind her back, head up. Captain Blake Djanou stood three heads taller than she, taller even than Treiner. His dark, leathery face and overarching brow gave him a brooding appearance.

"I have not yet received your report on the Miran incident. Is there a problem?"

"No, sir. Yes… I—I mean, no, sir."

"That did not sound very definitive, Officer. That leads me to believe there is a problem. What is it?" His short hair looked like black moss covering his scalp. His black eyes bored into her, holding her like irons, offering no chance to look away.

"I—I'm not sure my memory of the events is clear. Everything just happened so fast."

"And you're not certain everything was handled the way it should have been." His gaze never wavered.

She opened her mouth and tried to shut it immediately, but it was too late to hide her surprise from him. He had revealed no hint of approval or disapproval. What did he know? What had Moag and Treiner reported?

"No matter how much training an officer receives, shooting a live person is the most difficult thing an Enforcer ever has to face. It's never the way it is in training. There is no perfect scenario. If you don't question every move you made that day, then you are not an officer I want on my ship. That said, you need to schedule a visit with the ship's counselor, and you need to finish your report. I expect it on my desk by the end of your shift."

"But, sir, I don't think the ship's counselor—"

"You misunderstand me Officer d'Tieri. That was not a suggestion."

"Yes, sir." She turned toward the door.

"And d'Tieri…"

She turned back around and returned to attention. "Yes, sir."

"I expect your report to be the closest thing to the truth that you can write. No matter what."

There it was. The grenade, dropped at her feet and exploded. What would happen if she revealed that she'd fired reflexively, not a controlled reaction like she'd been trained to do? "Yes, sir."

She left the captain's office and went straight to her duty station. Treiner was already seated at the station next to hers.

She sat down and slipped her headset on without looking at him. The seat cushions form-fitted around her. They were designed for comfort for hours at a time, but her seat would not be comfortable for a long time, regardless of design. Her holographic view unfolded in front of her. Keyed to each user's own brain waves, the crew could not see each other's displays, though they could send and receive data from each other if needed. She sometimes stopped inside the door, amused by the sight of four or five people sitting in easy chairs, staring at nothing and waving their hands in empty space. None of it seemed amusing today.

"Got called into the captain's office," she said, her eyes still fixed forward.

Out of the corner of her eye, she saw the corner of Treiner's mouth twitch upward, though he didn't look at her. His eyes remained hidden behind his own headset. "Still having trouble finishing that report, huh?"

"You know why you son-of-a-runtboor. You know what happened was wrong!"

Treiner leaned back in his chair, which rolled back slightly with his movement. He pulled off his headset and looked at her. "It never feels right, Tess. I told you. You just have to come to terms with it and move on. Are you going to see the counselor?"

"Captain's orders."

Treiner cocked his head and nodded. "There's a reason. This was your first shooting. It doesn't get easier if it's the third, or the tenth. At least it's not supposed to. Did he tell you that?"

Hidden behind her headset, she gritted her teeth and glared. "More or less. Said if I didn't question what I'd done, he didn't want me as an officer on his ship."

"Makes sense. The thing is, you still have to put it to rest and move past it. Accept the fact that you did the best you could in that situation. Learn from it and figure out how to handle things better next time." Treiner reached over and laid his hand over hers. She jerked away and glared at him. Treiner left his hand on her thigh. She moved her leg away.

Treiner grinned, no, more of a sneer. His face looked almost ghostly through the holographic images of her own viewer. "What you have to realize is that the target put himself in that situation. He committed the crime. He had a laser, and he fired it, in spite of laws on Mira that prohibit civilians from carrying weapons. He's a criminal. Period. You are not at fault, he is."

"Moag shot him in the back before he ever tried to fire. You know that was wrong. I'll bet he hasn't had a moment's remorse over it. What's more, I'd like to read his report, because I'll bet pitfire and damnation that he claims that young man fired first!"

Treiner's smile disappeared and his deep brown eyes turned to stone. "As does mine, and Officer Delan Krugg's."

Her mouth gaped and she yanked off the headset. It took her a full minute to catch her breath and respond. "I don't believe you! You all collaborated to cover for Moag! You sons-of—"

Treiner put his finger to her mouth. She knocked it away and started to stand, but he pulled her back down. "Tess, you didn't see anything before he rounded that corner, and then Moag fired. That's all you have to write in your report. He fired at you, and you fired back. That's it."

"That's a lie, and you know it! I jumped when Moag fired, and I fired first." That was it. The truth that had haunted her ever since the incident. The truth she couldn't face.

"And do you want me to report that? Get you sent back for more basic training? I covered for Moag, and I'll cover for you, though I really don't think that's necessary. You fired in self defense. He *did* have a weapon. We're a team. We take care of each other."

Treiner's arms embraced her. "Tess, I care about you. You know that. Don't let this criminal that you met for an instant destroy your life, your career, and the careers of your shipmates. He's not worth it."

She bailed out of the chair and out of his arms so fast he couldn't stop her. She threw the headset behind her as she barreled out the door. What he said made a lot of sense, but she didn't want to accept it. She remembered those frightened, green eyes.

CHAPTER 05

By the time Tess returned to the investigations unit at the end of the mid-shift break, she had regained her composure. She stopped outside the unit and practiced an apology that she hoped would get Treiner off her back for the time being. *Dirk, I'm sorry I reacted the way I did earlier. I guess the shooting has me more upset than I realized. Hope you can overlook it.*

She took a step forward and the door slid open. Treiner was not at his station. She heaved a sigh of relief. She hadn't really wanted to bow down. Maybe if she could avoid him for a day or so the whole thing would just blow over.

Sinking into the flex chair, she donned her headset. A blank report template floated in front of her, and she pressed a key combination that solidified the image to make it easier to read. She couldn't even figure out what the first line should be. She closed her eyes, took a deep breath, and forced her mind back to the Miran marketplace. Step by step she traced her path through it, then opened her eyes and let her voice follow the flow of her thoughts.

"I left the ship and walked about half a ken into the market. Treiner, Moag, and Krugg had already left the ship and walked into the market ahead of me, and I did not see them. We were looking for supplies, and we had agreed to split up to seek out the parts we needed.

"The market was crowded and chaotic, so I did not hear or see my crew mates. I did not know they had identified a suspect and were pursuing him,"—no, delete the last sentence—"I received an alert that C-2 Treiner had identified a suspect, but I was not yet aware that they were in pursuit. I walked down a path between several stalls, looking for a trader who had igniters and some of the other parts on my list. I saw people running along a path parallel to the one I was on when a young man ran around the corner of a booth and stopped in front of me."

She deleted part of the next sentence and replaced it. "He was out of breath like he had been running, but I did not know he was the suspect that Treiner and Moag were chasing. I saw Moag come around another booth a few paces behind the young man. Moag lasered him from behind. He stumbled forward a step."

When exactly had she seen him draw his weapon—was it out when he came around the corner? No, she was certain he did not have it out when he first came around the corner. Maybe that was one reason she hadn't been afraid of him, just surprised when he appeared right in front of her. "The suspect did not have a weapon visible when he came around the corner, but after Moag fired on him, he pulled a laser out as he stumbled forward."

At this point she had to close her eyes again and study the remembered images. It all happened so fast that the exact sequence of events blurred together. He stepped forward. "I fired my laser and struck him in the chest. He staggered back and fired his laser. As he fell, his beam swung toward my head. He twisted his body"—no that was speculation—"his body twisted as he fell so that he missed me." Almost cutting off his own head in the process, but they wouldn't care about that, would they?

"I checked the suspect's pulse and found that he was still alive. Moag carried him to the shuttle, placed him in stasis, and we transported him back to the main ship. End of report. Signed EN-2 Tessiana d'Tieri. Send."

There, all facts, no emotion, no speculation, no opinion. What a good soldier am I. Even Treiner should be satisfied, although she doubted he'd ever see it, even as the team leader. The reports were confidential and read only by the Captain and second-in-command. Team members weren't even supposed to discuss an incident until after they'd filed their reports so they couldn't color each other's summations. What about her conversation with Treiner that morning? How did he know what was in Krugg's report? Had he dictated to them what they should write like he'd tried to do to her? That could explain Krugg's testy attitude yesterday. In a way, she could see Treiner's point. She didn't know the suspect. She hadn't seen what happened before he rounded that corner, and he did have a weapon, even if she hadn't seen it at first.

What if he was guilty of murder? Those soft green eyes and the light-complexioned, youthful face invaded her mind. Why did she have such a powerful reaction to him in that brief moment in the marketplace? Had to be those gorgeous eyes and that unruly mop of black hair.

The duty chime sounded the soft four-pitch tone that signaled shift-end. Tess stretched and pulled off her headset. She ought to go by the counselor's office and set an appointment for tomorrow. But first, she just couldn't resist swinging by the medbay again to check on the prisoner.

She moved through a crowd of crew members, some leaving duty stations, others arriving for second shift. Entering the medbay, she waited beside the door for a few minutes while Dr. Bruin gave orders to the personnel coming on duty.

When she had finished her instructions, Dr. Bruin walked over to greet Tess.

"Just can't stay away from him, huh?"

"No. I've tried. Treiner keeps reminding me that I don't know enough about him to trust how I feel, and in my mind I know he's right. But my heart keeps telling me different. Unfortunately, I was even kind of rude to Treiner."

"Well, I'm sure it'll be all right. Tess, you do have to be careful, and I'll admit I don't see any future between you and—oh, by the way, his name is Dahvin Tave."

"At last, a name! How did you find out?"

"He came around enough to say a few sentences. He's awake now—I'll let you talk to him, but just for a short time. He's still very weak."

Tess turned toward Dahvin's bed. Dr. Bruin caught her arm.

"Treiner is right from the perspective of ship regulations and common sense, but I've learned over the years that there's some value in a female's intuition, a perspective that males just don't seem to have. Be careful, but don't totally ignore your heart."

"Thanks. I really needed to hear that. I will try to be a little more discreet, and a little more—discerning."

Dr. Bruin winked. "Now you're talking sense!"

—

Dahvin was about to drift off to sleep when he saw Tess enter the medbay. He stretched as far as the restraints would allow and forced his eyes open, determined to stave off sleep until he had a chance to talk to her.

When she started toward him he smiled. Still tied down, he couldn't do much except turn his head. She smiled back, an impish grin that reminded him of old sailors' myths about dangerous supernatural feminine spirits. She couldn't get him in much more trouble than he was already in, so he was probably safe enough.

Tess sat down next to him, pulling the chair up to his eye level, and leaned forward until he could feel the brush of her breath against his face.

"So, I hear your name is Dahvin." Her low, soft, voice had an almost musical lilt.

"You can call me Dahv." His own voice was still husky, either from the drugs or from so much sleep. He caught a faint whiff of flowers, maybe a cologne she wore or the bath cleanser she used.

"My name is Tess."

He didn't tell her he'd already heard her name.

She grimaced a little. "I'm sorry I shot you. I...."

He tried to wave his hand to let her know he didn't bear a grudge, but his hand hit the restraint. He heaved a sigh. What he'd really like was to jump up and give her a hug. Where did that idea come from? Must be the drugs. She'd shot him. Why did he have such an attraction to her? Just because she was the most beautiful creature he'd ever laid eyes on. Good thing he couldn't hug her, they'd probably shoot him again. "It's okay. Things happened pretty fast."

"No kidding." She arched her pale blonde eyebrows, her blue eyes framed by dark lashes.

A lump formed in his throat. "They told me I'm charged with murder."

"I know."

How could he convince her it wasn't true? "I didn't do it. I've never even been to Gehren where Dr. Bruin said it happened. Would your people make something like that up?" It felt like a knife pierced his heart when she hesitated.

"No. The member planets issue our warrants. We use the DNA tracers provided to us to identify warrantees, pick them up and take them to the issuing planet."

"Would the Gehrens make it up?"

"Gehren is an advanced planet. I don't know much about it, but I think it has a reputation for justice."

He grimaced. He wanted to talk more, but he was already tiring. Even if they found him innocent eventually, he would still be jailed while they investigated. One day in a cage was more than he could face. Fog invaded his mind, making it hard to generate a coherent stream of thought. Images of flowers brought to mind by her scent blurred with her final words. Questions floated in his mind that he couldn't pin down.

He heard another voice. "Tess, time's up. He needs to sleep." He didn't get to say goodbye. He forced his eyes open one last time, but she was gone.

CONNECTED
RECIEVING....
CHAPTER 06

Tess checked herself over in the mirror before heading out to the investigations section. Four days had passed since she'd first seen Dahvin in that Miran marketplace. No matter how much others tried to convince her that her feelings were deceptive, she couldn't shake her growing attraction to him. What if he really wasn't guilty?

Maybe she could sneak a peek at the crime record from Gehren. She headed for her duty station, managing to avoid eyes she didn't want to meet. Once there, Tess opened the Enforcer suspect database. "Planet Gehren, Dahvin Tave." The computer's resonant female voice responded with *"no record found."*

No record? How could there be no record? Oh, yeah—his name hadn't been in the database, just a target code and a DNA tracer. His name would be on the Enforcer arrest record, but she wasn't looking for that. She was looking for a hint that he could be innocent.

Okay, try another tack. "Requests for assistance, Gehren." The holoview listed twenty-five files. Aiy karooba! But only one murder case. She tapped it, and increased the resolution so the view looked like a solid page.

Case Number: MD6525-2864

Date: ASD 2.16.5416. Local Gehren date: 16 Altan 2864.

Officer: Durren Murtry

Location: Alley behind Maxen's Market on Northport Street in the Olde Towne district of Durrand

Incident: Dom-el Maxillian Kittrend found dead on the scene.

Cause of death: Homicide.

Notes: The investigating officer found a DNA trace on the murder weapon belonging to an off-worlder, male, late teens by Alliance standards, not registered within Alliance and no matching identification in Alliance databases. Warrant filed with Enforcers.

Action requested: Apprehend for trial.

The report didn't include the actual DNA tracer. A note from the investigating officer indicated that a DNA trace found on the murder weapon belonged to an off-worlder. Without being able to do her own DNA scan, she would have to assume that the tracer transmitted to the Enforcer's matched Dahvin's. Dr. Bruin would have double-checked that.

A little bell rang in her mind. She looked back at the date—ASD 2.16.5416. Over three Alliance Standard years ago! Dahvin would have been just a kid. Or would he? His race could be one that aged slowly. Dr. Bruin had cell-tested him—even she thought he was still in his teens. Cells were cells. Even in races that had differing life spans, you could identify environmental traces that allowed you to compare ages.

Dahvin's young, frightened face drifted into her mind unbidden.

She just couldn't believe he was a murderer. A crime of passion, or self-defense, maybe? Not all societies defined murder in the same terms. Why was she trying so hard to defend him? She thought about her own youth, how her world had disintegrated into civil war. Roving gangs had wantonly murdered civilians and dragged young boys off to be slave-soldiers, including Joren, her best friend who lived next door. They dragged him from his home with his mother screaming and begging them not to take him. Then they shot his mother in front of him. She remembered the shock and terror in his eyes. Just like Dahvin's.

She had gotten a glimpse of Dahvin's chest in the medbay. There were scars across his body. Had he been a child soldier, enslaved like the boys on her planet? Tears stung her eyes and a breath caught in her throat. Slavery was illegal in the Alliance, but the Alliance hadn't done anything to protect the boy soldiers on her planet, or anyone else, for that matter.

Her parents were both dead by the time she was twelve, and a year later, she had watched in horror from a hiding place as her sisters were beaten, raped and murdered, leaving Tess to fend for herself in the chaos. She'd escaped rape that day, but had gotten caught later and learned how cruel it could be. At sixteen she'd made it off that hellish planet aboard a freighter, and at twenty had joined the refuge of The Enforcer corps. Some refuge! It was not a gentle life for a young woman.

Was that what she sensed in him, a kindred sufferer? Still, how could she sense that in the space of an instant without knowing anything about him? There was something deeper going on. She could see the logic in Treiner's warnings, but her instincts pulled her hard in another direction. If he had been enslaved and abused, and he'd murdered his captors, she would defend him with everything she had, even if it cost her career.

She reigned in her thoughts. The murder had happened on Gehren, a technologically advanced and peaceful planet in the center of the galactic arm—not some Fringe haven for outlaws. What kind of person had the victim been?

"Find file, planet Gehren, murder victim Dom Kittrend."

Pitfire and creation! He was the head of the wealthiest family on the planet. No wonder they had the Enforcers chasing across the galaxy for the murderer. But how would Dahvin figure into that? Had he worked for the guy? Had moneybags secretly abused him? Hard to believe for a planet like Gehren, but who knows what goes on in private anywhere? Seemed like money could cover up a lot of sins, no matter where humanoids went.

She tried to research more about Dom Kittrend himself. The files said very little about his personal life or his family. A footnote supplied by the data compiler explained that members of the Firstcaste, the wealthy upper class, never allowed their first names to be used outside of family and close friends. Dom and Doma were courtesies used in addressing them, so Dom wasn't even a real first name.

The man had two children, a son identified as Dom-yo and a daughter listed as Dom-ya, but those were obviously not first names either. Other than that, there were just hundreds of references to his business interests and political appointments.

Well, that made it easy to hide what went on in one's private estate, didn't it? She shut the computer down and headed out the door to grab something to eat, after a short stop in the medbay, of course. As she strode down the corridor toward the lift, she met a shipmate headed to the investigations unit.

"That's quite the scowl you have today, d'Tieri. Somebody harassing you?"

She hadn't realized she'd been scowling, but she did have a lot on her mind. "Nah. Just have to sit next to Treiner every day."

The crewman laughed. "I don't suppose you want me to tell him that, do you?"

"I doubt he would take it to heart anyway."

"Are you headed for the cafeteria or The Bar?"

"Hmm. Cafeteria, I think."

"If you'll head for The Bar, I'll meet you there in ten."

"Thanks, but I've got an errand to run, then I'll just grab something light before I go on duty."

"So I take it you're headed to medbay again?"

That brought her up short. He was obviously flirting, but he didn't have any reason to know where she spent her breaks. So how many crew members did know? Were her visits to medbay starting rumors? Tess cocked her head and gave him a crooked smile. "Mind your own business, and I'll meet you at The Bar in fifteen. Fair enough?"

He grinned wide. "Ohhh, you drive a tough bargain, but what's a poor schlupp like me to complain about? See you in fifteen."

She shook her head and waved a hand at him, then headed to the lift. They'd had a number of other prisoners on board since she'd joined the Enforcers.

She'd never had much direct contact with any of them. Two, prior to Dahvin, had been arrested when she was on field duty, and she'd never felt any particular remorse or interest in those, so why him? She had to quit conjuring up scenarios of imagined events on Gehren to justify her interest in Dahvin. She needed to get her head back on business and get her emotions under control, or she would end up conjuring herself right out of a great career.

—

The next time he gained consciousness, Dahvin had a keener sense of awareness than in previous awakenings. At the moment, there was a conversation in progress between the doctor and a man, and it seemed prudent to listen before those present noticed he was awake enough to hear.

"I'm not willing to release him to any authorities before I'm satisfied he's strong enough to defend himself." The doctor's voice shook with anger and defiance. "And besides, unless someone shows me strong evidence of his guilt, I'm not sure I'm willing to release him anyway. He's badly scarred. He's been brutally beaten, even tortured, in ways I've only read about in barbaric cultures. He's been brutalized sexually as well. There are even old internal injuries. The miracle is not so much that he survived our attacks, but that he lived long enough to survive them in the first place. I want to know who did this to him! If it was the person he's supposed to have murdered, I'll be the first to leap to his defense!"

"It's not up to us to decide anything, you know that," the man said. "Gehren is a member of the Alliance, and we're just the police, not the judges. We will have to turn him over to their justice system."

"Not if I don't give medical clearance. By Alliance regulations, I can hold him here as long as I determine it's medically appropriate."

"Don't overextend your definition of 'medically appropriate,' Doctor. Regardless of your personal feelings, when we reach Gehren, he *will* be turned over to them."

"Are you telling me we have no alternatives whatsoever? What if we can prove the Gehrens were the ones who abused him so hideously? Are we obliged to turn him back over to his abusers? He was just a child when most of this abuse occurred. Don't we have Alliance regulations that protect children? He's still a minor by Alliance definition."

The man was silent for a moment. "Are you certain of his age, or are you straining for an out?"

"No." The doctor's voice softened a little. "I've done a thorough genetic scan. He's not more than seventeen Alliance Standard years, and much of the abuse occurred between the ages of six and fourteen. He was still a child when this murder happened."

"Okay." The man sighed in resignation. "I'll check regulations and see what I can come up with. We won't reach Gehren for another twelve days."

So, he still had some hope of escaping captivity. And he had a little time to gain strength and plan an escape. Where in creation was Gehren, anyway? He'd never heard of that planet, so it must not be on The Fringe where he traveled. Could they have a connection with his former captors, the Pruzzians? He remembered the ape-lizard he'd seen on Mira. Was he accused of murdering a Pruzzian? Fat chance of that. He needed answers, fast.

The doctor approached, and he opened his eyes, allowing her to see he was conscious.

"Well, you look a little more alert," she said. "How are you feeling?"

"Better, I think. Why am I still tied down?"

"You've had nightmares. We had to keep you from fighting your way out of the therapy bath. And, you're in a good deal of legal trouble, it seems. Do you remember our earlier conversation?"

Though he'd admitted to Tess that he knew he'd been charged with murder, for the moment, feigning ignorance in the presence of the doctor seemed safer. "No. Most of what's happened since I got here is kind of a blur. What do you mean, legal trouble?"

"You've been accused of murder on Gehren."

"Never heard of it."

"It's a planet in sector seven, the center region of the galactic arm."

Her description placed it in the more populous part of the Milky Way, far from the region he'd plied his trade. The second arm had a large number of planets where space technology had been developed, the majority of which had populations that were descendants of a human progenitor race. Most planets in that region were members of the Alliance. He'd always kept to The Fringe, where the planetary systems thinned out, on the border of the Great Rift between galactic arms. Ships didn't travel across the Rift, where a lack of planetary systems and the possibility for repair and supplies could spell lingering death.

"I never go into that sector. I'm not an Alliance citizen. I trade on The Fringe."

"The authorities on Gehren have a genetic match for you. It would be highly unlikely for it to be an error."

Highly unlikely maybe, but not if the Pruzzians rigged it. Would they have gone to such extreme lengths? They never allowed their captives to live past puberty, and at his age, they would kill him anyway. Would they go to that much trouble just to make an example of him? It had been three years since his escape from the Pruzzian ship. Many of the other slaves from his ship would already be dead. Those that remained would not remember him. What would be the point? But who else would care about an unknown Fringe pilot like him?

"I've never been to Gehren, never heard of it. And I definitely never committed a murder there, or anywhere else, for that matter." The effort of talking was wearing him out. Would he ever regain strength enough to be able to help himself? "Will I be allowed to defend myself against the charges?"

"Yes, Gehren has to allow that, as a member of the Alliance."

It had been a short conversation, but he was tiring and the pain made it hard to speak. In spite of his best effort to control his response, a soft moan escaped.

The doctor ran a diagnostic instrument over his injuries. "I can ease your pain, but you will lose consciousness again," she said.

He had suffered enough for one lifetime and had a keen desire to avoid any pain whatsoever, but the prospect of being captive, unconscious, and unable to control his circumstances, terrified him even more. "No, please," he whispered. "I need to know…."

The pain intensified rapidly. His entire body contracted, cutting off his breath.

His obvious suffering answered the question in the doctor's mind, and in a few moments the room went black again.

CONNECTED
RECIEVING....
CHAPTER 07

After two tennights in the medbay, Dr. Bruin warned Dahvin that the Captain had ordered him moved to a secure holding cell. It would be another Standard tennight before they reached Gehren.

Two officers armed with lasers and braided metal restraining cords entered the medical bay to escort him. One officer was a canton, or team leader, named Treiner, identified by the code C-2 and name patch on his uniform. Dahvin thought he recognized him from the attack on Mira. He definitely recognized the other as the ape-lizard. Moag, according to the name on his uniform. Lower in rank, EN-2, the same as Tess.

He wasn't ready to go into a jail cell, but he had no choice. The main reason, in itself, that he dreaded the thought so much. Without turning his head he scanned the medbay. It presented an inescapable circle of panels with blinking lights and little beeping signals. There was no other exit. One wall had a grated vent, but not big enough for a man, even if he'd had a chance at climbing into it. Being again at the mercy and under the control of others was a frightening ordeal, even when his captors were humane. He shivered as a cold chill seized him.

"Is he ready to be moved?" Treiner directed the question to Dr. Bruin, not to Dahvin, another irritating reality of captivity.

Dr. Bruin, however, looked at him. "Are you ready for this?"

He looked into her eyes and recognized her genuine concern. It was pointless to resist, but he allowed his eyes to reveal his anger. With his back to Treiner and Moag, they could communicate silently. He would never be ready to submit to captivity. She sympathized, but neither one of them could do anything to prevent it.

He offered no resistance as the officers walked him out of the medbay, though anger and frustration seethed within him. Stay in control. Bide your time. Starting a scuffle with two armed guards while in restraints would just get him beaten to a pulp.

It took several minutes and a ride in a maglift to reach the security area. A lower deck he guessed from the initial sensation of losing the floor from underfoot. The maglift was round, not square like the one on his ship. The cargo lift on his ship handled shipping crates twice as wide as he was tall, and half again as high. By comparison, this one felt cramped with three humanoids. It was much faster than the one on his ship, however. From the size of the Alliance ship and the sensations of motion, he guessed it covered thousands of paces both vertically and horizontally.

Seconds later the lift slowed almost imperceptibly, and a soft whir descending in pitch signaled the end of the ride. The door opened onto a corridor that looked identical to the one they had just left. Boring. They could have at least color-coded different levels. It would have made it easier to plan an escape route. Perhaps the ship's designer had thought of that as well.

The trio turned right, and Treiner led them halfway down another corridor to an electrified gate similar to entries on secure cargo storage areas.

The holding area had a narrow hallway that branched into a T at the end, perhaps ten paces from the gate. Treiner pressed the com button on the outer wall.

"Requesting entry with prisoner."

Two guards appeared from around the corner and approached Dahvin and his escorts. The tall slender one had tan fur that blended into skin-tone on his long snout, and his floppy ears swayed when he tilted his head and nodded. The other had an exoskeleton, with large, bug-like eyes consuming most of its head, and six appendages. He stood on the back two and used the front two as arms. Dahvin couldn't tell whether the middle two were arms, legs, or could function as both.

Treiner pressed a button in the corridor at the same time Fur-face pressed one inside the holding area. The gate slid open. So, opening the gate required cooperation on both sides of the security barrier. A devilishly simple and effective precaution.

"Get moving." A none-too-gentle push from Treiner forced him into the secure hall. Dahvin clenched his hands. He shouldn't be stupid here. Treiner and Moag remained outside. Again, both pressed the panel, and the gate slid closed. That meant the jailers themselves could not enter or leave without another officer. The furry guard hooked a chain through the restraints and clicked it closed on a ring on his own belt, leaving Dahvin no choice but to follow.

Fur-face led him around the corner to the right and Dahvin faced another electrified gate to a holding cell. The bug stepped around them to the opposite side of the gate. Each guard pressed a panel on the side of the cell gate. It slid open, and Fur-face released the chain at his waist. He didn't have to be nudged. He was going nowhere but where they wanted him to. He stepped into the cell. The pair closed the gate. Then one of them pressed another switch and with a buzz, his remaining restraints fell off.

It would be impossible to escape without at least three accomplices, two in the holding area, since it took two guards to open the gate to the cell, and one in the outer corridor who could let the accomplices in the holding area out. The realization punched him in the gut.

The cell had its own lavatory and shower. Its most annoying feature was the gate across the front of the cell, which allowed his jailers a humiliating view of his every move, including dressing, toileting, and showering. At least the pale pink material coating the metal walls and the spongy covering on the floor made it seem less cold. The two guards had a small table and a couple of chairs in an alcove across from the gate. Though the cell afforded room to stretch and move around, it was as much a cage as the tiny, wire enclosure he'd endured on the Pruzzian slave ship.

A padded bench across the back wall served both as seating and a bed. He slumped onto it and leaned against the wall, which felt thirty degrees below his comfort level. He gave up on trying to control his shaking body. His chest tightened, and he had to focus on taking a breath.

Then he heard Tess's voice over the com link.

"EN-2 Tess d'Tieri requesting entry."

One of the guards stepped around the corner and he heard a buzz in the outer corridor. Tess entered the alcove with a small medical kit in her hands.

"Open the gate," she ordered.

The guard raised a hand laser to cover Dahvin while Tess was in the cell, but she waved him away.

"I don't need assistance. I need to speak with him privately, for medical confidentiality. Please activate the soundproof buffer and step out of view."

The guard started to protest, but was cut short by a look from Tess. She wasn't a high-ranking officer, so the guards must be the low men on the career ladder. The cell gate closed and they stepped around to the hallway between the cells.

"Aren't you taking an awful risk being in here alone with a murderer?"

"I can handle you."

She did have a confident air about her, in spite of the fact that her head only reached his shoulder. Petite and lithe, he imagined her as a young wildcat, her innate strength and speed magnified by years of training.

"Tough talk for such a little lady." It came out sounding a little snide, though he hadn't intended it to. He was totally captivated by her. The blue and gold highlights in her hair sparkled in the light. He'd always seen it pulled back and tied at the back of her head, like today, but he could close his eyes and picture it flowing behind her like the tail of a comet.

"How come they're sending you for medical duty? Are they really that afraid of me?"

"I asked to do it. I guess I feel a little like I owe you that much."

"Why? You did the job you were hired to do."

She seemed about to respond, but just looked at him. He couldn't read her face as easily as he could others, perhaps because of her training.

"You're shivering," she said. "Do you want the temperature higher?"

He was cold, but that was normal anywhere except on his own ship. "Yeah, I guess so." He shrugged his shoulders.

Tess spoke aloud to the room, "Seventy-five degrees ASTP."

"ASTP?"

"Alliance Standard Temperature. It will just take a couple of minutes, then if you want it warmer, all you have to do is say so."

"Alliance Standard this, Alliance Standard that, does everything around here have to be Alliance Standard?"

"Uh, yeah, it's an Alliance ship. What did you expect, Gorgan weird?"

Was there such a thing as 'Gorgan weird,' or did she just make it up? He snickered in spite of his stress. "Guess that's another reason I like living out on The Fringe."

Tess smiled back. "Sit down and take off your shirt. I'll change your bandages for you."

He hesitated. He didn't like taking off his shirt. He didn't like having others see the scars that crisscrossed his body. He'd taken the lash too many times trying to protect younger captives, and scars overlapped scars, leaving most of the skin on his upper body a lumpy white texture. Though he had gained weight and muscle since his escape from the Pruzzians, he couldn't do anything about the ugly, telltale scars.

"Dahvin, I've already seen your scars."

How could she read him so well? He was as practiced at hiding his true feelings as she. After a moment's more hesitation, he removed his shirt and sat on the bench at the back of the cell. She inspired a level of trust he had never felt for any other person, except one, but he couldn't figure out why he trusted her. He only knew that she seemed to have a powerful effect on him, making him happy to give in to her.

The burns were healing, though still tender. He braced himself for removal of the bandages, the more painful part of the treatments. It also hurt when the pads containing the salve touched the damaged skin, but that quickly changed as it soothed the burns with a cooling effect.

But when Tess removed the bandage on his back, he barely felt it. Her movement was quick and light.

"Tough lady with a gentle touch." He hadn't expected her to be so skilled with a medical application. Even the nurses in the medbay hadn't been so gentle.

Tess just smiled in reply. She had visited him several times while he was still in the medical bay, each time touching his hand or forehead in a soothing manner, but rarely speaking. Of course, for much of that time, he hadn't been able to talk much.

For him, her touch conveyed more than her words ever could have. He had learned to mistrust words, no matter how convincing they sounded. People revealed their inner thoughts through their eyes and body language, in ways most of them never realized.

Tess applied the salve to his back, then with a gentle tug on his left shoulder, turned him around to face her so she could doctor his chest. He found himself gazing into those captivating eyes, blue flame, or blue ice, depending on the emotions behind them.

Mesmerized by her eyes, he forgot to brace himself for the pull of the bandages. In spite of her best efforts, his chest was more sensitive and he flinched when she removed the old bandages. A slight catch of his breath gave him away, slight enough it probably would have been missed by the average nurse, but not by Tess.

"Sorry."

The burns on his chest were also more painful. He tensed, unable to breathe. Tess's fingers moved quickly and lightly, smoothing the ice-blue salve over the burn. In less than a minute the pain subsided, and he heaved a deep sigh.

"Okay, now close your eyes and relax." She placed her palms on his chest, below his shoulders. Her right hand lay as close to his heart as it could without touching the burned area in the center of his chest. With a delicate pressure, she eased him back against the wall. He could feel the warmth from her hands flowing into him. Did she know some psychic healing technique?

Unfortunately, her touch produced a radically different effect than she evidently intended. His body's reaction to the warmth of her touch terrified him.

"Tess, don't, please."

He pulled her hands away. He was shocked not so much by the sensation, as by his burning desire *not* to pull her away, to keep her there, to keep her touching him, to keep her warmth close to his heart. But the terror associated with arousal overpowered any desire to let her continue.

"Go away, please."

She lowered her hands, but didn't move away.

She frowned, confused.

"I won't hurt you. It will help you relax and sleep. You don't sleep well."

"No, you couldn't know what you're doing to me. Please, get out. Now!"

"Dahv, I understand more than you think. I understand some of what you've been through. I haven't suffered as much as you have, but I've been—*hurt*."

Her hesitation in the final word told him more than the word itself. Where he had been unable to read her earlier, now he read her clearly.

A cold chill shivered down his back, thinking of this beautiful, sensitive, young woman subjected to the horror of rape. Such kindred spirits were they, that a breath, a look, could convey a thousand words. His face burned with an instantaneous flash of stunned anger and sympathy.

"It was a long time ago, and I've had a lot of help in getting past it. I would like to help you, if you will let me." She took his hands. "Creation, Dahv, you're as cold as ice."

Colder than comfortable for him, the temperature in the cell was only partially responsible for the deep chill that had overtaken him. He struggled to keep from shivering. Too many conflicting emotions surged through him. Sexual arousal competed with fear and another unfamiliar power that nearly drove him to tears. He couldn't begin to cope at the moment. It terrified him to think what he might do if she pressed him.

"Tess, please, I can't—I can't do anything with you, not right now. Please, give me some time. I need you to leave. Now!"

"Okay. I'll be back later."

God, he hoped not.

God. Funny word. He didn't believe in any type of deity. The term had crept into his language from several cultures. If he had believed, he would have prayed that the horror he thought was coming would not come. But it did. He catapulted back in time to another reality.

—

Dahvin's entire body shook. Sleep deprivation and starvation had lowered his resistance to the pervasive cold of the Pruzzian ship. One of the crewmen knocked him to the floor for some unknown offense, and he crumpled into the corner. The brute grabbed him by the arm and hauled him to his feet.

"C'mon you little ass, the commander wants you."

The Pruzzians were the ugliest creatures alive, with gray-green, scaled skin. Even their genitalia had scales. They had three rows of small, razor-sharp teeth both top and bottom, ideal for clamping down on a victim and for ripping and tearing at their food. He'd never seen the female of the species, but they had to be just as ugly, or they would never mate. He wondered if mating was as painful for their own females as it was when they forced themselves on their human captives.

The crewman dragged him by one arm at a pace that made it impossible to get his feet under him and delivered him to the commander's quarters. There was no point in resisting. Resistance afforded the lower-ranked flunky with the opportunity to prove his superiority by inflicting additional abuse. The brute pressed a com panel and informed the commander his victim was in hand.

The door slid open, and he was heaved into the room. He had barely hit the floor before he was zapped with the blue fire stick. Paralyzed by its excruciating jolt, he couldn't scream, managing only a choked squeal. That suited the commander, who snorted his pleasure. Pruzzians didn't smile. The closest thing they had was a sort of toothy snarl.

If command of a ship was based on who was ugliest, the commander had earned his rank. Darker and scalier than the others, he shed scales during sex. While the other crewmen used female slaves to relieve themselves, the commander preferred boys, which caused no small amount of snickering behind his back. But his tastes ran as much to torture as to sexual release, and he used the former to achieve the latter. Dahvin was his favorite victim.

He chained Dahvin's arms up and behind him to the top of a frame over his sleeping mat, and chained his feet to the bottom of the mat's frame. The burning in his shoulders could not overpower the internal, ripping agony he endured over the next hour. The commander alternated between inflicting pain and sexual penetration until he had been temporarily satiated.

CONNECTED
RECIEVING....
CHAPTER 08

Tess headed out the door of her cabin and ran into Treiner. His cabin was on the opposite side of the level, and he took her by surprise. The look on his face spelled trouble.

"I thought you should know what that runtboor obsession of yours is capable of. Grippa's in medbay, unconscious, from a run-in with him!"

Tess stared at him, too stunned to make sense of his words. "What in pitfire are you talking about?"

"Tave, that murderous runtboor. He attacked Grippa! She's unconscious in medbay. You stay the pitfire away from him or you'll be next! Just thought you should know."

Treiner turned on his heel and stomped down the corridor before she could respond. Though she'd caught the gist of what he had said, it still sounded like gibberish. She'd better stop by medbay and get the story straight.

On the way, she tried to sort out what she'd heard. Grippa was one of Treiner's many fleeting affairs on the ship. Tess figured his conquests bailed out once they figured out the handsome devil was more devil than the handsome was worth. What if Treiner had attacked Grippa and tried to blame it on Dahvin? It would be a hard sell with Dahvin incarcerated under constant view.

But then, she'd already discovered the guards could be bribed. She had slipped them a week of her pay to keep quiet about her visits to his cell. They would back up any claims by Treiner.

She slipped into the medbay and spotted Grippa's form on the nearest bed. A quick look at the overhead display confirmed the nurse was unconscious. Tess walked over to Dr. Bruin, who turned around as she approached.

"Hiyo, Tess. I guess you heard about Grippa?"

"Oh, yeah—Treiner made sure of that. How bad is she?"

"It's not as bad as it looks. Her people have a way of going into a form of mental stasis that resembles a coma when they've experienced a psychic shock."

"Treiner is convinced it's Dahvin's fault. Why did Grippa go see him? I changed his bandages early in first shift."

"She didn't. A couple of crewmen saw her collapse in the corridor outside the holding cells and called for a medic. Given her empathic and telepathic abilities, and since she knew him from medbay, my guess is she tuned in on him as she passed the cells. We still don't know his history, but it's obvious from his scars that it was violent. She must have experienced something—psychic—first hand."

"But how would that be Dahvin's fault? Treiner's making it out like he attacked her."

"No one is blaming Dahvin. I doubt he has the mental blocking skills to shield his mind, even if he sensed her reaching out to him."

"You better tell Treiner before he kills him."

—

Dahvin felt someone shaking him. Expecting another round from the Pruzzian commander, he managed to look up enough to see a human standing over him. He'd never seen an adult human on the Pruzzian ship before.

"Tave. Tave, come to, damn you!"

How did this man know his name? The Pruzzians never bothered to learn their captives' names.

Black suit with red insignia—an Alliance uniform. Alliance? The fog began to clear, and reality shifted again. He was on an Alliance ship. Or was this the dream, interrupting the reality on the Pruzzian ship? No, no, he was beginning to remember, this was the reality, hopefully.

"What—*what*?" As often happened when he came out of his physical flashbacks, his muscles still ached with the strain of being contracted during the episode. At the moment, he could barely move. He still had trouble breathing and shivered from bone-chilling cold.

"Come to," demanded Treiner.

"What? What do you want?" Treiner had stopped shaking him, but still had a painful grip on him. Dahvin realized he was on the floor of the holding cell on the Alliance ship.

"What the hell did you do to her?"

"Do what? To whom?" Panic gripped him. What had he done? He remembered Tess being in the cell, remembered asking her to leave. But he couldn't remember her going out the gate.

"What have I done? Where's Tess? What happened? What did I do?"

"Tess? Tess is fine. It wasn't Tess. It was Grippa! She's unconscious in the medbay. Don't you even know who you're with?"

"Grippa?" One of the junior nurses on board. She had spoken to him once in the medbay. He couldn't fathom what was supposed to have happened. He hadn't seen her since he left the medbay.

He tried to straighten his body, but his muscles still cramped, and he flinched and groaned involuntarily. Extreme cold gripped him and wouldn't let go.

"You don't remember anything of what happened with Grippa?"

"I don't remember seeing her." When he was lost in a physical flashback, things sometimes happened that he couldn't recall. But Grippa hadn't been in the cell, at least not while he was conscious.

"Guard!" Treiner called to one of the two officers who manned the alcove outside Dahvin's cell. "Has anyone been in here today?"

"EN-2 d'Tieri was here a couple of hours ago changing his bandages, but she's the only one. He's been sleeping on the floor, having some sort of nightmare or something, since she left."

Dahvin tried to raise his head to see the guard, but cold still convulsed his body and his vision blurred.

"She must have been passing by in the corridor while you were unconscious." Treiner released his grip. "She's telepathic. She can control her contacts, but she might have tuned in to check on you. She must have experienced whatever you were feeling."

"Damnation, I hope not." Bile rose in Dahvin's throat. He would never willingly let someone experience what he had. He hadn't known she was there.

He shook his head to ward off the unwanted thought. He would not have wished such torment on anyone else.

Treiner tapped a portable com unit on his uniform. "Doctor, I'm in Tave's cell."

"How is he?" Dr. Bruin's voice answered over the com.

"He was unconscious when we arrived, but he's come to."

"Is he injured?"

"Not that I can tell. Disoriented, and shaky."

"I'll send a heated blanket through the delivery tube. Do I need to send a nurse?"

Dahvin shook his head no.

"He doesn't need one," Treiner answered.

A moment later Dahvin heard a swoosh and soft thunk. Treiner stepped over to a square panel in the wall of the cell. It opened and Treiner threw the blanket at him.

He unfolded the soft warm fabric and wrapped it around him. Though its comforting heat didn't halt his shivering altogether, it pulled him a little more into the present. "Could I see her?"

"Pitfire, no, you've done enough damage already!"

"Maybe I could apologize to her, tell her it was unintentional." Treiner's offensive attitude sent a hot flush across his face that cooled as quickly as it came. He couldn't do anything about the C-2's attitude, however.

"Stay the hell away from her, and I'll advise her, when she comes to, to stay the hell away from you."

No one else came to his cell the rest of the day. That night was a sleepless one. Terrified of allowing the darkness to overtake him, he forced himself to stay awake even when at last he felt drowsy. He spent a night of pure mental torture wondering how much harm he had inflicted on someone else.

Tess came early the next day with a medkit. He studied her face and movements, but couldn't detect any change in attitude. She expected him to remove his shirt as usual, but he hesitated, still trying to read her mood.

"Dahv, shirt off. You know the routine."

Her order seemed matter-of-fact, not harsh, but not friendly either.

"You know I didn't mean to hurt her. I can't control the flashbacks. They just hit. Sometimes I can sense them coming. That's why I sent you out of my cell. Please believe me, I would have killed myself rather than have someone else experience what I do."

"Dahv! I know. No one blames you. You were unconscious when Treiner found you. Even if you had known Grippa's telepathic, you couldn't have known she was nearby. She was in the outer corridor."

"Is she still unconscious?"

"No. Dr. Bruin said she woke up this morning. She understands what happened, it just took her by surprise, and she didn't have a chance to put up her psychic defenses. She's going to get a little therapy, but her people know how to deal with things like this. I guess it's a downside to being telepathic. But she'll be fine."

He heaved a deep sigh. "Still, she'll never forget."

"She's better off than you. It didn't happen in reality for her. She'll be able to cope. But you—*creation!* I knew from your scars things had been bad. I had no idea…. How did you survive?"

"You just do. It's not a choice."

Tess moved closer and laid one hand on his shoulder. As before, he could feel the warmth of her hand through his shirt. His entire body ached for that touch. But he couldn't risk a repeat of yesterday. He pulled away. "How much has Grippa told Dr. Bruin about what happened?"

"Almost nothing. Her people consider such connections to be confidential. She won't tell anyone anything. We can only gauge by her reaction, and the fact that the memories you were experiencing knocked both of you unconscious."

"Good. It needs to stay that way. No one needs to know."

"I do." Tess moved toward him, closing the gap he had tried to create.

He could feel the brush of her breath against his neck and smell her soft flowery scent. He was backed against the wall with nowhere to go.

"Talk to me. You can't keep that kind of abuse to yourself. You can trust me. I won't betray your confidence. Or talk to Dr. Bruin. Talk to somebody."

"No! It won't help me and it could hurt others. Do your job here and get out!" He looked away and gritted his teeth, regretting his harsh tone. But it still terrified him to think he might lose control with her.

Tess set the medkit down and folded her arms. Perhaps she was considering waiting him out, trying to force him to talk. She evidently decided she might be there the rest of her life.

"Fine. Now take off your shirt and sit down. I'm not afraid of what you might do, or say. I could pin you to the floor if I had to, you know."

He sighed in resignation. She was a spunky little thing, no doubt about that. And with her training, she might actually best him in a fight, if she had to, in spite of his superior size and muscle. He pulled off his shirt and sat down with his back to her. He preferred to let her do his back first, giving him more time to steel himself for changing the dressing on his chest.

Tess finished replacing his bandages, and when his breathing eased, pounced again. "Now, I'm not leaving. So talk."

"Tess…" He couldn't think of anything to say that would dissuade her.

"You don't have to talk about the painful stuff. Just talk. Tell me about something you like."

"This is stupid."

"Tough. Spill!" She crossed her legs and leaned back against the wall.

Why did she have such a hold on him? She could have ordered him to dance and he'd probably have done it. He heaved a deep sigh and tried to think of something "likeable" to talk about.

"I like—liked—flying my own ship, hauling cargo from planet to planet. I liked being my own boss, the freedom it gave me. That's why I stayed out on The Fringe, even though it was more dangerous out there. No one cares as long as you deliver the goods. I was a solo pilot. I didn't even mind the loneliness on long trips. It was—peaceful."

"Why do you say it in the past tense? You think you'll never be back?"

"What do you think? I've been accused of murder. You know more about Alliance justice than I do."

"Accused doesn't mean convicted. Are you guilty?"

He hadn't been prepared for such a direct question. She didn't pull her punches. Dahvin looked her straight in the eye.

"No."

"Didn't think so."

Well, that was the best news he'd heard in—forever.

CHAPTER 09

CONNECTED
RECIEVING....

Today had been a long one. Tess hadn't come to change his bandages. Maybe Dr. Bruin had decided it wasn't necessary. Or had Grippa told Tess what she'd experienced, and scared her off? Tess had said she believed him when he told her he wasn't guilty of the murder, but had she changed her mind?

He'd spent time studying the cell itself, to no avail. No object inside the cell would short out the electrified gate. Even if it did, he couldn't open it. That required two people on the outside working together. For an instant, he had considered enlisting Tess's aid, but dismissed it just as quickly. He couldn't do that to her. Such an effort would be bound to fail and destroy her life as well as his.

No. He'd have to be patient, bide his time. Not his greatest virtue. Another opportunity would present itself. He'd have to be ready when it did. Maybe when he got to the planet.

He rubbed his eyes. They burned and itched from staring at the holoview, the single source of information available to him in the cell. He had to figure out why he'd been identified as a suspect in a crime on a planet he'd never been to. He buried himself in the ship's library records, trying to learn everything he could about Gehren and trying to ignore all the reasons Tess might not have come.

Durrand, capital of the northern continent, unfolded before him.

Skyscrapers covered the landscape, wrapping in a crescent around a turquoise bay edged in white sand.

"What are the crime rates in Durrand?"

"*Eighty-five percent of all convictions in Durrand are for petty theft.*" The computer had a pleasant female voice, though not as musical-toned as Tess's. It made him miss her even more. "*Of those convicted, ninety-five percent are off-worlders. Most thefts occur in the sections of Durrand surrounding the spaceport. The remaining fifteen percent of crimes involve breaches of business law. There has been one murder in the past five years, Dom Kittrend. There has been no conviction in that case.*"

So Dom Kittrend must be the man he was accused of murdering.

Dahvin dug deeper into the reports of the case. Kittrend had been the patriarch of the wealthiest and most powerful family on Gehren.

But why *him*? How had they connected him to all this?

And where in creation did they get his DNA?

Dr. Bruin had told him his identity wasn't listed in the Alliance databases. If someone had killed off his worst political or business rival, it might explain the need for a scapegoat from off-planet. A bribe to Alliance officials would get you the information you needed to cover up the crime. What better choice than unidentified DNA?

So, how could he prove he *hadn't been there?*

The murder had occurred about three years ago, around the time he had escaped from the Pruzzians. On the brink of death from starvation and brutal beatings, he had stumbled aboard Marlon Tave's ship. He and Marlon operated on The Fringe, nowhere near Gehren in the center of the galactic arm. But without access to his ship's logs, how could he prove anything? The Enforcer crew had left his ship sitting in dock on Mira. The port authorities would have declared it abandoned by now and sold it for docking fees. There went his proof. That might have been planned as well.

"I need my ship's logs!" He kicked the wall behind the console so hard pain shot through his foot, earning him a frown from the guard in the alcove. Fur-face and The Bug weren't on duty this shift. Their replacements were both humanoid. "Skeleton" had a muscular build, milk-white skin, pronounced facial bones, and no hair whatsoever. His partner, whom he'd nicknamed Tubehead, was shorter and heavier with dark brown skin and odd tubular organs that extended from his forehead over his skull to the back of his shoulders.

Maybe the logs wouldn't help him anyway. If the true culprit could bribe someone high up in the Enforcers, he could certainly bribe a local judge. Would he be executed? Made sense. Or maybe he'd just be assassinated before there was even a trial. Dead men can't talk.

He swung his foot back for another kick, then thought better of it. "You're in a fine predicament this time. How the pitfire are you going to get out of this one?"

"Exit from the holding cell must be initiated by the guard." The computer sounded almost apologetic.

He rolled his eyes. "Yeah! Thanks for the help."

"You're welcome."

Aye-yi, for all their intelligence computers could still be really stupid sometimes.

Something on the viewer caught his eye and he panned the view to the right. Majestic trees lined some of the streets and were clumped in parks around the city. Their tops looked like ornate crystalline lifeforms. Ice! The bay remained liquid, so the planet had a warmer season, but now, during winter the temperatures would be well below his tolerance without special clothing. If he escaped the authorities while on the planet, he wouldn't have a thermal suit available.

Everything he investigated made his chances of escape and survival look bleaker. He'd been in many a tight spot on The Fringe, from outwitting pirates who outgunned him to having engines die in the vast emptiness between distant planets. But never had he felt as helpless as he did now. He was caught in a very well-orchestrated trap.

First shift had ended a while ago, marked by the changing of the guard at the front of the cell. Tess would be off-duty now. He ached for her healing, reassuring touch.

His heart skipped a beat at the sound of familiar footsteps in the hallway.

The guards had gotten used to Tess's visits and opened the corridor entry without her saying a word.

His heart missed another beat when he caught sight of her flowing, pale blue tunic. A dark blue band circled just below her bust, accentuating the soft curve of her breasts.

She entered the cell, and after closing the security gate behind her, the guard stepped around the corner without being asked.

He waved his hands and stuttered, "you—you look—uh, great."

Oh, real smooth. Why didn't he just *drool* on her?

"How are you doing?"

"All right, I guess. You're late today, is everything okay?"

He half feared she might be on her way to a date with someone on board. She had let her hair down, and it cascaded over her shoulders with all the colors of glowing fire.

He'd also never seen the tops of her ears before. From just behind and above her jaw line, they tapered upward until their delicate points nearly touched at the top of her head. The impulse to trace them with his fingertips almost overpowered his self-control.

She looked at him and smiled. "I just thought if I waited until the end of my regular shift we'd have a little more time to talk."

"Talk about what?"

"Just talk, *period.*"

Tess sat on the bench and opened the medkit, preparing to change his bandages. He'd grown a little less shy with the daily routine. But Tess's appearance had his senses tingling, and the memory of what had happened to Grippa was still fresh in his mind.

"Tess, I don't think this is a good idea."

She tilted her head and studied his face. "We've been doing this every day."

"Yeah, but…."

"I've told you before, I'm not afraid of you. You're more afraid of yourself. I have my medcorder with me. I'll keep an eye on your vitals. I'm not going to do anything to, uh… tease you. We won't do anything more than talk."

He'd never win an argument with her. Didn't want to. His desire to be close to her overpowered his fear of the consequences. He took off his shirt and sat next to her.

"Dahv, how old were you when you were first taken by the—Peruvans?"

"Pruzzians. I'm not sure by Alliance Standard, but by the dating system on my planet, I think I was about six years old."

"What's your home planet? Where's it located?"

"I have no idea. I wasn't old enough to even know I lived on a planet—it was just home. I had started school, but had to quit. Maybe because we were at war and it was too dangerous to go. I remember explosions near our house sometimes. I wasn't allowed to go very far from home. It was too dangerous for children to be in school, or maybe the school got destroyed."

"Your parents didn't talk to you about what was going on?"

"No. Sometimes my father would send me on errands, taking papers to other families in our neighborhood. I didn't understand at the time—he might have used me as a courier, thinking the Pruzzians would be less suspicious of a child. It obviously didn't work, since I was captured."

"What about your mother?" Tess smoothed the salve over the burns. "Didn't she object to you being put at risk by being used as a courier? Didn't people know the Pruzzians were taking children?"

"I think my mother passed away, or moved away, when I was younger, and my father didn't talk much. I do remember feeling lonely a lot of the time. I don't know what other people thought."

He had almost no memory of his mother and only vague memories of his father. In a distant hazy image his mother was there, and in later memories she was not. He couldn't even say what his father looked like, just an emotional impression of someone stern and quiet, more frightening than comforting.

"Were there other children taken?" Tess's hand continued to stroke his back in a circular motion as she spoke.

"There were a lot of us. In fact, as far as I could tell, they only took children as captives, never adults."

"How awful!" Tess stopped her ministrations. One hand touched his shoulder.

He resisted the slight pressure to turn toward her, struggling to control his breathing and his pounding heart, hoping she wouldn't notice. Her appearance and her questions aroused conflicting feelings he didn't want to deal with.

Tess moved around in front of him, her hair swaying as she passed, creating a slight flower-scented breeze. She sat down close enough he could feel the soft brush of her breath. It took every ounce of control he had to keep from grabbing her and hugging her to him.

With a deft move, she removed the coverings. He flinched. The burns were no longer as tender, but the skin on his chest was just—sensitive.

Her hand stroked his chest, smoothing on the icy salve. He held his breath.

"What about the other children that were taken, were they couriers too?"

He exhaled just enough to answer. "I don't know, we weren't allowed to talk to each other. I can't even tell you how bad it was, and I wouldn't want to anyway." He was desperate to turn the conversation away from his own childhood. Besides, he wanted to learn as much as he could about Tess.

"What about you? What was your childhood like? I guess I've always kind of wondered what it's like to be a normal kid." Maybe he shouldn't have asked. How old had she been when she was raped—or was that even what happened?

"Well, I can't say I would be a good example of that. Things were normal until I was about ten, and then my world disintegrated into warfare, too, although not because of an attack from off-worlders. Sad to say, we did it to ourselves. By the time I managed to get away, most of the planet's infrastructure and resources had been destroyed. There are few survivors left now, as far as I know, and it's a pretty meager existence. There's not much left to work with."

"What was it like before war broke out?"

Tess finished the treatment, gathered up the old bandages and salve, and closed up the medkit. Her head tilted to one side, allowing her hair to spill over her shoulder and one breast. He turned his head to stare at the wall.

"I lived in a large city with my parents and grandparents. I had two older sisters. I don't remember what my father did. He worked in an office of some sort, but I don't recall his job title. By the time I turned ten he had joined the army and had gone off to fight.

"My mother was a very loving person, and she laughed a lot. My grandmother was a little more stern, but still sweet."

"Where are they now?"

"They're all dead. My father was killed before I turned eleven. Then a bomb destroyed our house while my sisters and I were in school. My mother and grandparents were home, and they were all three killed. My sisters and I were left orphaned and homeless, living off of what we could beg or steal. We hid in abandoned buildings, or wherever we could manage. Eventually, things deteriorated to the point where there wasn't any effective government or police, just armed gangs roaming the streets, taking whatever they wanted.

"They would take the young boys and force them to join their gangs. And the young women, well you know what they took from them. When I was about thirteen, one of the gangs found my sisters and me in our hiding place. I managed to stay hidden, but I could hear their screams. They held my oldest sister, Zinya, down while they raped and murdered my middle sister, Marta, in front of her. By the time they were done with Zinya, she had died, too."

He dared to look back at her. Tess had leaned back against the wall, her head lowered. Her hair had spilled forward and he couldn't see her face, but she had to be reliving that horror in her mind. He wanted desperately to reach out and hold her, but he didn't dare. What if he had another flashback? What if he hurt her?

He could never live with that.

"I was on my own after that, just surviving as best I could. I wasn't alone, there were so many people homeless by then. Adults and children would sort of cling together in groups. But eventually, one of the gangs found me, too. At least I survived. I worked my way onto a cargo ship when I was sixteen, that's how I got away. I got accepted to the Enforcers about a year ago."

He reached out and slid one finger under her chin, raising her face so he could look into her eyes.

He stroked her face with his thumb, unable to find the right words to express his feelings. He couldn't conceive how any human could have done the things she described to a young innocent girl. His desire to reach out to her conquered his fear. He put his arms around Tess and pulled her toward him, embracing her as though he could ward off the memories.

"It was a long time ago, and I've had a chance to work with a very good counselor who helped me get through a lot of the fear and anger. But Dahv, you haven't had anyone. How did you cope?"

"Well, I did have someone who helped me tremendously. Marlon Tave. I wouldn't call him a counselor, but he was the closest thing to a real father that I've known. I took his last name after he died."

Tess sat up abruptly. "He died, too!"

"Unfortunately. He had a heart attack about a year and a half ago. There are times when I miss him desperately. He was my savior, in a way. After I escaped from the Pruzzian ship, somehow I stumbled onto Marlon Tave's ship. He saved my life, nursed me back to health, educated me, taught me everything, including how to run a cargo business."

"Do you know if any of the other children escaped from the Pruzzian ship?"

"I doubt it. I don't remember how I did. There's a gap between when I was on the Pruzzian ship and when Marlon found me. We never could find them and never found anyone who even knew about them. If we could have, I think Marlon would have tried to find some authority to help us rescue the other children. He was pretty amazing. He made me spend most of every day studying—history, math, science, cultures. He bought me a headset that enhanced comprehension. I learned a lot in a short period of time."

Tess moved a little closer in and sighed. "I guess I should spend a little more time studying some of those things. I went to school until my family was killed. But I never went back to it after I left Ramada. You'd never guess it by our history, but Ramada meant 'safe haven.'"

"I'll be your safe haven." He pulled her closer.

She leaned against him, placing one hand over his heart, careful to avoid the burned area. The heat from her hand soaked deep into his body, the warmth spreading throughout. He caved to impulse and buried his face in her hair, inhaling her intoxicating scent. His entire body tensed with a longing he'd never felt before. She turned her face toward him. He took her by the shoulders to push her away, but ended up pulling her into his arms. His lips brushed hers, then pressed against them. For an instant as they kissed, the rest of the world melted away.

Out of the corner of his eye he caught a flutter of movement in the corner of the hallway. He pushed her away and jumped up from the bench. What in pitfire was he doing?

The hallway was empty. Had he imagined it?

No, Tess had caught the movement as well. She stared wide-eyed at the corner where the two hallways intersected.

"I'm sorry. I shouldn't have done that." Her voice trembled.

He couldn't look at her. "It's not your fault." The heat of passion dissolved into intense shivering cold. "You need to leave."

The sound of a small bell announced the arrival of his evening meal. She'd been there for nearly an hour. It didn't take that long to change bandages. Damnation, what was he thinking? He should have sent her away sooner. He should have watched out for her. He knew better. He'd learned long ago the dangers of allowing his emotions to gain control. His lapse had endangered her.

He walked over to the automated chute and removed another large portion of meat with the same bland vegetable as earlier in the day. The single improvement was a piece of decent-looking bread.

"You don't care for that stuff, do you? I remember from the med-bay, you're a vegetarian, right?"

"Yeah, not that the kitchen seems to care."

"I think I can take care of that. Send it back."

He put the tray back in the delivery tube, but grabbed the piece of bread at the last moment before he pushed the send button. Tess walked over to the communication panel and punched in the com-code for the kitchen.

"This is EN-2 Tess d'Tieri. I need an order of steamed roquert, fresh danzi, and some dak cheese delivered to holding cell number one. And please make a note for future reference that the prisoner is vegetarian. Do not send any more meat dishes to the holding cell."

She turned back toward him. "There. If you have any more problems with the food, let me know."

"Thanks, but I don't want to antagonize the kitchen staff."

"Don't worry about it—the request didn't come from you. If they don't like it, they can deal with me. Let me know if you have any complaints, Okay?"

"Yeah, sure."

Tess walked back over to him and stroked his face with her fingertips, looking deep into his eyes. A bond had been forged between them, an understanding born of mutual suffering. He could read her more easily now, as she had read him earlier. A single look shared between them spoke volumes.

"I'd better go." Her voice was soft, low, musical. "I'll be back tomorrow."

He nodded. Tess turned and walked away. She pressed a buzzer to alert the guards that she was ready to leave.

He wanted to ask Tess if her visits would jeopardize her position on the ship, but she was already out the gate, and he didn't want to risk saying anything within earshot of the guards. He kicked himself again mentally—should have sent her away sooner. But it was so hard to resist her.

The delivery bell rang again. He opened the delivery chute and caught the savory aromas of the foods Tess had ordered for him. His stomach flipped in anticipation. He hadn't known what she'd ordered, but her selections were perfect. One was a sweet and tangy fruit, another a steamed vegetable with a spicy seasoning, along with his evening cup of tea.

Dr. Bruin had told him the herbal tea would help him sleep. He'd been sleeping so well the last couple of nights that he suspected there was more in it than just a simple tea. The aroma of the tea reminded him somewhat of Tess's scent and helped calm his jangled nerves.

CHAPTER 10

Tess hesitated outside the hallway as she left the holding cell, debating whether she needed to slip the guards another week's pay. That kiss! Had she lost her mind completely? She thought she'd caught a flutter of movement in the hallway. Had the guards caught them?

Even if they hadn't, making the guards go around the corner when she worked with Dahvin made her actions look suspect. How could she have been so stupid? There had been no reason to make the guards leave. She'd just wanted him to be able to open up and talk.

No, another bribe would just dig her in even deeper. She'd have to hope for the best. Rumors had started after she'd visited Dahvin in the medbay so many times. Pitfire and damnation. She should have been smarter.

Shaking her head, she turned away and walked down the corridor to the lift. This couldn't happen again. She'd even changed clothes to go visit him.

She'd *wanted* this to happen. A brutal realization, but she couldn't deny it.

A low, soft whir signaled the stop at Level 3B, where her quarters were located. The door opened, but her feet froze to the floor. Another crewman stepped onto the lift.

"Where you headed?" he asked, eyeing her outfit.

She took a deep breath. "Just out." She marched off the lift and down the corridor. In her cabin, she plopped into the chair and stared at the wall for a long time, battling competing scenarios in her head. She could keep seeing Dahvin, but let the guards view their actions and keep it professional. He would understand.

What she *should* do was stop seeing him altogether—she couldn't put her career in jeopardy. She closed her eyes. Every time she thought about not seeing him again it ripped her insides apart. She couldn't give him up. No—she had to. She buried her head in her hands. She couldn't!

Treiner had warned her. Now she understood why.

She'd never gone to see the counselor. She ought to. It was clear she needed help sorting this out. She changed into a sleep shirt and crawled into bed. An hour later she was still staring at the ceiling. She got up and ordered a hot sedative tea. Crawling back into the comfort of bed, she sipped it and planned conversations with the counselor.

She awoke to the musical tones of the wake-up call. The tea had done its job, but she still hadn't resolved what she would do. She kept looking for a legitimate out that would allow her to continue seeing Dahvin. There wasn't one. She would stop by the counselor's office on her way to her duty station. She got dressed still trying to find that elusive perfect solution that would allow her to do what she really wanted. Maybe she could make more use of the ship's vidcom system, allowing them to talk without being physically in the cell. She could code the transmissions to go directly to his computer.

"EN-2 Tess d'Tieri, report to the captain's office, immediately."

She jumped at Djanou's gruff, demanding voice over the com in her quarters. It wasn't often a crew member of her rank was summoned by the captain himself, let alone twice in two tennights. From the tone, she was in deep racca. Had the guards gotten fed up because she stayed so long and reported her? Good thing she had already donned her uniform and was ready to go.

She ran to the lift. The short ride gave her no time to reflect before the door opened on the cold, white walls of the command section. They seemed stark compared to the soft beige walls of the rest of the ship. Tess strode to the office door, her flat-heeled boots marking a brisk rhythm, passing two other crewmen on the way. Their faces yielded no clues. She didn't take time for a deep breath before pressing the buzzer. The door slid open and Tess took two steps in, still breathing a little hard.

Captain Djanou stood with his back to her, his size made more intimidating by the small, bleak office. He turned from the holo-wall consuming most of the area behind his desk, a flat metal surface with four slim legs bolted to the floor. Even a ship this size sometimes had to execute a sharp maneuver. The desk was pristine except for his holo headset. Two flex chairs sat on her side of the desk, She doubted she'd be invited to sit. Larger meetings were held in one of three conference rooms elsewhere on the command deck.

"Officer d'Tieri, explain your presence in the prisoner's cell."

The brusk challenge took Tess aback. Her fingers fidgeted behind her back "I—I just went to tend his wounds. I had permission from Dr. Bruin."

"That is not a part of your duties. Why did you request permission to do so?"

"I saw him in the medbay and he knew me. That's all."

"You visited him in the medbay and have now visited him in his cell to perform duties that are outside of your responsibilities. Tave is a prisoner, not a guest. You may be required to testify on Gehren regarding his capture. Contact between you is inappropriate. There will be no further contact between you."

She searched the Captain's face for some sign of reprieve. Harsh lines etched his forehead. His eyes bored through her like a cold ion beam. All of that was his normal demeanor. She'd never seen him smile.

The medical ruse had been a long shot. She'd hoped a generous bribe to the guards, would cover her. Why had she been so willing to risk censure for him?

"Yes, sir." Her voice was a whisper, her jaw clenched to keep back the tears threatening to humiliate her.

"A little louder, Officer!"

"Yes, sir!" She forced her voice to be bold and assured, though it must have been the voice of some other person.

"Dismissed."

She turned and marched out the door, then slumped against the wall just outside. Not see Dahvin again? Not only that—the implication had been clear. No contact. Not even voice contact. She wouldn't even be allowed to vidcom him. If Djanou had punched her in the gut it couldn't have hurt any more.

Her boots slapped against the floor in military rhythm, all her awareness focused on Dahvin—the warmth of her palms against his chest, the sadness in his eyes, and the relief he seemed to gain in her presence, the beat of his heart and the brush of his breath against her hair when she leaned against him. The guards must have informed on her, in spite of the bribe. Suddenly she found herself at the medbay. Her presence triggered the door, and her feet carried her in.

"Tess, what in creation? You look like someone slipped you a neuro-stunner!" Dr. Bruin hurried over to take Tess's hand.

"I can't see him again. Can't even talk to him. The Captain's forbidden all contact." She buried her head against the doctor's shoulder.

Dr. Bruin put her arms around her, steered her to an exam table, and helped her sit. A network of sensors across its surface came to life, the readouts displayed on a screen on the wall at her head.

"I can't do this. I can't."

"Yes you can. You have to. I should have stopped it before, but it was so clear that the two of you had feelings for each other. He needed you, Tess."

"I needed him, too! You don't understand. It's the first time I've been able to feel *right* with someone. What will I do?" She leaned against the doctor. Her entire body shook as a deep chill took hold.

"You will do what you have to do. You have orders. Do you want a sedative?"

"No, I'm due to go on shift." Tess pressed her palm against her forehead to push back the pain in her head.

"Attractions between security officers and prisoners are not unusual, hence the prohibition with contact following an arrest. Why don't you lie down for a while?"

Dr. Bruin put one arm behind her shoulders to guide her down on the bed, but she resisted and pushed the doctor away. "No, I have to get to work, or I'll have the entire ship batting rumors about."

"Okay, but take it slow. And, Tess," Dr. Bruin laid a hand on Tess's shoulder and looked into her eyes, "I'll send a discreet message to Dahvin and let him know why he won't be seeing you anymore."

"Thanks. I just can't believe it's going to end like this."

"Tess, it was going to end, anyway. He's headed to trial for murder."

She slid off the bed, still rubbing her forehead. Her feet landed, her legs feeling like barium weights. "I know, but I'm convinced he's innocent."

"We'll see what happens. Don't pin too much hope on that."

Why was it that no one else could see what she saw?

Or was she deluding herself?

She trudged down the main curving corridor, then turned right through a connecting strut and left into a corridor parallel to the first. She ran into Treiner just outside the door to her duty station. He draped an arm around her shoulders and pulled her to the side.

"I heard you got called into the Captain's office again. Trouble over the visits to Tave?"

She jerked away and whirled to face him. "You son-of-a-runtboor! I can smell your stench all over this! What'd you do, report me for collaborating with the enemy?"

Treiner threw up his hands in mock defense. "Hey, I'm just trying to sympathize. I tried to warn you he'd cause you nothing but trouble."

"*He* isn't the one causing me trouble." She turned toward the door and nearly plowed through it before it had time to slide out of her way. Reaching her station, she landed so hard in the seat that it enfolded completely around her before settling back to a proper shape. She shoved her headset on and activated the holo, but all she could see was a blurry haze. She'd have to get herself under control. Wearing her emotions like a frontal shield would cause her more trouble with the Captain, and generate even more shipboard rumors.

She took a deep breath as Treiner entered the room and sat at the next station. "Sorry about the outburst, Dirk."

"It's okay. Better you take it out on a sympathetic mate than some of the others. We've all crossed a line somewhere sometime." Treiner put his hand on her knee.

She fought the instinct to slap his hand through the bulkhead and out into space. She had to work with this man as part of a team. Finding a well of resolve somewhere deep inside, she brushed him off gently. "Give me some time and distance, okay? I'm not looking to jump into another arrangement."

Treiner moved his hand back and picked up his headset. "Suit yourself, but everybody needs a friend, and I won't wait forever."

Facing forward where he couldn't see her expression, she rolled her eyes. That kind of friend she would never need.

CONNECTED
RECIEVING....
CHAPTER 11

The buzzer at the corridor gate rang at mid-shift, but the footsteps coming down the hall had an unfamiliar beat. A short, plump nurse came around the corner. Dahvin's heart sank to the pit of his stomach.

The young woman, one he'd seen several times while in the medbay, showed a mini-tablet to the guards, who buzzed the cell gate open for her. Unlike their habit with Tess, they remained at their post. Was she afraid of him?

She smiled. "Hi, Dahv. Want to take a seat on the bench for me?" She walked straight over, sat down, and patted the seat next to her.

He hesitated, then strode over to the bench, pulling off his tunic as he went. He sat with his back to her. "I'm sorry, I don't remember your name."

"Oh, my name's Miki. I have a message for you from Dr. Bruin." She lowered her eyes and glanced at the guards out front, but they had returned to some game they were playing and paid no attention to the activity in the cell. Miki swiped her finger across the mini-tab and handed it to him.

> Dahv, Tess has had to focus on other duties and will not be able to have any further contact with you.

He frowned and looked over his shoulder at her, wondering if she knew the content. She was taking salve and fresh bandages out of her med kit.

"Is Tess in trouble for helping me?"

The young nurse focused soft brown eyes on him. "I don't know any details, Dr. Bruin just asked me to give you that. Are you ready for me to take the old bandage off your back?"

Dahvin nodded. She removed the old dressing with a quick, deft touch, but it just wasn't the same. Her fingers were cool, almost cold. She worked more quickly, probably more experienced than Tess. Or maybe Tess lingered for other reasons. In less than a minute she had finished.

"You can turn around now."

Before he could warn her about his chest she had the old dressing removed. Two minutes later she had packed up the kit.

"Thanks." He stood as she moved away from the bench.

"You're welcome. See you tomorrow." She smiled, warm and a little shy.

The guards got up from their seats as she reached the gate and buzzed it open. She turned and gave a little wave as she went around the corner.

And then he was alone.

Always before he'd had anticipation to tide him over. Now there was only the gut-wrenching certainty that he would not see Tess again, never hear the lilt in her teasing voice, smell her hair, or feel the warmth of her touch.

He closed his eyes, calling all the sensations to mind, caressing them, safely storing each one. Then came the questions.

Was she in trouble? Had her kindness cost her rank or trust among her superiors or colleagues?

They couldn't know—or could they?—the torture they were inflicting on him, perhaps on her, too, by denying them contact.

Perhaps it was better this way, though—for both of them. He faced an uncertain future, and she had a galaxy to travel. Besides, he needed to focus on potential escape options, and he had only a few days left before they reached Gehren.

He got up and moved over to the computer terminal. He hated this little stool. "Hey," he hollered at the guards, "any chance I could get a more comfortable chair in here?"

The taller guard looked up from the game and shrugged. "I can ask." Floppy ears swayed as he tilted his head and nodded. Dahvin had learned Fur-face was called Roamy, though he wasn't sure if that was a nickname or his real name.

While he wouldn't exactly call either of them friendly, at least they weren't antagonistic. They made a point of not looking when he toileted and showered. The bug-like guard went by "Gorp." He'd only seen him stand on two legs, but the middle limbs looked as if they could be used as either hands or feet.

The big fellow pressed a com button near their table. He couldn't hear the conversation, but a few minutes later a crewman arrived with a flex chair. Much better! He recalled Tess's face once more for reassurance. Time to get down to business.

"Show me the trajectory from Mira to Gehren." The computer displayed a star chart between the two planets. A green dotted path marked the route with three red dots showing the artificially-generated wormholes. Every spacer hated them and loved them at the same time. Without them, travel between star systems was infeasible. They were relatively stable. If one started to collapse, engineers could usually detect it in advance, warn ships off and re-establish balance. But once you were inside, the slightest micrometeorite could disintegrate a ship in the blink of an eye. You didn't suffer, you just didn't ever know you were dead.

Filters at each end of the wormhole were supposed to catch anything larger than a micron, but still, once in a rare while a ship disappeared never to be seen again. Robotic "cleaners" went through to mag-vacuum all debris. It was a reality of space life that pilots didn't talk about.

From their current position, the Enforcer ship had already crossed two of the wormholes. In his little cargo ship, he could feel the subtle shift in the hum of the ship's engines as the timbre of the vacuum shifted inside the vortex. Small ships groaned and creaked with the mutterings of ghosts and bounced about as they crossed through the spherical singularity. But the Enforcer ship was too big, or he was not familiar enough with its engines. He hadn't noticed the jumps. The next one was scheduled for the night shift. With any luck, he would sleep through it.

He stretched and looked at the guards. They had finished their game and were munching down their midday meal. The little bug-eyed guy balanced on two legs and his tail-end, eating his favorite seething mass of black-and-brown worms. The big guy was chowing down on a chunk of solid meat and a biscuit. Though he should be hungry, neither fare did much to encourage his appetite. What was it Tess had ordered for him? Oh yes, danzi and dak cheese. No one seemed to object to a special order from the jail cell, and in a few minutes his choices arrived in the chute.

He sat back down to the com terminal while he ate. Odd that the ship's computer had let him see the current star route. How much would it allow him?

"Computer, display ship's diagram."

"Which ship?"

Duh. *"EN238."*

"I'm sorry. That information is not available." Soft spoken, so apologetic.

No surprise the Enforcers would have security-conscious AI. If he tried really hard he could pretend it was Tess. "Okay. How about schematics for the atmospheric shuttle."

"I'm sorry. That information is not available."

Not to him, anyway. Now it was time to get creative and see what he could con the computer into revealing without breaking the algorithmic rules. "What deck is the shuttle bay on?"

"I'm sorry. That information is not available."

"What deck is the jail cell on?"

"The term 'jail cell' is not recognized."

Hmm. "What deck is the prisoner holding cell located on?"

"Deck five."

Well, at least he could get *that* information. The lift had gone down from the medbay to this level. The shuttle bay would most likely be in the belly of the ship, but without knowing the layout of the ship, he had no way of knowing how many decks lay between the cell and the shuttle bay. Not that it made a lot of difference. His chances of getting to the lift in the first place were null and void.

He stood up, stretched, yawned, and took a stroll around the cell. Better shoot for the planet, where security might not be quite so professional.

He strolled back to the terminal. "Computer, can you tell me if Dahvin Tave's trial will be held in the city of Durrand, on the planet Gehren?"

"Yes."

AI, but not sense enough to elaborate. "Where in Durrand?"

"In the Union courthouse. Would you like a map?" The ship's AI didn't seem concerned about security on the planet. That was some other computer's problem.

"Show the entire city with the courthouse highlighted."

The map took up the whole view and still showed the courthouse as a tiny dot. He studied the streets in general and gradually zoomed in to get a fix on the precise location. The courthouse was six Alliance Standard kens from the bay—a long hike in freezing temperatures.

He also studied the local police force, the Durrand Ministry of Security and Public Assistance. Since the city had a low crime rate the officers might be more trained in public service than in criminal control and apprehension. That could work in his favor.

The planet had two moons, the smaller one visible only one month out of the year, in the spring. Its pull contributed to the weather shift to warmer temperatures. It also pulled the bay tides out farther, leaving a full quarter of the bay only a couple of paces deep, with myriad sand bars. He couldn't swim, but he could hold his breath a good while. If he could get to the bay, and the weather was warmer, maybe he could crawl along the bottom, surfacing occasionally, and elude hunters long enough and far enough to escape.

"Show location of the Durrand spaceport." Right next to the bay.

Perfect.

It was getting late and his eyes ached. Tomorrow was another day. Two days left until they reached Gehren. As if on cue, the delivery bell chimed with his evening cup of tea.

"Good night, computer."

"Good night. Sleep well." A poor approximation of Tess, but his imagination could fill in the feel of her against his chest and the scent of her hair.

—

Tess pressed the buzzer outside the door of Ship's Counselor Brie Tammer.

"Come in."

She entered trying to look confident without being rude. Counselor Tammer had long blonde hair, fair skin and blue eyes, pretty by human standards. Her long slender fingers, with long nails, were folded on her desk. She smiled as Tess entered and sat in the deep-cushioned chair facing her.

"Nice to see you Tess. How're you doing?"

"Fine. Captain Djanou asked me to come see you. I assume you heard about the incident on Mira?"

"Yes." Tammer leaned forward on her desk. "Plus, the captain told me he had asked you to make an appointment. It's been over a tennight since the shooting. I was planning on contacting you myself. You're not nervous about talking with me, are you?"

"No." She smiled and her face warmed a little. "I'll admit, I wasn't exactly looking forward to it."

Tammer chuckled a little. "I have such a hard time convincing crew members this is no more painful than having a tooth pulled without anesthetic."

Tess snickered in response and eased back in her chair. "Yeah, I guess us law enforcement types aren't so comfortable getting in touch with our inner feelings."

Tammer just smiled and waited for Tess to begin.

"I'm not really sure where to start. I think the captain's concerned because this was the first time I had to fire on a suspect."

"Even seasoned officers question their actions after a shooting. Why don't you start by just walking me through what happened from your point of view? I've talked to a couple of the other officers who were on that detail, so I have some idea of the event in general, but each person's perspective is different."

The fact that Tammer already knew the basics helped her find a starting point. "Yeah, I just kind of came in at the end. Treiner had alerted me that they had identified a suspect and were in pursuit, and then all hell broke loose in the market. People were running every which way. There were even birds of some kind flying around, and some kind of little fat animal got loose and almost ran me down.

"He—Dahvin Tave—stopped when he saw me, and for a minute we just stood there looking at each other. I didn't know he was the one Treiner was after, I just thought he was running because everybody else was. Then Moag came around another stall a little farther away and shot him in the back. That knocked him forward a step and startled me, I fired at him, and then he fired at me."

"And how did you feel after you fired?"

"Horrible. Worse because Moag had already shot him, and I shot him again. That was unnecessary."

"Humans tend to feel guilty when they have to shoot someone. Training helps us separate appropriate reactions from inappropriate ones, but sometimes it takes some help to accept it. As you know, Moag's species does not have the surface emotions that humans have. It would not have affected him the way it affects you. But you have to deal with how it impacts *you*. Do you accept the fact that you acted in an appropriate manner, given the circumstances?"

Tess hesitated and looked down at her hands. "I—I'm not sure 'appropriate' would be the right word. The problem is, I didn't mean to fire. I jumped because Moag fired and I pulled the trigger."

"Tess." Tammer looked her in the eye. "You were in a life-threatening situation with an individual identified, at least by your team leader, as a criminal suspect. That suspect tried to elude capture, not the behavior of an innocent man. Moag fired, Tave moved toward you, and you fired in self-defense. To an objective mind, you were justified."

Okay, that did make sense, so why did her heart still reject it.

"The thing nobody believes, is that when he fired, his laser beam was aimed so it would have cut off my head, but he twisted his body to miss me. In fact, he almost cut off his own head. Moag claims it was a lucky muscle spasm, but I was looking right into his eyes. It was no accident. He saved my life."

She paused to take a breath.

Tammer leaned back in her chair and nodded. "You mentioned that he fired his weapon. Did you notice it when he first came around the corner?"

She crooked her mouth and frowned, trying to run the scene through her mind. "I don't remember seeing it until after Moag fired. We were kind of standing there looking at each other, I think I would have been more…" she shrugged, "more scared, or on guard, if I had seen a weapon. I think that's why it startled me so when Moag shot him. It looked unprovoked."

Tammer nodded. "So you hadn't seen Tave at all before he came around that corner?"

"No. Treiner told me that Dahvin had fired at them, but I didn't hear any laser fire. Although I have to admit, as noisy as that market is, and especially with so many people running and screaming, I wouldn't have been able to hear a laser. And, now that I think of it, everybody seemed so panicky, it does make sense that somebody was shooting. I guess it's just hard for me to accept that it was Dahvin who fired first."

"Why is that?" Tammer tilted her head to one side.

She took another deep breath. "I don't know. I just—haven't seen him act in any way that is the least bit aggressive. If anything, he's—passive, sort of. Do you know anything about him? Has Dr. Bruin told you anything?"

The counselor pursed her lips and shook her head. "No. There's no reason for me to know anything about him. It's not within my purview to counsel a prisoner, unless I'm requested to do so by the captain. Why do you ask?"

"Dahvin was held as a slave during most of his childhood. He was horribly abused. He's a victim, not a killer." The emphasis in her voice had been more than she'd intended.

Tammer raised her eyebrows. "It sounds like you've gotten to know him pretty well. Officers are not usually allowed to interact with prisoners once they're aboard. Have you been talking with him?"

She hesitated. She'd already opened up the subject, but she wasn't at all sure she wanted to dive in further. The counselor waited.

Several seconds passed.

How long she could wait her out? With Tammer's training, the counselor would probably win that contest.

"I've been changing his bandages for him in the holding cell. I asked Dr. Bruin to let me do it. I saw his scars while he was in medbay. You should see him—his entire upper body is covered in scars. I couldn't help but feel some sympathy for him. I wanted a chance to learn more about him."

"Well, that would explain why Captain Djanou made a point of asking me to talk to you. You violated procedures."

"I know." Tess heaved a deep sigh. "The captain's forbidden me to have any further contact with him at all."

"I'm not surprised. He is headed to trial on Gehren, for murder. We are only two day-cycles from Gehren. You might have to testify at Tave's trial, and your testimony shouldn't be compromised by personal feelings, although it appears you've already crossed that line."

A shiver ran down her back. "Yeah, I will admit it's hard for me to be objective. But what if objective is wrong in this case? Just because he's a suspect doesn't mean he's guilty. From talking to him, I can't see him murdering somebody. Well, maybe the ones who abused him. But from what he told me, they wouldn't be on Gehren. In fact, he says he's never been to Gehren. And we did arrest him on The Fringe, nowhere near where the crime was committed."

"None of which is up to us to speculate on or decide. His guilt will be determined on Gehren." Tammer leaned forward and looked Tess in the eye. "May I make a suggestion?"

Did she have a choice? She nodded.

"Try to distance yourself emotionally from Tave. Let events run their course on Gehren. Either he will be found guilty, and perhaps that will help you see him in a different light, or he'll be found innocent, as you seem to believe. If that happens, there will be no further obstacle to developing a relationship with him.

"And Tess, the feelings you have toward him are not unusual. I'm going to send some literature to your com for you to read. Sometimes, women especially, begin to build prisoners up and feel sorry for them, wanting to help them out. It's part of our nurturing instinct. Understand?"

She understood the theory, just didn't accept that how she felt about Dahvin was nothing more than misplaced sympathy. Regardless of her feelings, she had to accept there would be no further contact with him, for now.

She left the counselor's office with a lighter step, more at ease and calmer than she'd been in a long while. But as she got closer to her cabin, the heat of anger crept back into her veins, driving out the calm. Everyone seemed determined to undermine the feelings she had for Dahvin. Real feelings, not just the product of some misplaced inner turmoil. She had to protect her position in the Enforcers. But secretly she would do what she could to protect and defend Dahvin. She was all he had. She would not let him down. Whatever she had to do, even sacrifice her career, she would do it to help him.

No one—*no one*—was going to stop her.

CONNECTED
RECIEVING....
CHAPTER 12

The day Dahvin dreaded had arrived. He sat alone on his bunk, arms wrapped around his knees and head tucked between them. He'd spent hours trying to contrive a means of escape during his transfer to the planet, but had never come up with a feasible plan. Even if he escaped, how would he survive Durrand's frigid temperatures? He would have to hope an opportunity presented itself. At the moment hope eluded him.

The past two days had dragged by slowly. He no longer needed bandages, so he'd had no visitors from medbay. There was only one he cared about anyway, but he didn't dare even ask about her, for fear he would jeopardize her position.

The entrance bell sounded. His heart leaped. Maybe she'd gotten a reprieve from the captain, or had decided to sneak in and see him one last time. A moment later, Moag and another enforcer, both unarmed, stepped into the cell. Pain stabbed through his chest.

"Turn around and face the back wall." He'd only heard Moag speak a few times, always the same snarling growl. Did the brute have any other tone of voice?

He glanced past Moag. The gate was closing, and besides the two men in his cell, there were three armed Enforcers on the other side of the gate. He would never have made it more than a step or two.

He turned and faced the wall. Moag fastened his hands behind his back with metal wrist bands, then bent down and added a pair of wire ankle restraints that would allow a meager shuffle at best. He attached two short woven metal cords to Dahvin's wrists and attached the end of one cord to a buckle on his own belt. The second cord was fastened to the other unarmed guard. He wouldn't be going anywhere except where they wanted.

The guards led him down the corridor to the left, instead of to the maglift as he'd expected. Three-quarters of the way down the hall, they turned right facing a massive, sectioned, metal door. One of the guards pressed a control button, and the door rolled up and across the ceiling above them. The group marched across a large, open, cargo area, containing a few large crates along the sidewalls. The echo of their footsteps beat out the rhythm of a small army.

At the far side, Moag raised another large door, identical to the first, and they entered the shuttle bay. The cell had been only paces away from it. The launch area held four large troop shuttles and three smaller ships. From their low-sitting stance, two of the three smaller shuttles were locked down. Only the one in the center sat raised on its landing feet, with the entrance ramp awaiting boarding. Together, the seven shuttles could have delivered a sizable landing party.

Moag led him to the center vessel. Smooth and sleek, painted a stark white with the signature Enforcer red lettering and shield insignia, it looked tiny in the massive landing bay. As they walked up the ramp, he spotted the launch command center through a window on the deck above.

He was an expert pilot. If he could overcome the guards and get to the controls, he could escape. Moag and the other unarmed guard each gripped an arm and marched him onto the shuttle, the armed guards watching from a slight distance. Treiner was already in the pilot's seat.

Moag shoved him hard into a seat facing the pilot console. The instant he hit the seat, a solid metal frame came down over his head and locked into place at his waist. Moag and the other guard released the cords from their belts and took the two seats at the navigation station. With both hands still bound behind him, he was snapped in so tightly he couldn't even wiggle, let alone get a hand free. His nose started to itch. It would be a long, miserable trip.

The Enforcers were so skilled at controlling their captives, no matter what he imagined, he just couldn't come up with a way out. Even if by some miracle he wiggled free, Moag and the other guard sat three lengths away looking straight at him. He wouldn't be gaining control of the shuttle. Maybe when they landed he could wrangle a chance at it.

"Hey Treiner, mind telling me where in Durrand we're going? Am I headed straight for prison?"

Treiner glanced back over his shoulder. "An evaluation center. That's what they call it anyway. But don't get any bright ideas about escaping. They're ready for you."

He couldn't hear the instructions from the command center, but he heard Treiner's reply.

"Acknowledged, command, initiating launch sequence."

He watched Treiner's fingers fly across his control panel in a practiced sequence. The shuttle's engines hummed louder. Through the front viewport, he saw, rather than felt, as the ship lifted off the deck. He did feel the thump when the landing gear and ramp tucked themselves into the craft's underbelly. The sensations made him homesick for his ship and The Fringe.

Minutes later, he saw the red glow across the nose of the shuttle as it hit the planet's upper atmosphere. The shuttle must have been well-shielded from the heat of entry, for less than a quarter of an hour later they started their landing approach. His freighter would have taken twice as long.

He watched the craft swoop in over a huge city. Off in the distance a bay shaped like a waxing moon opened into a sea. The irregular skyline of a sprawling metropolis disguised the natural lay of the land, but a general rise in the foundations of the structures hinted at low hills bordering the bay to the east and west. To the north, the city stretched out like a giant amoeba before yielding to low, vegetation-covered hills where the density of structures thinned out. Even from the stratosphere he hadn't seen another landmass across the sea to the south, although his research had shown a southern continent. At the bayside edges of the city, glistening white-capped waves slapped against golden sand beaches. In spite of its deathly threat to him, he was mesmerized by Durrand's beauty.

He studied the vista. It was winter in the northern hemisphere, but there was no ice in the bay. Patches of white gleamed on the distant hills, but from this distance he couldn't be sure they were snow.

It took him by surprise when the shuttle landed on the roof of a building, a wide two-story structure. Two humans with light gray skin met the Enforcer crew. Their short-cropped hair covered elongated skulls, arching over each brow and coming to a sharp point in the center of their foreheads.

Each time he encountered a human species he searched for similarities to himself. Kidnapped as a child, he had never known the name of his planet or what his native people called themselves. These two were not his species. This was not home.

The older of the two, marked by stark white hair and age lines around his eyes and mouth, stepped forward and bowed slightly toward Treiner. Dahvin rolled his eyes. He'd never willingly bowed to anyone, and didn't intend to start now, especially not to Treiner.

"Good morning, Canton Treiner. I am Doctor Marken Blaine. This is Orderly Ramon Bunzi." Blaine used a formal version of the Alliance language, a little strange to Dahvin's ears, but understandable.

A slight breeze with a hint of salt ruffled the thigh-length white tunics the men wore. A blue patch arched across Blaine's right shoulder, marked by an insignia of a circle with an eye in the center. The younger man's outfit was plain, except for a small pin with the same insignia on his collar.

"Good morning Dr. Blaine." Treiner faced Blaine as he bowed, but did not show the orderly the same level of respect. There was clearly a social hierarchy here. Bunzi stood half-a-head taller than Blaine, his youth apparent from smooth facial skin and darker gray hair,

Blaine turned and addressed Dahvin, but did not bow. "This is the Blaine Mental Health and Evaluation Center. You will be staying here until your trial. I will conduct your pretrial evaluation. I trust you have been advised of the reason you were brought here to Gehren?"

He wasn't sure how to respond. "I was told authorities on this planet issued a warrant for my arrest on a murder charge."

Behind Blaine, he saw a metal door in a raised box-like structure. A fence of flexible, tightly-woven metal surrounded the roof, reaching above his head. He suspected it was tougher than it looked, and the tight weave would make getting any sort of handhold impossible, even if he wasn't restrained.

Dr. Blaine unlocked the metal door and led the way in to a flat area large enough for the entire party to stand. Past the landing an enclosed staircase led down to another door.

Once the outer door closed behind them, Dr. Blaine insisted that his restraints be removed. "I believe we can handle it from here, Canton Treiner." Blaine inclined his head toward the rooftop door.

Moag grumbled, then unlocked the restraints. Treiner scowled, but held his tongue. Blaine stood with his hands folded in front of him, polite, but resolute. After a few tense seconds, Treiner and Moag turned and exited back out onto the roof.

The dim lights in the stairway gave little detail to the plain, metallic stairs and walls. It could have been headed into a dungeon, but they exited the stairway into a well-lit, pleasantly scented interior. A textured, pale, blue material covered the walls, with sections that offered realistic three-dimensional views of garden spaces. He touched one, expecting to find a window, but it was solid, just a part of the wall. The floor had a smooth surface with a spongy feel. The effect surprised him. Homey for an institution.

He didn't see any doors anywhere along the hall. It continued unbroken for perhaps a hundred paces, then widened out into a sitting area, judging by what furniture he could see. Blaine led the party a couple of paces from the stairway door and turned to face a blank section of wall. A rectangular section soundlessly dematerialized into a door.

Looking back over his shoulder, he realized the stairway door had merged invisibly into the end wall. Blaine motioned him into the room about the same size as his cell on the ship, but outfitted with comfortable furniture, including a bed, dresser, desk, and chair.

"There's a bathing room through that door." Blaine pointed to a visible door near the back of the wall opposite the bed. At least it would be a nice change from toileting in full view of the guards in the ship's cell. Definitely not the jail cell he'd been expecting.

"And there's a closet here." Blaine hooked two long fingers into a small indentation in a panel set off from the wall by a deeper tone of beige, and slid the panel open into a space in the wall.

"I don't have anything to put in the closet. All I have are the clothes I had on when the Enforcers captured me and one jumpsuit they gave me. Everything else got left on my ship."

"I'm sorry," said Blaine, his already wrinkled brow showing a deeper series of creases. "Maybe we can get you some extra clothes. There's a computer module here, too. You can use it to access our library and the public library, and some entertainment sites." Blaine pointed to a flat square a little larger than his hand propped at an angle on a small desk with a comfortable flex chair. Would it tell him how to escape? That was all he was interested in.

"The evening meal will be served in about an hour, and I will send an orderly to show you the way to the dining hall," Blaine said. "Is it all right if I call you Dahvin, or would you prefer Misyer Tave?"

"Misyer" must be a polite prefix. It sounded affected and effeminate. "Dahvin is fine."

Blaine stepped back through the opening to the corridor, and the wall turned opaque. He eyed the wall, memorizing the precise location of the opening, though no hint of a door was now visible. He stepped forward, keeping his gaze locked in place, and ran his fingers along the wall where the edge of the door should have been. Not even a hint of a seam. He pressed his palm forward, trying to sense a force field, but it felt solid. He hit it with his fist, which bounced back at him. He ran his hand slowly over the surface. A force field normally produced a tingling sensation, even if it couldn't be seen. He felt no tingling. He was completely baffled. He'd never seen this technology before. He was now on a planet much closer to the center of the galactic arm, and therefore presumably a much older and more developed civilization with more advanced technology.

He checked all around the perimeter of the door for an activation switch.

Either there wasn't one, or it was deactivated. The room didn't have any mirrors or windows to the hallway, so he couldn't tell whether anyone outside would be able to observe him while he was in the room.

On the opposite wall a window looked out onto a yard, dotted with trees and sets of tables and chairs. Some trees looked winter-bare, while others still had silvery-aquamarine foliage. Another high fence like the one on the roof surrounded the yard. He did spot a small black circle next to the window. As he reached for it, the window turned opaque, blending invisibly into the wall. He waved his hand over the button a second time, and the window reappeared. The next time he moved over it, the window stayed, but he could now hear chirping sounds, some type of native animal outdoors, and could feel a faint cold breeze. Pleasant enough, but he was only interested in whether he could get out.

He held his hand over the surface of the window, feeling the breeze, but again no tingling sensation. He raised his hand to try to punch his fist through it, then hesitated. A broken hand would not be helpful. He tried pushing his fingertips gently forward, a trick that sometimes foiled an energy barrier designed to stop fast-moving projectile weapons. But the surface of the window was as solid as the door had been, even though air and sound could penetrate. He looked around and spied the desk chair.

He picked up the chair and swung hard at the window. The chair bounced violently back and clobbered him in the head, knocking him flat on his back. The chair bounced a couple more times and landed right side up, perfectly unscathed.

"Won't try that maneuver again." He rubbed the dent on his temple where the chair had taken its revenge. No doubt about it, he wasn't getting out of here. He was a prisoner in every sense of the word that mattered to him. He picked himself up off the floor and glared at the offending window. He raised both fists and pounded it, then laid his head against it. Tears burned the corners of his eyes, but he pushed them back.

If you're panicking, you're not thinking clearly. He could hear Marlon's voice in his head. *Remember the five steps to crisis solution. OAPPE. Observe, analyze, plan, plan again, execute.* Dahvin turned back to examine the room itself. He wondered if all the "patients" in this mental center were prisoners, or whether it was a true mental hospital. The room appeared outfitted for long-term use.

He tapped on one of the walls. Plastic? Wood? Covered with a flowered-pattern material, it didn't have the cold feel of metal. He punched it once with the side of his fist, not wanting to risk breaking his knuckles. His hand rebounded off the wall. Whatever it was had a resilient quality. He would not break through it easily—or dig through it.

He sat down at the computer and tried to decipher the alien symbols. A while later, he heard a voice come through the invisible doorway.

"Dahvin, it's Ramon. We met earlier. Dr. Blaine would like to meet with you briefly before the evening meal. May I open the door?"

How polite. As if he really had much choice in the matter. "Suit yourself," he answered, somewhat curt.

"With your permission."

The doorway appeared, and Ramon motioned for him to exit the room. Dahvin followed him to Dr. Blaine's office. Along the way, he watched for an escape route, but couldn't spot any exits between his room and the office. The hallway appeared to be an unbroken wall, though given their disappearing door technology, there probably were several other doors hidden along the way. There surely was another way out other than the roof. But where?

Sunlight filtered into the hallway from the left farther down the hall, but he couldn't tell whether it came from a door or a window. Before they reached the sunlit area, Ramon stopped and pointed him toward the wall.

"Dr. Blaine, I have Misyer Tave here." Ramon addressed the blank wall.

"Please, come in," said Blaine's voice from the other side. He hesitated, confused as to how he was supposed to walk through the wall. An instant later the opening appeared. Must take new orderlies a while to figure out where the doors were.

Blaine sat in a flex chair behind a massive old-world desk covered with a busy clutter of cubes and data squares. He motioned for Dahvin to sit in a similar chair facing the desk. With his snow-white hair and pale gray eyes, the doctor looked rather like a quintessential tribal healer of a primitive culture.

"What is your native language? We have lingual processors, if your language is in our databanks, we might be able to use your native tongue instead of Alliance, if you would be more comfortable with that."

That was a difficult question. He didn't remember the name of his planet. After years aboard the Pruzzian ship, he had lost all but a few words of his native tongue, and the only other language he knew was a smattering of the one spoken by his slave masters. He had no intention of using that language for any reason.

The child captives were never allowed to speak to each other, and consequently had no real verbal language. They had created a few discreet eye and hand signals, but none of what he had used for communication during his captivity existed in any Alliance database. Marlon had taught him the Alliance language, along with galactic history, mathematics, and other subjects.

"Alliance will do." He didn't intend to do a lot of talking anyway.

"My purpose is to find out more about you, to help determine whether you did or did not commit the crime of which you have been accused, and if you did, reasons why you may have committed it. Here on Gehren, the crime of murder is a rare one, and we generally find that when it occurs, there are extreme circumstances surrounding it."

Blaine's demeanor was matter-of-fact, neither ingratiating nor threatening. In other circumstances, he had an approach Dahvin could have trusted. He had learned to read voice tones and body language and to assess people's intentions by signals other than what they said. The doctor didn't seem to be hiding anything, for now.

"Well, I didn't commit murder here or anywhere else. I've never been here before, never even heard of this planet until after I was arrested." His fingers beat a rapid rhythm against his legs. He folded his hands in his lap and confined his movement to his right thumb scratching against the palm of his left hand, a motion he could manage unseen. He would not allow the doctor to sense any nervousness.

"Then how did your DNA get to the crime scene?"

"Who knows? My guess is someone had a purpose in rigging that."

"I see." Blaine remained stoic, but obviously unconvinced. "Perhaps we could start by talking about events that led up to the situation."

"There were no events, at least not involving me."

Blaine leaned forward and folded his hands on the desk, looking him in the eye. "All right, let's start with, where do you remember being approximately three Alliance Standard years ago?"

That one was easy. He was enslaved by creatures nobody in Alliance territory has even heard of, half a galaxy arm away from where they sat, hours or days away from death by starvation and torture. True—but not believable to anyone in this part of the galaxy. On the other hand, a Standard tennight less than three years and he would have been on Marlon Tave's ship.

"Check my ship's logs, they should be able to tell you. The Enforcers left my ship sitting in dock on Mira." He folded his arms across his chest.

The doctor seemed unruffled. "Perhaps we can arrange that. There will also be an ombudsman assigned to your case, Art Stohne, from the Ministry of Security and Public Assistance. He is responsible for the legal investigation and will present all of the facts in your case, including my findings, to the judge during trial."

That much, except for the man's name, he had already learned from his own research aboard the Enforcer ship.

He dodged most of Blaine's other questions with the same diffidence. After about half an hour the doctor gave up and summoned the orderly to escort him to dinner. The dining room turned out to be adjacent to the sitting area he had seen from a distance on his arrival. On the way, he spotted one transparent panel, on the opposite side of the hall and nearer the dining room from Dr. Blaine's office. It was the height and width of a door, but had no visible handle. Given the portals in this place, which disappeared and reappeared with no hardware, it could be either a door or window.

"You people sure have strange doors here." Maybe he could sneak in a question about the transparent panel.

"Really? How so?" Ramon's gray eyebrows tweaked up.

"They're solid, and then they just disappear. I've never seen anything like that before."

"You're joking! You don't have doors like that on spaceships?"

He pitied the orderly, who'd obviously never been off this planet. Poor guy. "No. Ours slide, sideways in most cases, except cargo doors, which lift up sometimes or fold out into a ramp. How do you know where the doors are?"

Ramon shrugged. "You get used to it. This is an old building, and it used to have old-style sliding doors until they refurbished it about twenty-five years ago." He chuckled. "We were one of the last buildings, except the historic ones in Olde Towne, to get Chechire doors. Did you notice the window in your room? All you have to do is wave your hand in front of it and you can close it, have view only, or have air coming in."

"Yeah, I did discover that—and the bouncy material on the walls."

Ramon frowned again. "Hmm. I don't think I ever noticed they were 'bouncy.'" He sidestepped to a wall and pounded on it. His fist bounced back. "Huh. What do you know about that? Learning new things keeps life interesting."

More like *dangerous*. He decided to broach the subject of the transparent panel. What about the clear panel across from Dr. Blaine's office. Is that a window or a door?"

"It's a door. It doesn't change like a Chechire door, so it doesn't let air in, but it makes it easier for visitors to find their way back out."

Ramon had unwittingly revealed an escape option. *Thank you very much.*

"How do you get the doors to open?"

Ramon looked at him, perhaps becoming a little suspicious. "You sure have a lot of questions about doors."

"Always curious about different technology. Part of life in space, I guess."

"Well, here we are at the dining room." Ramon sidestepped the last question.

The room had ten round tables with four form-fitting chairs at each one. There were only a couple of other individuals eating together at one table, both of whom looked like native Gehrens. Ramon pointed to an open buffet line at the front of the dining room. Although he didn't know the local fare, Dahvin managed to find what looked like some appetizing vegetable dishes. One, an orange mashed vegetable, had a pungent, tangy odor. It had a tantalizing savory flavor. Another pale yellow, bland-looking tuber turned out to be a sweet fruit.

He found it easier to identify cheese and breads, and the ones he selected were very tasty. The cheese had a deep golden color and a rich, barely sharp flavor. The roll he'd chosen was still warm, a thin brown crust and a soft-but-firm center. He wouldn't go hungry here.

Ramon waited in the dining hall while Dahvin ate, then escorted him back to his room. He would ask about opening the doors another time when the orderly's suspicions weren't already aroused. Maybe he would figure it out on his own.

CHAPTER 13

CONNECTED
RECIEVING....

Art Stohne had no more than stepped inside the front door of Durrand's Ministry of Security and Public Assistance when Junior Officer Tal Quint tapped him on the arm.

"The Security Superior wants to see you in his office right away."

A junior officer delivering the message must mean nearly everyone on duty in the building was watching for him. What could be so important?

In spite of the apparent necessity that he get to the Superior's office quickly, he bypassed the lift and took the stairs. He always took the stairs. He loved the wide arching stone steps with their view of the entire interior of the ancient building. Three stories high, the main hall was open from the first floor to the domed roof. Windows around the circumference of the dome allowed light to penetrate all the way back to the first floor.

Massive stone columns supported the stairs. Two sets of stairs began near the front door, arching in opposite directions upward to the second floor, and beyond wide landings on both sides of the hall, continued on up to the third. Their supporting columns progressed taller and taller as the stairs curved toward their final destination on the third floor. The two tallest columns stood like magnificent colossi at the back of the hall.

In spite of a heart-stimulating hike to the top, he was well-conditioned and made it to the Security Superior's office still breathing lightly.

He opened the door and greeted the receptionist, Madra, a trim middle-aged woman who'd been the Superior's assistant for the past fifteen years. She sat behind her half-moon table, hands poised over a com-board.

"Good morning, Master Stohne. The Superior wants to speak with you. He is available now if you'd like to go in."

"Thanks." He walked the few steps toward the inner office and opened the door, a heavy, ornately-carved, antique, bluewood that the Superior had preserved when much of the interior of this building was refurbished a decade ago. He preferred the old wood pieces which had graced the original building over their synthetic replacements.

Superior Harken Strohm sat behind his console watching six different holo displays. Five rotated views of more than a hundred locations in Durrand. The sixth provided intra-office communications. Strohm's thick white eyebrows scrunched together as he studied the displays on his right. He was twice Stohne's age, shorter, and a veteran of over fifty years in the Ministry of Security. Stohne waited quietly, watching out the windows to the east as a spacecraft glided over the sea into a landing at the city's busy spaceport.

"Ah, Master Stohne, I see you got my message."

"Delivered by a junior officer the instant I entered the building. The entire force must have been on the lookout for me." He grinned. As one of the security force's most experienced and respected officers, he had little reason to worry about why he'd been urgently summoned. Still, it was unusual to alert the juniors.

"Is there a major problem brewing?"

"No. In fact, I hope we're going to resolve a very old one. There's been an arrest in the case of the elder Dom Kittrend's murder."

That set him back on his heels. Probably the most famous case in the history of Gehren. Patriarch of the planet's most influential family, Kittrend had been found murdered three years ago in an alley in Durrand's old historic district, far from his usual haunts in the business and financial centers.

"I thought we'd figured out the killer was an off-worlder who'd left the planet."

"That is what we had determined, and apparently we were correct. An Alliance Enforcer crew identified the killer's DNA and arrested him on one of The Fringe planets."

"The Fringe! I didn't think their authority extended out there."

"It doesn't. But apparently the local authorities didn't object."

"I'm not sure how the judge will view that."

Superior Strohm didn't speak for a moment, but looked at him long enough to make his insides begin to squirm.

"I know you understand how important it is for us to close out this case," Strohm said at last. "I trust some minor points of law will not be a problem."

He hesitated, not sure he'd correctly interpreted what the Superior was saying. Perhaps he hesitated a moment too long.

"Master Stohne, let me make it clear. We have the right man. There is no reason for this case not to be resolved quickly, quietly, and efficiently. I know you are the man for that."

"I understand, sir. Though I'm not sure about the 'quietly' part. This will be big news in Durrand, you know that."

"I don't intend for the public to be aware of the situation until after the trial. The Kittrends suffered enough from the loss of their patriarch and our inability to resolve the matter from the beginning."

"They surely can't fault us for that, when he'd left the planet. We don't control the universe."

"Nonetheless, it *will* be concluded now. You are the man to do it, correct?"

It would take a fool to turn down this opportunity.

He bowed. "I am the man."

He left the Superior's office, tossing a smile to Madra as he left, and headed down the left-hand staircase, the opposite of the way he'd come up. On the second-floor landing he stopped to gaze out the huge window that faced west toward the center of Durrand. The object of his gaze was easy to spot—the expanse of perfectly manicured green surrounded by stone walls that shielded the mansions of the Firstcaste families from the vagaries of Gehren's midcaste and nethercaste residents. The private enclave encompassed a diameter of about thirty square blocks of the city. Fifteen of Durrand's Firstcaste families had their homes there, adorned with stately interconnected domes, like billowing clouds forming over a green sea. In the center, reigning supreme over all, stood the biggest, grandest home of all, the estate of the premiere family of Firstcaste, the Kittrends.

Laws had changed over the last one hundred years, and many of the limitations of the caste system had been outlawed. The term "caste" was no longer socially acceptable, and these days, in theory at least, any citizen had the right to apply for or occupy any job or government position.

Tal Quint passed him on the landing. "Daydreaming or scheming?"

"Trying to figure out what I need to do next. How is everything with you?"

"Very well, thank you for asking." The junior officer responded with a slight bow. Stohne nodded back, and the younger man continued on his way.

Quint was a perfect example of just how much had changed on Gehren. A child of common laborers, he would have been considered nethercaste under the old system, denied the opportunity to become a public assistance officer. Yet he had proven to be a great asset, one of the Ministry's most promising juniors. What a loss it would have been a hundred years ago, both to the society and to the individual, if he had been denied this opportunity.

But practice is not the same as law. While laws can influence overt behavior, they cannot change the hearts and attitudes of people. The Firstcaste families still had an unbreakable grip on the majority of the planet's wealth. True, midcaste citizens had at the very least made it into the upper levels of management of the most powerful companies, but Stohne had yet to read of a marriage between Firstcaste and midcaste. Things were now more fluid between middle and nethercastes, but the Firstcaste families managed to remain aloof. Even to this day, anyone from a middle or nethercaste family would never use a Firstcaste person's familiar name in conversation, and most of the older history tomes still omitted the familiar names of Firstcaste members, except as footnotes to avoid confusion.

His Superior's implication was clear, but it raised the hair on the back of his neck. He expected Stohne to secure a quick conviction of the suspect in Dom-el Kittrend's murder. There was no other acceptable outcome. As ombudsman, his legal responsibility was to collect all the facts in the case and present them to the judge. That included thoroughly investigating the suspect, his psychological state, motive, opportunity, and how and why he committed, or didn't commit, the crime. With the investigative technology available to him, he had little doubt that they already had the right man. But still, there seemed in the Superior's orders little concern for justice for the suspect. He had always considered the Superior one of the most just and fair men he'd ever known.

Strohm hadn't mentioned whether the Kittrend family had been notified yet. Surely they had a right to know the investigation had been reopened.

He headed back up the stairs to the Superior's office to check. "Madra, I thought of one more question I needed to ask him. Is he still available?"

"Yes, I believe so. Let me check." She waved her hand over a small black circle on her right.

"Superior, Master Stohne wanted to speak with you again briefly. Do you have the time?"

"Yes, of course, Madra. Send him in."

He stepped back into the inner office.

Superior Strohm looked up immediately. "Is there something else?"

"I was wondering if the Kittrend family has been advised that there's been an arrest made."

"No. I wanted to be sure we had the investigation under way first. Would you like the honor?"

"I'm not sure that would be appropriate news for me to deliver."

Superior Strohm looked at the floor, but hesitated only a moment.

"I think perhaps the man heading the investigation would be the one in the best position to put to rest any concerns they might have. And Master Stohne, I presume you will remember that with the death of Dom Kittrend the elder, his son now carries the title of 'Dom,' not Dom-yo. His father should now be referred to as Dom-el."

Stohne grinned. "I'm not that young. I remember the Firstcaste protocols all too well."

"I really had no doubt."

"And Superior, I neglected to tell you before how much I appreciate your confidence in me."

"My confidence is well-earned, Art. This could well put you in position to take over when I retire."

He raised his eyebrows. "Not something soon forthcoming, I presume."

"Unfortunately for you, no." Superior Strohm grinned at him.

He grinned back and bowed.

Leaving the Superior's office, he headed back down to his own office on the second level. Before talking to the Kittrends, he wanted to look over the photographs and video from the Kittrend crime scene. His office was programmed to project a holographic image of an ancient library, walls lined with physical books, never seen anymore except in the high-end antique stores. Beyond his finances in reality. In the center of the room sat a desk, holographically enhanced to resemble a massive old wood desk and a comfortable armed desk chair.

The sound-dampening system gave him more of a sense of quiet and privacy than the bustling Ministry of Security and Public Assistance would afford otherwise. He breathed in the scene before him. Alas, only the chair was as it seemed. Perhaps he should add a scent program, something mindful of polished wood. Well, that was for another day. Stohne stepped over to the desk and waved his hand over a button. A holo display module and controls appeared in front of him.

"Computer, load visual record of the murder of Maxillian Kittrend, arranged chronologically."

A matrix of over two hundred photo tiles filled the viewing area in front of him. He touched the display, highlighting the first twenty frames. All twenty showed the prone body of Maxillian Kittrend, lying on his back, legs crossed, arms folded across his chest with the fingers interlocked. The man looked more like he'd laid down for a nap than been victimized by violent crime.

He spread his hands apart across the scenes to enlarge the view. Kittrend's body lay in a narrow alley between two ancient buildings in the city's historic quarter. He'd already known that, but seeing it before him in three dimensions still struck him as strange.

The area around the body showed no signs of a struggle. The murder weapon lay beside him, less than an arm's length away. Who murders someone, and then just lays the weapon down right beside the body? And how did a murdered man land in such a perfectly posed position? So now, question number one—was he already in that position when he was murdered, or did the murderer pose the body afterward?

Something else caught his attention—Kittrend's clothing. The patriarch of the top family of Firstcaste wore rumpled, dirty brown pants, a filthy shirt, formerly white but at the time of death a patchwork of gray and brown smudges, and an old sweater with several holes and tears. The poorest farmer in rural North Continent wouldn't be that badly dressed.

"Computer, load crime scene simulations."

A new set of three frames appeared before him, indicating three likely scenarios the computer had generated from the facts of the case entered at the time the crime was first investigated. He hated the simulations, though he was forced to admit they were a useful tool. They allowed the investigator to see the event from different angles and track movements of all the players and objects. But he didn't like having the computer decide for him what was most probable based on statistics. It took out the human and emotional factors, which in his experience were sometimes more critical.

"Computer, end office décor program ten."

The library faded out of existence, replaced by humdrum white walls and the single window on the south wall, now framed simply by plaster. The desk transformed into a half-moon shaped table with a slight recess in the center where the holo projector and control terminal could be folded into a flat desktop. Only his chair remained unchanged. He stood and turned to face the wall behind his chair, slightly left of center from the holo display module. The vantage point would allow him to be an active observer of the three-dimensional holographic simulation.

"Run the most likely simulation first."

—

Stohne shivered slightly as the computer lowered the room temperature to simulate cold autumn air. Northport Street in the heart of Olde Towne was deserted. Durrand's city lights created a pink glow in the darkened sky, punctuated by a few of the brightest stars of the Milky Way. The shops would not reopen for hours.

Across the street to his left was a grocer, and on the right was one of the many antique shops that were the mainstay of Durrand's historic district. Between the two an alley allowed access to the rear of the shops for deliveries and disposal units. The only light on the street came from antique-style lanterns standing at the intersections of Northport and the cross-streets at either end of the block. They left the alley in impenetrable darkness.

Kittrend tottered down the street with an uneven gait that betrayed his age and failing health. He wore simple tan pants and a white shirt, mostly covered by a dark brown sweater that looked like it had been salvaged from a resale shop. In his left hand he clutched a single shopping bag, heavy with the treasure he'd purchased. Stohne could just make out the label on the bag. It was from one of the most expensive antique shops in Olde Towne.

The patriarch lumbered past the grocer and crossed in front of the alley. Just as he reached the sidewalk near the antique shop, a hooded figure stepped out of the alley darkness and grabbed him from behind, his powerful grip pinning the old man's arms at his sides. Kittrend yelped and gasped as the attacker's arms tightened and cut off his breath. The assailant was taller and more athletic in build than his victim. He wore a solid black shirt, pants, gloves, and a hood that had made him invisible before he stepped into the light. Kittrend squirmed and wriggled, but was no match for this surprise attacker.

The black figure moved his hand to his pants, then shoved it hard under the old man's chin. Stohne balled his hands into fists, unable to stop what was coming. The flash of a laser lit up Kittrend's skull like a lantern. He arched momentarily, then sagged limp. The killer gripped his lifeless victim with one hand, catching the shopping bag with the other. He dragged the body into the alley. Fabric ripped as the body was dragged across rough-hewn stones preserved as part of the original street paving. He wanted to rush in and tackle the assailant, but was frozen in place. The computer raised the ambient light just enough to allow Stohne to follow the activity in the alley. The killer laid Kittrend down, folded his arms across his chest and crossed the legs.

The black figure searched Kittrend's pockets, taking his victim's money purse and a few other items that Stohne couldn't identify. He casually tossed the weapon, a small black personal laser, beside the body. He gave a quick furtive look around, his gaze fixing for a split second straight at the spot where Stohne stood. Then the killer confidently strode off with the loot.

—

Stohne took a deep breath, having to consciously remind himself to breathe. He looked at his palms, expecting to see blood. No blood, just a row of small, deep impressions from his bone-hard fingertips. He would never get used to seeing a crime, let alone a violent murder, played out right before his eyes, while he stood by, helpless to prevent it or interfere in any way.

"Computer, start office décor program ten." He walked over to the window and gazed out, needing to refocus his mind and regain composure to achieve an objective analytical view. Once again computer-enhanced, his single office window was framed with intricately carved albassa wood. No window covering. He had the good fortune to have a south-facing view that looked out toward Durrand Bay. The sea rose in the distance to meet the sky, looking higher than the near shore—an optical illusion created by the curvature of the planet.

A seacaw flew past his window, heading back out to sea after an inland feeding expedition. On the ground seacaws were ugly and ungainly prisoners of gravity, with too-long legs that created a stilted waddling gait, giant wings that were hard to fold neatly, and beaks that looked too heavy to hold up. In the air, the legs tucked invisibly away, the beak pointed out ahead parting the wind, and those magnificent wings spread wide, allowing the caws to float and glide effortlessly. Unfortunately for the fish they targeted, they were also efficient dive-bombers. Their underbellies of soft aquamarine fur camouflaged them against the Gehren sky.

The seacaw looked right in the window at Stohne, as if inviting him out for a fly. He chuckled. He wouldn't mind if he only had the wings.

The bird turned and drifted toward the bay. How did such a massive bird manage to soar so effortlessly? What the blazes was Maxillian Kittrend doing walking the streets of Olde Towne in the middle of the night?

CHAPTER 14

Dahvin awakened to find himself completely entangled in his bedding. He had a vague memory of being pursued by some unseen being, aware that it was gaining ground on him, but never catching a glimpse of the monster. With the stress of arriving on Gehren, and without Dr. Bruin's nightly cup of tea to relax him, his night terrors had returned.

The clock read 5:25 in luminous green numbers, but not knowing the local day-cycle, it didn't mean much to him. It was night—the yard outside his room illuminated by the planet's larger moon at full phase. He kicked his way out of the bedding and walked over to the window.

He hadn't noticed the ice on the trees the previous day, but he'd been preoccupied with other concerns. Now moonlight sparkled and glinted off the branches. He waved his hand over the window and got a whoosh of freezing air—crisp and clean, not the distinctly unpleasant odor of most planets he'd been to. Air on spaceships recycled constantly, and Dahvin had grown used to the scent of the sterilizer used in the recycler. Unfortunately, the air was too cold to enjoy for long. He cycled the window back to where he could see out but not feel anything.

It took a few minutes to sort out and straighten his bedding. He stared at the bed, trying to coax himself back under the covers, but he didn't relish the thought of another round of fleeing from his nighttime assailant. He gave up and walked over to the slender, square computer module on the desk. A small icon blinked in the lower right corner. Intrigued, he sat down and touched the symbol. Tess's face sprang to life in front of him. Of course, it wasn't a real-time communication, but just seeing her face raised his spirits.

"Hello, Dahv. Wish I could talk to you in person, but for now, this will have to do. I have a code to give you so you can send me a private message back. If you use this code, no one should be aware that we are communicating. Please do not try to reach me by any other means, at least for the time being. It would cause trouble for you as well as for me."

So, his suspicions about her sudden break with him on board the Enforcer ship had been correct.

"Here's the code: E-N-2-3-8-D-T-1-5-7-3-2-P-V."

He found a symbol that looked similar to "pause" on Alliance Standard equipment and halted the recording. His hand went to where the pocket on his flight suit would have been, where he kept his complet, but of course, not only did he not have his flight suit, the miniaturized personal computer had been confiscated when he was arrested. He searched the drawer in the desk for something to save the code on and found a small, flexible, plastic device, probably something comparable to his complet. It activated when he picked it up, but he couldn't figure out how to use it.

"Alliance Standard symbol set."

"*Gondo net ponymat.*" It had a robotic tone, nothing like the feminine voice of the Enforcer ship, or the one on his own cargo ship.

He tried a shorter version. "Alliance Standard."

"*Gondo net ponymat.*"

Local technology that didn't adhere to Alliance protocols. He'd have to memorize the sequence. That was safer anyway—no one else could find it. He ran the sequence over in his mind several times, then touched a forward arrow on the desk module to restart Tess's message. He would need to get someone to help set it up for Alliance Standard commands.

"*I hope everything is okay with you for the time being.*" Tess's image leaned forward. "*I'm following your case as well as I can. Nothing has been released to the public news media yet, so all I have is what's in the Enforcer database. According to our records, you are being evaluated at the Blaine Mental Health and Evaluation Center. Your trial is scheduled about three tennights from now—about one mooncycle on Gehren, I think.*

"*I hope you're sleeping all right. I worry about you. I know how difficult this must be. Try to stay calm and don't do anything stupid that will get you in more trouble. I will send you any information I can along the way.*

"*Dahv, I love you. Hold on to that. Stay strong.*"

Her features froze in place with the end of the message.

He sat, too stunned to move. The phrase "I love you" kept replaying in his head. She had never said that when they were on the ship. Maybe she didn't dare. Even though the guards were supposed to have activated a sound barrier, they might not have. She might have feared that they would hear.

I love you. No one had ever said that before. His parents, maybe, but he couldn't remember. Marlon Tave had treated him with love and kindness, but he never actually said it. Did he love Tess? How could he be sure? He didn't really know what love felt like. He loved Marlon, but more like a father. Wouldn't love for a woman feel different? He couldn't tell Tess he loved her if he wasn't sure, he couldn't risk hurting her. Would she expect him to say he loved her? Would she be hurt if he didn't?

He sat in the moonlit room, his heart pounding. It would be better if she just believed he didn't love her. She would be angry, or hurt for a while, but she would get over that. Besides, if he ended up in prison, she couldn't waste her life waiting for him. No, it was better if he just didn't tell her. Maybe he shouldn't respond to her at all. That idea sliced through his heart like a longknife. He wasn't sure he had the strength to do that.

He buried his face in his hands. The same arguments kept wrestling around in his mind over and over. He didn't want to hurt Tess, but the thought of not communicating with her terrified him. She was his lifeline, the only spot of hope that kept him going. He *needed* her. She knew that. That's why she had said she loved him, why she warned him not to do anything stupid. She really *did* know him. She must know he was thinking about trying to escape. He couldn't keep from communicating with her, but he would not tell her he loved her.

When he finally raised his head, the first glimmer of light was beginning to show on the horizon, painting the bottoms of a low-hanging bank of clouds a soft yellow. He went back and laid down, but there was no hope of getting any more sleep. He couldn't get Tess out of his head, or figure out how he would respond to her message.

The bedside clock read 7:42 when the buzzer at his door sounded. "Come in." He still didn't know if he could open his door from the inside. The door dissolved, activated from the outside. Ramon, the orderly he had met when he arrived, stood just outside.

"Are you ready for sunfare?"

He cocked his head. "Sunfare" was not an Alliance Standard term. "The morning meal I assume?"

"Oh, yeah, sorry, that's what we call it." He chuckled. Ramon always seemed to have a jovial air about him.

Dahvin was in no mood to be upbeat. "I'm ready, I guess. What are they serving this morning?"

"Eggs and fried purken strips. And of course they always have a selection of fruits and different kinds of rolls each day. Today they're having mita balls—a little ball of baked bread drizzled with sweet syrup." Ramon held up one hand and made a circle with his fingers, demonstrating the size of the rolls.

"I don't eat meat, so I'll pass on the eggs and purken strips. I'm guessing that's a meat, right?"

"Right. Comes from an animal called a purken, a fat little short-legged thing with almost no head and no tail. Basically looks like a round ball with puny legs and a lump on one end that passes for the head. They have eyes but can't see very well and don't hear very well either. Guess I need to direct you to some sites so you can learn a little about the plants and animals here."

"Except for the plants I'm likely to be eating, I don't plan to waste much time doing that. And I can usually sort out what to eat by look and smell."

"Suit yourself. If there's anything else you need help with, just ask. I'll help with anything I can."

"Actually, when we get back to the room, I could use some help figuring out how to get the computer set up for Alliance Standard."

"Oh, sure. No problem," Ramon said. "If you just say 'Alliance Standard' it will change everything to commands you recognize."

"I tried that with the little flexible plastic thing I found in the drawer, but it didn't work."

"Ah, sorry about that. I can get you one that uses Alliance. But the computer won't have any trouble converting."

"Thanks. I hadn't tried it on the computer yet. And, I have a question. Can I open the door to my room from the inside?"

Ramon shook his head. "No, sorry. For the time being you'll have to rely on one of us to come and escort you to and from the cafeteria and Dr. Blaine's office. You can also go into the lounge on this floor during certain times of the day, but you have to be accompanied."

"Is that because I'm charged with a crime?"

"Yes." Ramon nodded, then waggled his head from side to side as if he wasn't sure. "But also because you're an off-worlder, and we don't have any information on your race in our database. I think it's just a precaution at this point. When you talk to Dr. Blaine, if you can tell him what planet you're from and a little more about your race of people, that might help."

Great. Things would be staying the way they were, then. "I don't know what planet I'm from. I was kidnapped as a child and never returned. The Enforcers told me my racial profile isn't in their database, and I doubt if it appears in yours either."

"Kidnapped! Wow. I'm sorry to hear that. So, did your kidnappers raise you, or did you get rescued?"

"I didn't get rescued, I escaped eventually. And I wouldn't call what they did raising me. It's not a period I like to talk about."

Ramon raised his eyebrows and tilted his head, but didn't say another word. There were more people in the dining room this morning, so they apparently were not trying to keep him isolated. Three Gehrens sat at one table. One of the three looked like she might be female. A telltale bulge in the chest of her tunic indicated the presence of breasts. Dark gray hair, a few crons longer than her companions, covered her head with fine curly fuzz.

Another Gehren, a Rigan, and an individual of a species he couldn't identify sat together at a second table. Even seated, the Rigan was head-and-shoulders taller than the Gehren, with the bluish skin, artificially elongated earlobes and patterned haircut typical of his world. The third individual had a round head with eye stalks that bobbed when he spoke to his companions. The three had finished their meal, evidenced by small scraps left on their plates, and had started some sort of a game.

He decided to try the mita balls and a small, pale blue fruit. It had a sweet and tangy flavor. It might turn out to be one of his favorites here. He also went back for a second helping of the mita balls, which seemed to please the cook. She smiled broadly and gave him a slight bow, the only person to do him that courtesy so far.

After sunfare, Ramon brought one of the flexible plastic personal computers with a Standard symbol set and two outfits of lightweight tunics and pants.

"Will these work for you?" Ramon asked.

"These should be fine for the time being, thanks."

"Dr. Blaine will be meeting with you later today. Would you like to stay in the recreation area for a while? I could teach you one of the local chacca games."

"No, thanks. Dr. Blaine said I could use the computer for some research and entertainment sites. I think I'll check that out."

Ramon nodded, and they walked side-by-side back to the room. He watched carefully when the orderly stopped where the door would appear. Ramon waved his hand over the wall and the door opened. He wasn't holding a device that he could see, so maybe the orderlies were chipped.

He stepped into his room and waved to Ramon, who grinned and waved back as the door closed. When he thought the orderly was out of earshot, he replied to Tess's message.

"Tess, I can't tell you how wonderful it was to hear from you. But please do not waste your love on me. I don't think there is any chance of me getting out of this situation. I would..."

What should he say? He didn't want to sound too formal or uncaring, but he didn't want her to believe he could return her feelings. "...like to be able to communicate with you, but I don't want to make things difficult for you. The personnel at Blaine Mental Health and Evaluation Center have been very kind so far. I have a private room where no one is watching me, at least I don't think they are."

He clapped his hands in front of the tablet. He figured she knew that having some privacy was important for him.

"The technology here is very strange. They have doors that—" he paused, trying to figure out how to describe them, "—are invisible when they're closed and sort of dematerialize and then rematerialize. The window in my room works the same way, except I can set it so I can see out, or to allow air in from outside. It's too cold to do that for now, but I did try it once.

"I have met the doctor I will be working with. I can't say much about him yet. He seems fair and honest, but I've only talked with him once."

He hunched toward her artificial image. "I got your code and will send messages now and then, as I find out more about what is going to happen, if you want me to. But, Tess, please don't get too wrapped up in my affairs. There's no future for you with me."

He had to stop the recording after the last sentence and leave the console. He fought back tears, and he didn't want her to get any hint of his inner struggle. He walked over to the window and opened it for a blast of cold air. Taking several deep breaths, he choked down the emotions surging up from somewhere deep inside.

There was nothing more to say. He returned to the console, hit send, and closed down the display. He walked back over to the window and opened it to the air again. Leaning against the window with his forearms he buried his face against them, gasping short breaths from the cold and from the choking sensation in his throat. He stayed there until the freezing air numbed his arms and face, but he couldn't numb the agony in his heart.

Tess saw the message icon blinking the instant she walked back into her cabin. *Dahvin!* She ran to the console, not even taking time to change clothes. She studied his face in the image. He looked all right, his skin color was good, and he looked at ease. She tried to look past him to his surroundings, but couldn't see much except a wall with what looked like a small table.

"Please do not waste your love on me," his image said.

She tensed. Had she misread his feelings for her?

"Tess, please don't get too wrapped up in my affairs. There's no future for you with me."

She studied his face. It was harder to read him when he wasn't sitting right next to her. He seemed calm when he said the last sentence. Then she smiled. Of course, he was trying to protect her. Typical Dahv. She should have expected that. It only made her love him even more.

That last statement must have cost him so much. She leaned back in her chair and pictured him there. If she had any doubts about his feelings before, she was certain now. If he didn't love her and wanted her to leave him alone, he would have just said that. What he *did* say told her he was willing to let her go for her sake. That was love, the willingness to sacrifice his feelings to protect her.

"I'm as tough and determined as you are, my love. I will find a way." She grinned and the hot flush of triumph warmed her cheeks. "I promise."

CONNECTED
RECIEVING....
CHAPTER 15

Stohne arrived at his office early in the morning. He needed to have a talk with Daks Kittrend, who had inherited the title Dom and the reins as family patriarch since his father's death. It took half an hour for his automated cruiser to reach the walled mini-city of Firstcaste mansions. Simply called "The Estates" by locals, it had originally been built at the edge of the city, but with the growth of Durrand in all directions, it now sat almost dead center in the sprawling metropolis.

Energy-producing, uni-cellular protiki covered the buildings of the city's business and financial district. The streets were also covered with a durable plant, since cruisers had no need for wheels. As he neared The Estates, however, the glistening, pearlescent protiki and grass-covered roadways gave way to older paved streets and stone buildings.

The Kittrend homestead still incorporated about six city blocks in the center of The Estates, with expertly designed and maintained grounds. Too ostentatious for Stohne's taste. The gate to The Estates had opened automatically as Art's vehicle approached, but when he reached the Kittrend's grounds, he had to stop at a private gate and wait for a guard to let him in. A show of power since there was little need for such security in modern Durrand.

In spite of the police markings on his cruiser, the guard asked for his ID. He complied, and the guard scanned his ID across a com panel in his booth, then pressed his palm to it, opening the great carved metal gates. Stohne started through, then stopped as a question popped into his mind.

"Excuse me, does every vehicle that comes through the gate get logged in?"

"Yes, sir." A billed cap obscured the man's eyes. His dark gray tunic was accented with a red stripe down each sleeve and a patch with the Kittrend family crest at the top of the sleeve.

"And how about when they leave?"

"Logged out," said the guard.

"And what about as the Kittrends come and go?"

"Well, of course, I don't check their ID, but I *do* record when they leave and return."

"Have you always done it that way?"

"Well, for about the last four years or so, since some time before Dom-el Kittrend's death."

"And before that, no one logged vehicles?"

"Oh, we've always done that, since this gatehouse was built, some one hundred years ago. We just didn't keep track of the Dom's family."

"I see. Who changed that procedure, Dom-el Kittrend?"

"No sir. His son."

Odd for the son to have had that authority prior to his father's death. He drove on to the front door of the massive home. Well-pruned trees lined the drive, munchans that maintained their foliage year-round. They created an almost solid visual barrier between the driveway and the grounds. But here and there along the way he could catch a glimpse of a vast grassy expanse beyond. Rumor had it that the Kittrends had once kept quite a collection of exotic animals here, including a few from other planets.

He drove out of the treed lane and onto a circular drive, adorned with shrubs that flowered during the spring and summer. The driveway circled a fountain, turned off for the winter, with a stone statue of a mythical cariote, its mothy wings spread wide above its snarling, horned head and fish-like body.

He didn't see any specified visitor parking, so he stopped in front of the main door. There was no doorbell he could discern, but the door had a knocker with the same mythical beasthead. A single knock was quickly answered by one of the employees, who told him that Dom Kittrend expected him. He tried to quell a sense of intimidation, but he remained acutely aware of his own social position as he approached the planet's wealthiest and most influential man.

The employee led him to a spacious library, its walls lined with perhaps a thousand or more antique books encased in environmentally controlled shelves, the only thing in the whole estate that he envied. Daks Kittrend, Dom of the most powerful clan in Firstcaste, was seated in a huge antique-style over-stuffed chair, one of four surrounding a small table. He wore, not the typical tunic and pants of the working professionals, but a coral shirt with a high rounded collar and a dark red V-necked jacket. Both the shirt and jacket buttoned in the back, requiring the assistance of a servant. Kittrend did not speak, but motioned to another overstuffed chair near him. Stohne hated those chairs.

"Good day to you, Dom Kittrend." He said, executing an obligatory bow.

"Good day to you, Master Ombudsman. What can I do for you today?"

"I am sorry to remind you of a tender issue, but someone has been arrested in the death of your father." Stohne watched for Kittrend's reaction to the news.

Kittrend nodded, but showed no other emotion. "I was aware of that. I assumed your visit was related to his arrest."

"The Superior of the Ministry of Security and Public Assistance had told me you had not yet been informed."

"I am hardly reliant on MSAPA for such information. I was advised a tennight ago by business contacts in the Alliance Enforcer Corps that an arrest had been made."

"I see. My apology for an erroneous assumption." It took conscious effort to hide his irritation. So much for having the upper hand. He should have known better.

The door to the library opened and Dom Kittrend's sister Amalya flowed into the room. Firstcaste women never seemed to walk. They had a practiced carriage that made them seem to float. She wore a floor-length flowered skirt that swirled around her ankles as she moved. Her hip-length blouse puffed at the shoulder and tapered to her delicate wrists.

Firstcaste women were raised to be feminine perfection, and Doma Kittrend was first among the first. She was, indeed, the perfect woman. She was a few years younger than her brother, in her late twenties, but she could have been eighty and Stohne figured she wouldn't have looked much different. Her platinum curls cascaded onto her shoulders, framing her porcelain face. She was far out of his league, but he lost his heart all the same.

Stohne bowed, lower than he had for her brother. "Good day, Doma Kittrend." He did not rise until she responded.

"Good day Master Ombudsman." Her voice flowed in musical tones. "Would you care for tea?" A servant bearing a pearlescent tray with an antique ceramic teapot painted in delicate soaring birds and winding vines followed at her heels. Three matching cups completed the ensemble. He straightened from his bow as she took a seat in one of the overstuffed chairs. The servant poured the first cup of tea and handed it to Amalya, who balanced it artfully just above her lap.

"Sister, this discussion is perhaps not for your ears."

"This is in regard to the investigation into father's death, is it not?"

Dom Kittrend frowned. "I am sorry, I did not know you had been made aware of recent developments." He seemed to almost admonish his sister for her upstart response.

"I also have my sources. We women do love to talk among ourselves." She tossed a hint of a sly smile at Stohne.

It provided the opening he needed to proceed. "Alliance Enforcers have arrested a man who had the genetic imprint found on the weapon alleged to have been used in your father's death." As he spoke, he took a seat in the chair Dom Kittrend had designated earlier. "He was found on a distant planet beyond Alliance territory. He is very young, about seventeen years of age now."

"That can't be!" The Doma's hand trembled just enough to splash a drop of tea onto her skirt. With a quick dab of her napkin, she tried to disguise the loss of composure. In an instant she appeared as poised as ever, but Stohne could sense an internal struggle to maintain the façade.

Dom Kittrend directed a stern glance at his sister and touched his hand to his mouth. "That is somewhat of a surprise. That would mean he was just a child when Father was murdered. Still, experience has taught us that off-worlders do not share Gehren's civilized discipline." His tone remained cold and unreadable.

"He does match the DNA trace that our investigator picked up off the weapon. We have already checked that."

Doma Kittrend gave her brother a stricken look.

"I don't know what we could tell you that would be of any help." He did not return his sister's look, instead maintaining eye contact with Stohne.

"Well, for one thing, do you have any idea what your father would have been doing in the part of town where he was found? Was there any indication that he might have been kidnapped prior to his death?"

The Doma started to open her mouth. Her brother shot her a harsh look, and jerked his head a little sideways toward the door.

"Ah, forgive me," she stammered. "I believe I have some business to attend to in my study. If you don't need me specifically, perhaps my brother could answer your questions."

"Actually, if you could spare a little more time, I would appreciate both of you being present. I never know when one person might remember a detail that the other one doesn't."

"Of course, my sister and I both will do whatever we can to cooperate with your investigation."

If it was possible for a tone of voice to freeze the air, Dom Kittrend had just succeeded. Stohne had no doubt he had wanted his sister out of the room. And him, too, for that matter.

"Your father was found early in the morning, about eighth hour, as the shops were opening up. Do you know where your father was the day before he was found, or in the pre-dawn hours that day?"

"No. My father always started his day very early, often at work before the rest of the family had sunfare. It was not my place to keep track of his actions. I served as a senior officer in the company at that time, but my father had not been expected to retire for many years yet."

"So you don't remember anything about his whereabouts that morning or the previous day."

"I did not know where he was at any given time."

"Would any of his employees have known his whereabouts? Did he have a regular routine?"

"I don't know if any of them would have known where he was that early in the morning. He spent the early morning hours alone studying market reviews and other business documents before meeting with his business appointments."

"Would he have done that here or at an office?"

"Our offices are here on the grounds. It allows us a full range of options to provide for the comfort of our business associates without the bother and inconvenience of traveling to and from hotels and restaurants."

"I would like to speak with any of the employees who would have worked with him at that time, someone who would know his regular routines and possibly when and under what conditions he left the house that morning."

Dom Kittrend took a sip of his tea. "I'm afraid that would be impossible." Kittrend was losing patience with the questioning, and Stohne half expected to be summarily dismissed at any moment. "The only one that close to him would have been his personal assistant Lane Coutier, and he is no longer employed by us. Another company offered him a very lucrative position and he relocated to South Continent. I'm afraid I don't know the name of the company or the city. I'm sorry."

Of course he wouldn't. Or wouldn't divulge it. For someone who claimed he was willing to cooperate, Dom Kittrend was less than forthcoming. Or was Stohne just fishing for answers that didn't exist? "I presume if there had been some indication that your father had been taken away against his will, one of the employees would have noticed and said something to you?"

"As you may have noticed, all visitors have to check in at the gate, and we do keep a log of those who visit. Would you like to see the log for that date, if we can find it?"

Finally, a hint of cooperation. "Yes, please, and perhaps two or three moons leading up to it and one moon after, if possible. That would be very helpful."

Kittrend pushed a button on a small console on an end table next to his chair. "Edmund, contact the gate monitor and ask him where the visitor logs are kept. See if he can come up with the log for 1 Maritane 2864 through 50 Altan 2864."

"That would be three years ago, Dom Kittrend," a voice answered back.

"Yes, I know, but they keep the logs for a while. See what you can find. It is very important for Ombudsman Stohne. He's doing some follow-up investigation related to father's murder."

"Yes, Dom Kittrend, I'll see what I can come up with."

"That may take a little while, Master Stohne. In the meantime, is there anything else I can answer?"

Stohne shifted in his seat, feeling swallowed by the too-soft upholstery, and took a drink of tea, trying to sort out what he'd heard and what he needed to follow up on. "Back to a previous question, do you know of any reason your father would have been in Olde Towne where he was found?"

"It's hard to say. My father did like antiques, as you can see from this library. He also liked to collect bottles of vintage wines and other odd bits of antiquity. There may have been a shop there with something that had caught his interest."

That was logical enough. The shops in that part of town catered to off-world tourism, but there could have been a shop with unique pieces. Dom-el Kittrend might have made frequent trips to that part of town.

"Is there anything you can think of that seemed out of place, or out of the ordinary, either that day or the day before your father's death?"

"No, not really."

Doma Kittrend shot her brother a look that Stohne couldn't quite decipher. The Dom raised his nose another notch, but continued unabated. "We got the call from the police just as we were getting ready to sit down to sunfare. Of course everything after that was, as you can imagine, quite disruptive."

Tears welled up in Doma Kittrend's eyes. "It was horrible," she whispered in a choked voice. "To just find him lying in an alley in a place like that. So... so humiliating!"

For her or for him? "So you don't know of anything in that time period that seemed unusual?"

"No. As senior officer, I was already beginning to take on more responsibility in the company, preparing for eventual succession to my father. It was not unusual for him to come into the offices late, or not at all on some days. None of us would have thought anything of it if he had not shown up early that day, unless he had missed an important meeting, and we did not have any scheduled that day. I do remember that."

"How did your business associates react to the news of his death?"

"He was very well respected, both in business and politics, as you well know. Everyone was devastated."

"Did you have any problems stepping in as successor?"

"There were some quick adjustments that had to be made due to the suddenness of his death. As I said, we did not expect the succession to take place for many years. There were still some aspects of the business, relationships with particular associates, on which I was not yet well versed. But everyone was very cooperative. We made as smooth a transition as could be expected under the circumstances."

"You don't know of any business associates who would have a reason to hurry things along?"

Dom Kittrend took a deep breath. "I think I can honestly say all of our business associates would be offended by such a suggestion. As I said, he was deeply respected. That is nothing like being disliked."

Doubtful Kittrend could say the same for all of the Dom-el's political rivals. Stohne had watched the Doma out of the corner of his eye, but she now sat with her eyes lowered, offering no further reaction to her brother's responses. Back to the dutiful Firstcaste symbol.

"Did he have many business dealings with off-worlders? They don't always have the same values as we do."

"Not directly, as far as I know." Kittrend's tone seemed honest. "We have a division of the company that handles off-world trading, and the director of that division would be the one to handle those negotiations. As you noted, that requires someone with some expertise in the laws and customs of the planetary trading partners."

A ping from the console next to Kittrend alerted him that someone was trying to contact him. He pressed a button.

"Edmund here. We did find the log you requested, Dom Kittrend."

"Thank you, Edmund. Please thank the gate monitor for me as well. Bring the log disk up here to the library, please."

A few minutes later an employee in a dull brown labor uniform appeared, bowing to Daks and Amalya as he entered the room. Kittrend motioned to Stohne, and the employee handed him the small, flexible-plastic recording, bowing again.

"Thank you, I'll look over this a little later, if that's all right with you. Would you mind if I keep it for a day or so? Would you like it copied before I go?"

"You are welcome to it." Kittrend gave a dismissive wave.

"Thank you. One last thing, do you remember any meetings or activities that may have involved your father the day before his death?"

"Hmm. If I remember correctly, we did have a business meeting with some representatives from Emdac, but my father did not participate in that meeting. It was a routine planning meeting that I handled. As I mentioned, he had begun to pull back from the business a little, and would have only attended the important sessions. The rest I was expected to handle."

"All right. Thank you both for your time. I am sorry to have to raise these issues with you again. I hope I haven't upset you too much, Doma Kittrend."

"It's all right." Dom Kittrend cut off any response from his sister. "We understand you have to be thorough in your investigation. As I said, we will do whatever we can to cooperate."

Stohne wasted no time reviewing the Kittrends' visitor logs that same afternoon. On the day prior to Maxillian Kittrend's death, an entry showed two vehicles arriving at the estate, both identified as carrying representatives of Emdac. The log also noted the coming and going of family members by vehicle ID. Doma Kittrend had left the property the morning of the meeting, and had not returned until early evening. Her brother had not left the estate.

On the day that the former patriarch was discovered, there were no log entries prior to eight in the morning. None—not even for the patriarch himself. Nor was there an entry for him the previous day. Odd. When and how did he leave? Did he have a private back way out? After about nine in the morning the day of Maxillian Kittrend's death, there was a predictable flood of visitors, including three separate visits by police officers, the coroner, and two other visitors whose names he recognized as close acquaintances of the Kittrend family. All reasonable entries given the circumstances of the day.

He checked entries for several days prior to Maxillian Kittrend's death. It seemed Amalya Kittrend went out almost daily. Her brother, on the other hand, rarely left the estate and then usually in the company of business associates. A fairly constant stream of visitors came to the estate, many of whose names he recognized as prominent Gehren business people. None of the names seemed to suggest visits by off-worlders.

The one name conspicuously absent was the deceased patriarch's. Where had he been? Perhaps, as had occurred to him earlier, he'd had a private back way out. Or perhaps, he'd had another apartment somewhere with a mistress? That would be something the family might have reason to hide. But the suspect DNA was an off-world male, so a mistress would have had little bearing on his case.

If there was something strikingly odd about the case, Stohne wasn't finding it. Perhaps Dr. Blaine would have more luck investigating the case from his work with the alleged suspect. It was getting late, and he needed to meet with the young off-worlder.

CHAPTER 16

Late on the second day after his arrival, Dahvin heard the slight buzz signaling someone was at his door. Orderlies had escorted him to morning, midday, and evening meals, always when there were only a few other people in the dining room. The rest of the time the staff left him alone. If it was supposed to be some sort of solitary confinement, or intended to make him uncomfortable and more willing to communicate, it was lost on a man who had spent most of the last year-and-a-half totally alone on a one-man spacecraft.

"*Misyer Tave, Dr. Blaine would like to meet with you. May I enter?*"

He recognized Ramon's voice over the intercom, polite as always.

"Come in." The door opened and Ramon stepped in and to the side to allow Dahvin to walk out ahead of him. At least they didn't force him to wear any physical restraints.

They walked side by side to Dr. Blaine's office. Dahvin kept a keen eye out for anything that would tell him how the doors opened, but still couldn't find a key. After Ramon announced their arrival, the door to the doctor's office opened. He couldn't spot any action by Ramon triggering it.

Another man sat in one of the chairs in front of Blaine's desk. He swiveled around and stood up as Dahvin entered the office, but did not bow. Though

Dahvin wouldn't bow to anyone, it rankled him that the professionals on this planet did not consider him worthy of the same courtesy. They'd already decided he was scum.

Blaine introduced him as Art Stohne, the ombudsman who had been assigned to his case.

The newcomer was taller and slimmer than either Blaine or Ramon, more official-looking, with the same gray hair and eyes as everyone else he had met. He wore a dark gray tunic with a high collar and matching pants. A thin red stripe ran from the left side of a plain black belt up to an imprint of a blazing sun on the left shoulder, then down the back. Blaine and the other Center staff all wore a somewhat similar style of white tunic. The tunic colors and insignia must have designated individuals' respective professions.

Stohne leaned back in his chair. "What I will attempt to uncover is whether a crime was indeed committed causing his death, and if so, by whom. If a crime was committed, and it appears you committed it, I can also present additional information regarding your mental state at the time and any other mitigating factors, such as the possibility of self-defense." Stohne sat straight, but relaxed, his slender hands folded across his belt. The body language gave Dahvin little clue as to the man's true character or intentions. "Dr. Blaine will be working with you to develop a complete and detailed psychological profile, which will be admitted as evidence. The judge makes the final decision. There is also an appeal process, if necessary. Do you have any questions about the procedures?"

"What if I'm found innocent?"

"Then you will be released."

"That will work out very well, since my ship is several tennights' travel from here, and may have already been sold to pay docking fees. That was my home and my livelihood."

Stohne's eyebrows shifted upward a tiny bit. "I see. The Alliance Enforcers should have taken care of that. Perhaps they have impounded your ship."

Dahvin shrugged. "If so, no one told me, and I don't have any of my personal belongings off the ship. How am I supposed to defend myself if I'm not allowed to prove where I've been?"

"Dr. Blaine mentioned to me that there would be logs aboard your ship. I will send a message to the authorities on Mira requesting that your logs be obtained and forwarded to us as soon as possible."

Stohne stood up and motioned for Dahvin to follow. The two men stood and eyed each other for a moment, each one trying to read the other. Stohne was harder for him to read than Blaine had been. While the ombudsman spoke with a straightforward manner, he was more reserved than Blaine, and Dahvin did not totally trust him. Stohne seemed to be trying to figure out the same about him.

Stohne showed him into a small meeting room that opened off of Blaine's office, furnished with soft comfortable chairs separated by a square table. The floor had the same spongy feel as the rest of the center, except that in this room it had a fuzzy texture. One wall had a picture of the city and the crescent-shaped bay. It was flat, but looked three-dimensional. The opposite wall had a metal sculpture of a bird with a long neck and wide, outstretched wings.

Stohne pulled out one of the small chairs and left it for Dahvin to sit down. Then he took a seat on the opposite side of the table. As he settled into his chair, Stohne pressed a small gold square in the center of his left palm. A recording device? "Let's talk about where you would have been three Standard years ago, what you would identify as ASD 2.16.5416."

Dahvin recognized the Alliance Standard date of Kittrend's death, but without his ship's logs and some frame of reference, it was difficult to know how to answer the question. It was too close to the time that he had escaped the Pruzzians and first stumbled onto Marlon Tave's ship.

"It's hard to remember where I was on an exact date three years ago. I have spent the past three years hauling cargo on The Fringe. At that time I would probably have been flying with Marlon Tave. I learned my trade from him."

"And where were you prior to that?"

He held his breath, striving to maintain an air of calm indifference. Stohne eyed him keenly. "What difference would that make?"

"Just trying to figure out where you were at what time, in relation to the incident I'm investigating."

He noticed the ombudsman's carefully chosen words, avoiding the term "crime."

"That's easy enough. I've never been to this planet in my life. Never even heard of it until the Enforcers assaulted me without provocation and hauled me halfway across the galactic arm for a crime I couldn't possibly have committed!" He would have to watch himself. He was losing his cool too easily.

Stohne looked him in the eye for a moment, then waved one finger over the square in his palm. An opaque holographic square appeared in the air above it and Stohne's fingers flew across it. "We have a DNA match that links you to the scene of the death of a local resident," he said, without looking up.

"So I've been told."

"How do you think it ended up on Gehren, if you've never been here?"

"How much do you know about doing business on The Fringe? Just about everybody out there has made an enemy somewhere. I'm guessing the DNA was planted."

"Seems like a lot of trouble," Stohne said, still with that same unemotional tone, "to plant evidence that far away."

"Don't ask me, you're the investigator." He shivered, though he could feel sweat beading on his forehead. He dug his nails into his palms. Deep breath. Keep cool.

"All right. Well, it seems it would be best to see if we can obtain your logs, and then perhaps we can get some more definitive answers."

Stohne rose, motioning toward the door for Dahvin to precede him. Blaine had left his office, but Ramon waited just outside in the hall, and escorted him back to his room. Dahvin didn't get a chance to see Stohne leave the building. He still didn't know how to activate these damned doors.

—

Stohne left the Blaine Center with a rock in the pit of his stomach. This was going to be one of those cases that wasn't quite what it seemed. Over the years, he had learned to trust his instincts. Not something an objective professional should do perhaps, but once he had learned not to ignore them, they served him well. Facts didn't lie, though sometimes they could lead to the wrong conclusion.

The facts in this case seemed straightforward. Maxillian Kittrend had been found murdered in a Durrand alley. The murder weapon was lying next to the body, and only Kittrend's and the off-worlder Dahvin Tave's DNA had been found on the weapon. Tave's responses to his questions had been defensive and a little testy. Stohne would have expected him to be more cooperative and eager to answer if he was innocent.

Still, something nagged at him. The facts seemed a little too straightforward. What was Kittrend doing in that alley, a far distance from the high-society areas he would have been likely to frequent? The shops in that section dealt in odd bits of junk and souvenirs designed to appeal to off-world tourists. There were better places to find high-end wares. And what about the way Kittrend had been dressed in the photos he'd seen? Not the clothes the planet's most wealthy and powerful man would wear. Did the man enjoy getting out and seeing how the lower castes lived? That was difficult to believe.

He'd found no indication Kittrend had been kidnapped. No signs of a struggle, according to the police report. In fact, the position of the body indicated no struggle at all. As the investigator had described it, "It looked like he just laid down and went to sleep and woke up dead."

He still had time to drop by the coroner's office. Perhaps there were details not included in the autopsy that would lead in another direction. He covered the short distance between the Blaine Center and MSAPA headquarters in just a few minutes. The coroner's office was on the lower level. MSAPA was a five-hundred-year-old stone building close to the bay and the spaceport. This part of town included a mix of centuries-old stone buildings and newer flexkrome buildings that had replaced wood structures. Though not as colorful as natural protiki, flexkrome was beautiful. Iridescent pastels shifted in color as he drove past and the light struck them from different angles. But the old stone monoliths, with their ornate carvings over doors, windows, and on the parapets, held a special place in his heart. Thankfully the governing council had the foresight to acknowledge their historic value.

When he reached headquarters, he bypassed the elevator and trotted down the stairs. Master Coroner Keem Dorton wasn't in his office, so he poked his head through a back door into the examining room to look for him. A row of super-cooled cadaver storage units lined the right wall, and three examining tables sat in the center of the room. Sinks and storage cabinets lined the back wall.

Dorton, a short, stocky man with a bushy mustache, his head sprinkled with the white hairs of advancing age, was overseeing his young apprentice as he worked on a female cadaver. Orange blood spatters covered the white aprons they wore over MSAPA's gray tunics.

The profession held no attraction for Art.

"Good day to you, Master Coroner."

"Good day, Master Ombudsman. What brings you down here today?"

Dorton pulled off the bloody apron and motioned toward his office as he headed in that direction himself.

"Continue as you are, Misyer Marks," Dorton said over his shoulder to the young man.

"I need to talk to you about Dom-el Kittrend's murder case. I read the autopsy report. I wondered if there were any minor details that didn't seem pertinent at the time that might help me with it."

Dorton held the door to the office open and allowed Stohne to precede him. The office was downright dingy, the furnishings indicative of Dorton's dedication to his work, not budget constraints. Dorton pulled out a dilapidated office chair, and motioned to a solid plastic one on the other side.

Old-style filing cabinets lined the wall, the only other furnishings in the office. The Master Coroner insisted on parchment backups of all documents. The extent of the paper filings was startling. Stohne had known the man long enough to accept his eccentricities. Not many midcaste men could grow a mustache like Dorton's. Some nethercaste heritage? That might also explain his penchant for poor decor.

Dorton landed heavily in the old chair, which squealed a protest. "All the details would have been in the report, minor or otherwise. I doubt I could tell you anything else."

"I did not mean to question your thoroughness, of course, Master Dorton." Stohne slid into the plastic chair, testing its sturdiness. "I thought perhaps you might have noticed something about his clothing, or something else that would not ordinarily be included in a coroner's report."

"Nothing notable, or it would have been mentioned."

Dorton was indeed a consummate professional. He would not be the Master Coroner otherwise. Nonetheless, the man's answers seemed a bit too quick and defensive. The Coroner was always a quiet and reserved man, and seemed to prefer the isolation and autonomy of his job. But Stohne had expected him to be a little more forthcoming.

"Did your apprentice assist in the autopsy?"

"No, I performed that one alone."

"That's a bit unusual, isn't it, especially with someone of such importance?"

"He had other business I needed him to attend to, and I thought it best for the family if as few eyes as possible viewed the body." Dorton leaned forward and rested his elbows on the desk, eliciting another squeak from his chair. He looked down at his folded hands.

Avoiding eye contact. "Yes, of course. I'm certain they appreciated your discretion. I am curious as to why Dom-el Kittrend might have been in the part of town where his body was found. I assume you agree with the police report that there was no indication of a struggle, or of him being drugged, or taken to that area against his will?"

"I can not tell from an autopsy what a man's interests or intentions might be. As for signs of a struggle or drugs, I would have noted it in my report if anything like that had been apparent."

"Yes, of course."

The young apprentice entered the office. Stohne looked him over with a subtle, practiced glance. About twenty-four years old, the man had a slight build, angular facial features, and stood half a head taller than Dorton, with quick, almost furtive movements. Stohne clamped his teeth together, suppressing a smile as it occurred to him that the assistant resembled a rodent.

"Excuse me, Master Coroner, I need to get some forms from the filing drawers."

Dorton nodded at the young man but did not speak to him. The apprentice edged over to a cabinet and began sorting through one of the drawers.

"What kind of clothes did he have on, a suit or something more casual?" He was fishing, and Dorton was rapidly becoming the fish.

"More casual, I would say. As I recall, he had on a white shirt, brown slacks and a matching sweater. I believe that information was in the report."

"Ah, yes, I remember. Anything in his pockets that might indicate whether he had been shopping in that part of town?"

"No, his pockets were empty."

"Doesn't that seem odd for the Firstcaste patriarch? Wouldn't you expect him to be carrying at least a wallet, or some identification, perhaps a purchase-card?"

"It's not up to me to decide what's strange for a man like Dom-el Kittrend, except as to his physical condition in death. I don't speculate on a person's personal habits."

Out of the corner of his eye he caught the apprentice watching them keenly. The man still shuffled papers in the drawer, but he didn't seem to be paying attention to what he was doing.

"I'm trying to determine why Dom-el Kittrend might have been in that part of town, whether he was there of his own volition."

"You'd have to ask his family about that."

"So you didn't notice anything unusual, and it seemed to you that he was in fact killed by another person?"

"As I stated in my report."

It was interesting that Dorton seemed to remember so clearly what he had written in a report three years ago, even if it was a high profile case. It seemed he wouldn't glean anything new from the Master Coroner. The young apprentice kept looking for a form he should have had no trouble finding. Surprising that the Master Coroner hadn't noticed the young man eavesdropping.

Nothing the coroner had said conflicted with the police report he had read. How did a murdered man end up lying flat on his back, with his hands folded over his chest? From the simulation he had run, the most probable scenario was that the body had been posed after death. Why? If the murderer had wanted it to look like a suicide, he or she would have placed the laser in the dead man's hands.

Why did Dorton seem so defensive? In all the time he'd worked with the man, he'd always been professional, courteous, and honest. Today he'd seemed more like a man with something to hide.

And what about the apprentice's suspicious behavior? Did he in fact know something about the autopsy in spite of what Dorton had said?

None of it made much sense, and again his instincts hinted things were not as they seemed.

CHAPTER 17

Dahvin hadn't seen Blaine for the past two days. Ramon had told him the doctor was out of town taking care of another patient. During the interim, he'd spent the time researching everything he could think of relevant to his case, though he already knew most of it. Gehren did not have a death penalty, but it did impose mandatory "lifelong monitoring" of persons convicted of murder. In most cases, those accused of crimes were remanded for rehabilitative therapy. The Blaine Evaluation and Mental Health Center headed the list of facilities providing that type of therapy. That explained the security measures he'd experienced.

Only in severe cases, where the criminal was considered unwilling to cooperate with therapy, or was beyond rehabilitation for some other reason, was the convict sent to a prison. So maybe he'd be sent back to the Blaine Center after the trial. Though it wouldn't be a prison, it wouldn't be freedom either.

A sigh welled up from deep within. He would have no more control over his life and his movements than he did now. And he wouldn't have the opportunity to earn a living.

He studied the layout of the city of Durrand. In the financial district the streets were neatly laid out in squares, with streets numbered in sequence. In the parts of the city along the bay and near the spaceport, however, several parks scattered around interrupted the flow of the streets. Many of the streets had names instead of numbers, and without a better knowledge of the Gehren language, he had no hope of working out any pattern to the names. The Blaine Center was on the north side of Durrand, and the spaceport was on the west side, kens apart. In winter conditions and without adequate clothing, he would have to move fast to cover the distance before hypothermia set in. His chances of getting someone to pick him up when he looked like an off-worlder, didn't speak the language, and was dressed in mental hospital garb, were slim to none.

His best bet seemed to be to try and escape from the courthouse, located much closer to the spaceport. That cut his time frame dangerously close, however. He wouldn't be at the courthouse until the trial started. He hated the thought of leaving his safety to chance. He'd prefer to have a plan, but a reasonable plan eluded him.

He looked out the window. The sun was well up and his stomach told him it was time for sunfare. Ramon usually showed up earlier than this to take him to the dining room.

As if on cue, the buzzer at his door sounded. Ramon's always-cheery voice rang through the com. *"Hey, Dahv, sorry I'm late. Had to show a new patient around. Are you ready for sunfare?"*

"Definitely."

The door opened. Ramon stood waiting, a big grin on his face.

"Is Dr. Blaine back yet?"

"Yes. He got in late last night. He told me this morning that he wants to see you after you eat."

Dahvin nodded. He would have preferred to avoid Blaine for a while longer.

Ramon didn't stay to eat with him as he sometimes did. He excused himself saying that he had a chore to attend to. The orderly returned as Dahvin finished and escorted him to Blaine's office.

Ramon waved his hand in front of the door and it disappeared, showing Blaine seated at his desk. He snuck a peek at Ramon's hand, but he wasn't holding any kind of device. If the door was heat-sensing, it would open for anyone, yet thus far it seemed only the staff could control the openings. He hadn't yet dared to ask again how they did that, but he was beginning to suspect the staff had control chips implanted in their hands. Or maybe the doors were programmed to the staffs' DNA.

Ramon waited outside the door, leaving him to enter alone.

"Dahvin, please sit down." Blaine waved toward the chair in front of his desk.

"You can just call me Dahv."

"All right. I wanted to talk to you a little more about your life as a whole, who you are, where you are from."

He would have done almost anything to get out of this conversation. He glanced behind him, but the door had already closed.

"Is that really necessary? It basically boils down to whether or not I was here when your man was murdered. I wasn't here, and I'm pretty sure I can prove that eventually, so why bother with a life history?"

Blaine sat in silence for a moment, and Dahvin could feel the older man studying him. Trying to read body language? He folded his arms across his chest.

"It may not be quite that simple." Blaine stroked his chin. "I have received your ship's logs. The trouble is, the section of the logs that includes you begins on the day that Dom-el Kittrend was murdered. And, it begins here on Gehren."

Blaine could have pulled the chair out from under him and he probably would not have moved. He sat frozen in place by Blaine's words. It took several moments for him to recover enough to begin to think defensively. Could Blaine be lying?

"Show me the log."

"I thought you might ask to see it. I have it cued up on the console here in my side room."

Blaine stood up and motioned toward the door at the side of his desk. Dahvin preceded Blaine into the same small room where Stohne had interviewed him the day after he'd arrived. A small square module similar to the one in his room was set up on the table in the center of the room.

"I'll let you look at it alone, if you wish," Blaine offered. "Take as much time as you need to review it."

He sat down at the table and pressed an arrow at the bottom of the module to begin the replay of the log. He'd never seen Marlon Tave's logs from the time when he had first entered the ship. He had never wanted to revisit that time. Marlon had cared for him, educated him, become a father to him. Eventually, he had taken Marlon's last name.

The log recording was cued up to ASD 2.16.5416—the same Alliance Standard date Kittrend's murder had been reported. Marlon described finding a young boy passed out in the cargo bay just after his ship had left the planet.

"*The boy was unconscious when I found him. He doesn't have any ID on him that I can find. No electronic chip I can detect. I've moved him to the medbay.*"

The audio sent a shiver down his back. It was so strange to hear Marlon's voice again. His heart skipped a beat. If it had been a video log, he could have seen his face one more time.

"*The medibot reports his wounds are partially healed, but badly infected. The boy has multiple long lesions on his back, chest, abdomen and ribs, as well some on his arms and legs. He also has deep hematomas, especially on his back and buttocks. There are tears and scarring in and around the rectum. He had cuts on his feet, and the medibot found and removed bits of broken glass from his feet. The bot reported some older internal injuries that are already healed over and do not require immediate attention. The boy was also emaciated and dehydrated.*"

Dahvin dug his fingers into the sides of the chair. Marlon's voice trembled with emotion. What had he been feeling? Anger? Sympathy.

The log continued uninterrupted. "*The injuries to the boy's feet occurred during the tennight or so before he showed up in the cargo hold. The most recent of the wounds to his torso were apparently inflicted approximately four Alliance Standard tennights prior to showing up on the ship. The bot's analysis indicates that wounds were inflicted continually over the past several years, the oldest ones having scarred over and more recent ones in progressive stages of healing. The bot is administering antibiotics and nutritional supplements and has placed him in a deep recuperative sleep. I don't expect him to wake for at least a couple of days.*"

Marlon had added daily descriptions of Dahvin's progress to his log. He had regained consciousness two days after Marlon found him on the ship.

The entry for that day said Marlon had asked him his name, but he hadn't responded. He had a vague recollection of the first time he saw Marlon's kind, caring eyes, and of struggling to remember a name he had not been allowed to speak for over eight years.

Dahvin doubled over in the chair, his arms folded across his abdomen, struggling to hold insides that felt like they would explode out through his skin. Deep sobs shook his entire body.

He didn't know Blaine had entered the room until he felt a hand on his shoulder. He tried to stifle his tears, but his breath still came in jagged gasps.

"I'm sorry, but this was necessary. We have a great deal to talk about." Blaine's voice was quiet and gentle.

He fought to catch his breath and clear his mind. Could they have fabricated anything that accurately? Could they have tampered with the date on the log? But it was so seamless and accurate. He hadn't known what planet he was on when he stumbled onto Marlon's ship. Was it possible he had been here?

"Do you want to review more of the logs now?" Blaine asked.

He shook his head no.

"Then come back into my office. I want to ask some questions."

"Not now," he whispered. His whole body shook.

"I'm afraid I must insist." Blaine said, his voice assertive but quiet, not forceful.

Dahvin needed time to gather his thoughts, time to plan what he would say. He had to be able to think defensively. Clearly, the doctor had no intention of allowing him to do that. Blaine pulled his chair back slightly and nudged him by the shoulder just enough to get him to stand up. Then he guided him back through the door to his office.

He landed like lead in the chair across from Blaine's desk and waited for the first question. He stared at the floor, afraid to look up. Blaine's eyes, practiced at getting to know—maybe even *manipulating*—patients, studied him, trying to discover how best to pry into him. More than ever before, he resented Blaine. Years of his own life had been spent disguising his true feelings, concealing pain and fear. Since losing Marlon, he had even learned a few tricks of his own for manipulating others. But he was no match for this man.

"Dahv, I am most concerned with how you received the injuries that were described in the logs. I knew from the Enforcer ship's medical records that Dr. Bruin had noted severe external and internal scarring."

He sat in silence, digging the nails of his right hand into his left palm, struggling to hold on to some measure of composure. He did not want to discuss the brutality of the Pruzzians. It was none of their business. It had nothing to do with what they really wanted to know.

"What you really want to know is whether I murdered Dom Kittrend." He stared at his knees, still unable to look at Blaine. "I did not. That's all we need to talk about." In spite of his best efforts, his voice was still little more than a choked whisper.

"No, that is not all that we need to talk about." Same even tone, insistent, but gentle at the same time. "I am a physician. I deal primarily with mental illness, but I am a physician first and foremost. You may have been brought here for a mental evaluation related to an investigation, but you are my patient now. No one can suffer the injuries you did and not be mentally injured, as well."

Blaine leaned back in his chair.

"Physical injuries are sometimes much easier to heal than the emotional injuries that result from them. I do not believe the type of injuries described in Marlon Tave's logs could have been accidental. I want to know who did that to you."

"It doesn't matter, honestly. It wasn't here." It was so cold. Why couldn't they raise the temperature just a little?

"Dahv, answer me. Did Dom Kittrend, or any member of his family, have anything to do with the injuries you suffered?"

Ah, so that was it. That would have been an easy out, indeed. He could have claimed self-defense. For a moment he considered lying about it. Kittrend attacked him, he fought back, the laser discharged.

That wasn't believable, even to Dahvin.

"I never even knew Dom Kittrend. If I was ever here, it was only for a short time, before I found my way onto Marlon Tave's ship." He faltered. How do you describe a horror that no civilized being could conceive? "I was... a long way from here. A prisoner."

"A prisoner? Of whom?"

Blaine was not going to release him from this hell. He had no alternative but to turn and walk into it. He took a deep, shuddering breath, dug his nails in deeper, and looked up, though his eyes only made it as far as Blaine's desk.

"Pruzzians. The creatures... weren't human. Not even like some of the weird human-animal hybrids that have developed on some planets. These were pure, I don't know, more like pure reptiles. They walked upright, but they balanced on their back legs and short powerful tails. And they were scaly all over with reptilian eyes and heads. They just weren't human."

If Blaine was shocked, he did an admirable job of concealing it. Was he familiar with the Pruzzians?

"Please tell me as much as you can about your captivity."

"I was taken from my home when I was about six. I think we were at war with them. I couldn't really understand what was happening, but I remember a sense of danger. My father only allowed me to go outside our home at certain times. I heard huge explosions sometimes near where we lived and in the main part of the city. I had to quit going to school. My father sometimes gave me papers to take to someone else's house. I think they were messages. My father said adults couldn't go–it was safer for a child. I guess not safe enough, because they took me."

He had to stop and force himself to inhale. It was so cold in here.

"How did they take you, Dahv?"

"I don't know. A flash of white light surrounded me, and then I was on their ship. I never saw my home again."

"What did they do with you on their ship?"

"They used the children to do simple jobs, like cleaning things. We also were tied to a chair in front of a console for long periods of time. We were just supposed to watch the lights on the console. If the lights changed, we were supposed to call them."

"And the beatings?"

Deep chills shook his whole body. "They punished us. For the least little thing. Sometimes just because we spoke. Sometimes because they would say something in their language that we didn't understand, and when we didn't do what they wanted, they would beat us. Some of them tortured us just for fun. We were kicked, whipped, beaten with sticks, whatever suited them at the moment. And they used this stick, or rod thing, that shot out a blue streak. The pain was—" his breath caught in his throat, "—overwhelming. It would just flatten you. You couldn't move. One of their favorite toys."

"Dahv, there were other injuries, internal injuries."

"No! There is no point in going into any more of it! It has nothing to do with what you're investigating. I almost wish it did. I wish I could use it as an excuse. But it didn't. I never knew any Dom Kittrend. Why can't you just accept that?"

"I may not have all the pieces put together yet, but you were here on Gehren when the murder took place, and the investigator found your DNA on the murder weapon. How that came about I have yet to uncover."

Blaine leaned forward and folded his hands on his desk. Dahvin chanced a quick peek at the old man's face. He had developed a skill for reading others' faces, even aliens he'd just met. In Blaine's face he saw concern, compassion even. He wished he could ignore that. Any excuse not to cooperate.

"For now," said Blaine, "let's try something less traumatic. I saw later in the logs, Marlon Tave became very important to you, didn't he?"

"Yes. He was the closest thing to a father that I had. I barely remember my real father."

"And he died suddenly, about a year and a half ago?"

He closed his eyes hard, trying to stem the rush of tears that threatened to engulf him. Grief. Overwhelming grief. That was what had driven him to tears earlier. Not the fear, or the pain, but losing Marlon. The dark mass within him that he had held at bay for the last year-and-a-half threatened to swallow him. He had become so practiced at suppressing it he'd almost convinced himself he'd conquered it. But it was there, just below the surface, now threatening to break out and destroy him.

He took a deep breath, fighting to hide his internal struggle.

"It's all right Dahv, take your time. It takes a long time to recover from the loss of someone important to you. In your case, this man was clearly more than just a father to you."

He nodded. The term "savior" was used in many cultures to define a being, usually supernatural, always historical and not physically present. But his savior had been real, present, and very, very personal. The loss was excruciating.

Blaine waited patiently while he regained composure.

"Dahv, how did you escape?"

He tried hard to remember. "I'm not completely sure. I was in pretty bad shape by then, close to death. We were supposed to load some crates onto a Rakshi ship. I was too weak at that point to move the crates, but the Pruzzian crewman just kept whipping me. I don't remember much except that at some point I realized I was on a different ship, behind some crates. I think I must have collapsed on the Rakshi ship while we were loading. I actually never knew whose ship I was on, but since we were loading a Rakshi ship, I assume that's where I was."

"What happened there?"

"I just stayed there, I guess, until… we landed somewhere. Then I got off. I remember that I ran, but I don't think I could have gone very far. I hid in a dark place. That's about as much as I can remember. Like I said, I was in pretty bad shape."

"Do you remember boarding Marlon Tave's ship?"

"No. I don't remember much of anything before just being there and him taking care of me. A lot of what happened in that time period is just a blank, sort of. There are gaps."

Blaine sat in silence for perhaps a full minute. Dahvin could imagine him trying to sort out whether he was hearing the truth. Who would believe such insanity? He kept his head down, still avoiding the man's face. Those eyes looked deep into his soul, it seemed. Down to that darkness, just waiting for an escape. He didn't dare look up again.

"What you've told me is consistent with the ship's logs and the medical facts in your case," Blaine said at last. "It's not surprising you have trouble remembering details, considering the trauma you've experienced. All right, I think maybe that's enough for today. This has been difficult for you, I know."

No. He couldn't possibly know. "What happens next?"

"Well, there is still a considerable amount of investigating to be done. There are key details that you seem to have trouble remembering. That leaves a lot of questions unanswered."

He finally caught his breath. Maybe the interrogation was over for now.

Blaine touched a module in front of him. "Ramon, could you please come and escort Dahvin back to his room?"

Ramon's voice sounded like he was standing right next to Blaine. "Yes, Doctor."

Ramon guided him back to his room. He didn't touch him, never made any move that could be interpreted as forcing him to move. The orderly just walked beside him. Quiet today, not his usual joking self. Perhaps he sensed that his charge was in no mood for humor.

Back in his room, he sat on his bed, paralyzed by the memories from the logs. He had to pull it together. Had to think defensively. *To fight!*

He tried to focus on where the log entry started. He wished now he'd been able to control his emotions and spend more time studying them. He needed to know exactly how the entries read. He closed his eyes and focused on the first entry. He could almost see the text floating in front of him. Gehren was only mentioned in the time-and-place stamp at the beginning of the entry. If someone had tampered with his logs, someone who knew what they were doing, that would have been easy enough to change.

Mira, where the Alliance had captured him, was the central, most important trading post on The Fringe. Between twenty-five to thirty ships docked there each day. What if the Alliance bribed the Miran space authority? They could have searched ships' logs until they found one that had been in port—any port—on the date of the "murder." Then they would have altered the port ID to match Gehren, pulled the crew's medical records, and picked a DNA tracer to add to the crime data.

Of course! Why hadn't he seen that? Because he'd let his emotions get the best of him. Given enough time, he could probably have found some of the old cargo delivery records that would prove Marlon wasn't on Gehren on that date. But in his current situation, he didn't have the resources to do that research. Of course, they already knew that too. That's why his ship had been left sitting on Mira.

He had to get away. Regardless of whether they normally executed or imprisoned criminals here, there would be no soft sentence for him. He was a danger to whomever wanted Dom Kittrend dead.

And he was completely expendable.

CONNECTED

RECIEVING....

CHAPTER
18

Before sunfare the next morning, Blaine summoned Dahvin to his office. He watched carefully when Ramon closed the door to his room. The orderly held no device. The interior doors had to be activated by imbedded chips. The door across from Blaine's office with the transparent panel led to a stairway and down to an outside door. The stairway atrium rose two stories, with another transparent door at the bottom of the stairway leading outside. Above and beside the outer door more transparent panels allowed natural light to filter into the stairway all the way into the second-floor hall.

Through the windows, he could see the sidewalk, landscaping, and street beyond. The sidewalk, paved with some type of smooth, unbroken, stone material, led from the door of the evaluation center and branched to a *T*, continuing in each direction along the street. Bushes that retained a pale blue-green foliage in spite of the surrounding snow lined each side. A dark blue-green plant covered the roadway. He'd only gotten to see one or two vehicles go by, but they looked like cruisers that floated slightly off the ground—no need for pavement.

He hadn't had the opportunity to see anyone come or go through the outer doors. Were they accessible to non-staffers who might not be chipped? Did outsiders have to request entry? Or was everyone on this damned planet chipped?

Ramon opened the door to Blaine's office with a wave of his hand, and Dahvin discovered Stohne already there, seated in an extra chair added in front of Blaine's desk.

"Dahv, please come in." Blaine's greeting was warm and welcoming as always.

"Have a seat." He motioned to a chair next to Stohne.

"Hello, Dahvin." Stohne was cordial, but other than that his demeanor was as impassive as usual—so hard to read.

"I wanted to ask if you would give your permission to have Master Stohne review the logs from your ship."

"Do you need my permission?"

"There is another legal approach if you refuse, and under the circumstances, I would probably recommend to Master Stohne that he pursue that approach, but I would much rather that you give him permission to view the logs. They are private logs from your ship, so it requires either your permission or an order from a judge."

He thought about making it as difficult for Stohne as possible, but in the end he knew it would be pointless, and would most likely only serve to antagonize the one man on whom his defense rested. Not that he expected any defense from him. But antagonizing him or Blaine at this point would only encourage them to tighten their control of him.

"I will allow him to view them, as long as I don't have to sit through that again."

"You don't have to, Dahv. Master Stohne can view them alone if you give your permission."

"I don't even want to discuss it any further."

"Eventually, that will be necessary. But perhaps we could allow a few days before you have to deal with that."

He nodded. He was not in control of the situation, not in control of his own future at the moment, and that made him extremely uncomfortable. But the best he could do was go along with things for now and keep looking for a way out. He *had* to figure out how to get those outside doors open.

"All right," said Blaine. "It will take a while for Master Stohne to go through the logs. I understand that afterward he wants to take you to see a certain area of the city. Why don't you get something to eat in the dining hall and then wait for us in the recreation lounge. I'll let you know when he's finished."

At last, maybe he'd get a chance to see how those outer doors operated—and be out of the building. He nodded again, and stood up to leave. Blaine rose from his chair and stepped to the door to open it. Unnecessary, since he could have just opened it from behind his desk. He'd seen him do that. Perhaps Blaine was just going out of his way to be polite. Stohne remained seated.

He'd finished eating and was in the recreation lounge, playing a local card game Ramon had taught him, when Stohne stepped into the room. He tried to avoid looking him in the eye.

"I take it you're done," he said without looking up. "Dr. Blaine mentioned there was something else you wanted me to do." He stood up, trying to look at Stohne without really looking at him.

"Dahvin, I want you to know, I have the greatest sympathy for what…"

He waved his hand, cutting him off mid-sentence. "I don't want to discuss it—not any part of it—nothing. Let's just get on with whatever's next."

Stohne nodded. "Are you ready to take a little sight-seeing trip?"

"Sight-seeing?"

"There's an area of town I need you to see. I want to see if it will jog any additional memories."

Now that he knew he had been on Gehren at some point, and possibly the day Dom Kittrend was murdered, he feared going anywhere and learning anything. On the other hand, it would get him outside the Center. And through that door.

As they left the lounge, Stohne stopped him in the hall.

"Dahvin, I'm sorry to have to do this, but I will be required to put restraints on you, since we will be leaving the Center."

He nearly bit his tongue trying to keep his cool. He shouldn't have been surprised. For all their courtesies, these people weren't stupid.

He nodded his consent. Stohne secured a thin plastic strip around Dahvin's wrists, then knelt down and wrapped a similar piece around one ankle, across, and around the other, leaving him enough length in between to walk comfortably, but not to run.

Blaine stood in the hall waiting for them as they came around the corner from the recreation lounge. He accompanied Stohne and Dahvin to the door across from his office, and used a small laser light to release the lock on the door. It was the first time he'd seen that device. He still didn't see any lock mechanism, but he heard a slight click. Blaine pushed the door open for Stohne.

Another man wearing a suit similar to Stohne's came through the outer door as he and Stohne were headed down the stairs. That door was evidently not locked.

He had learned that most of the professional people in Durrand, the capital city of Gehren, wore a similar style of suit, a hip-length tunic with a stand-up collar and straight-legged trousers. Different professions had different color codings. Legal professionals like Stohne wore a medium gray suit with a dark stripe on the arm and down the sides of the trousers.

Those who had obtained a certain level of expertise in their field, were addressed as "master" and had a colored patch over their shoulder and the emblem of their profession on the patch. Subordinates in each field wore the emblem with no colored patch and were addressed with a simple "misyer" or "apprentice." Everything was always very polite on Gehren. He remembered that Blaine had offered to address him as "Misyer Tave" when he first arrived. It still sounded ridiculous.

Stohne opened the outer door, and they stepped out into the sunlight. He glanced back over his shoulder to get a look at the front of the building. It had a pearlescent finish that reflected several pastel hues of blue to gray to slightly pink. It almost gave the building a sense of motion, for as he moved away and looked at it the color patterns shifted. It was really quite beautiful.

Stohne touched his arm a little impatiently. "We need to get going."

The door of the evaluation center had opened onto a walkway paved in smooth white stone. Up close, he could make out the fine lines between stones. Across the front of the building a well-kept garden bordered the sidewalk beyond the bushes. Dark red, star-shaped blooms on some of the plants braved the winter cold.

The walkway and the street were all one level, with only the edge between the living street-cover and the stone sidewalk marking the boundary between them. A solid black transport vehicle with a sunburst insignia waited in front of the center. The lettering on the insignia must have been in a local language, for he couldn't read it. The cruiser had three doors on the side facing them.

As he and Stohne approached, the driver's door opened, sliding up and disappearing into the roof of the vehicle. The driver stepped out and pressed a button, raising the middle door. He wore the same style of clothing as Stohne with the same sunburst insignia on the right shoulder.

Stohne guided him into the middle seat of the cruiser and closed the door behind him. A metal mesh material ran from floor to ceiling in front of him, securely separating him from the driver. The same material behind separated his seat from the one that Stohne had taken. He figured that material was a lot tougher to tear through than it looked. It might be the same mesh that he'd noticed surrounding the roof of the evaluation center when he first arrived.

"Where are we headed?"

"I thought it might help if you saw the area where the crime was committed."

A few days ago he would have steadfastly insisted it was pointless, that he wouldn't remember a place he'd never been to, or an event he'd had no part in. Now, his stomach clenched in a hard knot.

The cruiser rose up slightly as it moved forward. He couldn't tell if it was riding on an air cushion or an anti-gravity maglev, but the ride was very smooth.

As they drove, he noticed that most of the surrounding buildings were faced with the same type of material as the evaluation center. There were a variety of colors, some in darker shades of the pearlescent finish that the center had, some in more opaque colors. A network of sidewalks bordered the city's well-spaced, straight streets. He spotted at least one small park in a square among one group of buildings.

Everywhere people crowded the sidewalks. Most wore the same professional garb he'd become familiar with, but here and there he spotted one in more colorful, casual clothing. No one paid any more attention to them than to the professionally dressed natives. A few aliens made their way among the pedestrians, evoking no particular interest from those they passed.

Stohne had evidently been watching him. "Admiring the view?"

"Looking at the buildings. What are they built out of—is that metal?"

"No. It's actually a living covering, a type of uni-cellular plant called protiki that grows here. Like many plants, it absorbs energy from the sun, but it releases almost as much as it absorbs, making it an excellent energy source. We discovered a couple of centuries ago that we could face the buildings with it. The superstructures of the buildings are metal frameworks. The energy conduits are laid over the metal, and a porous fabric mesh is laid over that. The protiki are planted in the mesh.

"It takes a couple of years for the protiki to completely cover the exterior, but it's worth the wait. Once it has formed a complete covering, it provides all of the energy required to operate the building. In some cases it provides a surplus that can be transferred to other uses."

Dahvin fell silent for a while. A living power source. Amazing. Spaceships used matter-antimatter reactors, but they were too dangerous for use on a planet. He'd known more than one pilot who'd had to dump his main engines and use backup digtali crystals in the reserve thrusters to high-tail it away when the matter-anti-matter mix became unbalanced.

"And those plant things can stay alive on the buildings?"

"Yes, in fact they seem to thrive. Maintenance bots have to peel excess layers off every five or six years. The excess strips are then used to start colonies for other buildings. We are gradually covering every building on the planet with them. Most of our commercial buildings have already been coated, and we're beginning to convert individual homes."

"Why are they different colors? Is that just natural?"

"Yes. So in addition to their useful properties, they are also incredibly beautiful." Stohne's voice dropped a little, deep awe and admiration audible in his tone.

After driving for what seemed to be about half a Standard hour, they reached a broad circular intersection with a huge stone statue in the center.

"That's a statue of Dom Kittrend's fifth-generation paternal ancestor," Stohne said.

Dahvin decided not to comment on that issue.

"The spaceport is just a short distance there to the right." Stohne pointed out the window.

The street on which they'd been driving had been wide enough for two lanes of cruisers in both directions. The road they intersected was the same width, but on the opposite side of the intersection the street narrowed, barely wide enough for two cruisers to pass each other.

The cruiser half-circled the intersection and exited onto the narrow street on the opposite side. The architecture changed dramatically here. Old stone structures lined the street. It was difficult to determine their age, but he guessed they had stood for several hundred Standard years. Although the street was only a short distance from the high-tech realm of the spaceport, it looked like another world. The area had a vaguely familiar feel to it.

The cruiser slowed down near the middle of a block-long row of merchant shops and glided silently to a stop in front of a small grocer's with fruit bins in front and signs in the windows advertising the wares. The grocer bordered a narrow alley that divided the block in half. The alley was blocked from sunlight by the surrounding buildings and so dark that he couldn't see more than a couple of paces into it, but he somehow knew that it was where the merchants kept their waste disintegration bins.

"This is one of the oldest parts of the port city of Durrand, capital of Gehren." Stohne opened the back door and stepped out. "It has been maintained in its original style for historic purposes. It's also a favorite tourist spot for off-worlders."

The driver got out and opened Dahvin's door. Stohne motioned to him to come out. As he leaned over and looked out of the cruiser, a wave of familiarity punched him in the stomach. Flashes of cruel memories and their physical sensations assaulted him. The now-familiar blackness that preceded his flashbacks overtook him too quickly to fight it.

—

Dahvin shivered in the cold, dim alley. He shrugged, trying to ease the pain of the half-healed whip-welts on his back. His oversized shirt stuck to the bloody scabs, then pulled loose as he moved, ripping the scabs off with them. Hunger drove him to examine every bit of trash in the alley, hoping some scrap of food might still cling to it. His bare feet burned from cuts, scratches, and blisters.

How long had it been since his last day aboard the Pruzzian slave ship? Beaten to a bloody pulp and starved nearly to death, he'd fallen behind a crate on a Rakshi ship the Pruzzians traded with. When he came to, the Rakshi ship was already in hyperspace. It had landed here—wherever here was, and he'd stumbled into this dark, cold, cruel place. But at least he was off the Pruzzian ship.

Where was Max, that crazy old man? Out hunting for bits of useless trash and broken objects he called "treasures?" What about food? He needed food, and without Max he had a hard time finding it. When he'd first met him he had the feeling the man would have willingly cut his throat for a few scraps. But he'd followed Max around, learning how to scout out the few scraps that had kept him alive. It was a brutish existence, but he was still alive, and free.

Now they had a sort of partnership where each would scavenge, and if they found enough, they would share. When there wasn't enough, Dahvin went hungry. He was hungry now. And cold. So cold.

He laid down and curled up, shivering. He wrapped his arms around himself, trying to conserve what body heat he had.

—

Unaware of Dahvin's violent reaction to the scene, Stohne turned to ask him a question, and saw only feet protruding from the open door of the car. When he peered inside, he caught his breath. Dahvin was curled up in a tight ball in the backseat, shaking violently. He touched the young man's foot, then shook it, but got no response at all. He motioned to the driver to return to the cruiser. There was no sense in trying to question Dahvin in this state. They would have to return to the evaluation center.

He shook his head and hesitated for a moment before climbing back in the cruiser. He had half hoped the young man wouldn't recognize this place, the alley where Kittrend was murdered. But with the logs from Dahvin's ship to explain the condition the boy had been in at the time of the murder, and his extreme reaction to the site, Stohne had little doubt now that Dahvin knew this place.

Back at the Blaine Center, an orderly took Dahvin to his room and administered a strong sedative to ease his shaking.

Stohne followed Blaine and the medical assistant to Dahvin's room, and waited in the corridor while Blaine made certain Dahvin was settled into his bed. As Blaine came back out, he stopped him. "What does this mean?"

"I don't know yet, I'll need some time to work with him a little."

"How long do you think it will be before you can talk to him?"

"I don't know. I actually expected the sedative to calm him enough so that I could talk with him. But I don't think that's advisable just now. We'll just have to wait and see."

"Please let me know as soon as you've had a chance to talk to him." He turned toward the hall. There was nothing more he could do tonight.

"I was so sure—"

"I know." He placed his hand on Blaine's shoulder. The doctor had clearly developed a strong rapport with Dahvin. He understood how much Blaine had wanted to believe the young man was innocent, and no doubt Blaine would still do everything he could to prove it, or alternatively, to justify Dahvin's actions. Though his own job demanded more objectivity, he'd also come to believe Dahvin's story and had been looking forward to proving it.

"To be honest, I thought he was innocent as well. But his reaction to that street...." He shook his head at the image of Dahvin in the back seat of the cruiser, curled in a fetal position, shaking and unresponsive.

He slid his hand off Blaine's shoulder and headed down the hallway, now empty except for Blaine and the assistant still standing at Dahvin's door. His footsteps sounded louder than normal, beating a steady funeral drumbeat.

CONNECTED
RECIEVING....
CHAPTER 19

Early morning light created a gray rectangle on the opposite wall, but failed to illumine the blackness of Dahvin's room. Images from the previous day's flashback flooded back into his mind. Dreams, or memories?

Dreams were imaginary creatures, products of stress or unresolved problems, but the monsters in them were not real. Flashbacks were physical memories, demons that yanked him out of the present reality and back into his tortured past. He tried to sort out the confused images overlapping, battling each other for primacy in his mind.

He closed his eyes, demanding order from the chaos. An old man, skulking around in back alleys, grabbing discarded food from disposal chutes, hoarding bits of broken objects as treasures. Crazy old man. Memory, not dream. Dark alleys between buildings—memory. But memories of this place, or some other place? That merchant, the one with the fruit bins out front—that was here. He'd seen it clearly yesterday when he first looked out of the cruiser. He remembered that very shop. He'd stolen food from that shop, been chased away from that shop. Chased to... Marlon's ship!

Oh, damnation!

It was all true. He'd been here. He remembered the place, though not

Dom Kittrend. He searched his mind, trying to call forth a memory that matched the photos of the wealthy patriarch he'd seen in his research. No, there was nothing familiar about Dom Kittrend. The man he had known here, in the back alleys, called himself Max. Crazy old man—dirty, living like a homeless animal.

"Dahvin, are you awake?"

Crazy old man was calling to him—no, a real here-and-now voice. Dr. Blaine's voice. The doctor had never come to his door before, always an orderly.

"Dahvin, can you hear me?"

He debated whether to answer. He wanted more time to sort things out. The doctor didn't want that. Blaine wanted to probe his mind before he had a chance to get his mental defenses up.

A whispered hiss signaled the disintegrating door. He kept his eyes closed, slowed his breathing, laid perfectly still.

The overhead light flicked on and quiet footsteps approached his bed. "Dahvin, I can tell from your vital signs that you're awake."

Of course he'd have a medical scanner with him, stupid. He opened his eyes. Blaine pulled the desk chair over to the bed and sat down, too close for comfort. Ramon stood near the door.

"How are you feeling?" Blaine ran his little black disk over Dahvin's head. "The sedative is out of your system, that's good. Do you feel like sitting up?"

Not really. He shook his head no.

"Let's try it anyway. I'm going to slip my arm behind your head and...."

He threw up his right hand and blocked the doctor's offending move. "No. I'll do it myself."

Blaine pulled his hand up, raising both hands in a show of surrender. He leaned up on one elbow. He wasn't dizzy, as he'd expected. Physically, he felt fine. He pushed up from the bed and slid his feet to the floor. He sat, hands braced against the side of the bed, refusing to look at Blaine.

The doctor ran his instrument over his chest. "Physically, you seem to be fine, no side effects from the sedative. Do you feel groggy, disoriented at all?"

"No. I'm fine."

"What do you remember from yesterday?"

He kept his head down. He knew he couldn't avoid the questions indefinitely, but if he could only have a while to try and gather his wits. "Please, leave me alone, at least for a while."

"All right. We'll meet this afternoon. Dahv, believe me when I tell you that my main concern is for your welfare, both physical and mental."

He jerked his head up and glared at Blaine. "You work for them. You...." He needed to *shut up*. He had time. He needed to shut up and get his head together. He looked away from Blaine at the far wall.

"I'm not sure who the 'them' is that you are referring to, but this center is a private facility. My recommendation to the court will be based on my honest assessment of your physical and mental state at the time Kittrend died, and whether or not, in my expert opinion, you planned to murder him, if it was an accident, or you believed it was self-defense, or," Blaine paused, "whether you had nothing to do with his death."

He was breathing hard, his teeth clenched. He didn't dare allow himself to believe anyone was on his side.

"Dahv, you *must* deal with these memories. I would like to help you do that, if you'll let me."

"I was dealing just fine until Enforcers shot me down on a planet beyond their jurisdiction, dragged me here in chains, and then you and your ombudsman started messing with my head. Leave me the pitfire alone, and I'll be way better off!" Dahvin gritted his teeth so hard they ached.

Blaine leaned back and eyed him for a moment. "All right. We won't make any progress this way anyway. Take some time to cool off. We'll meet this afternoon." He stood up and motioned to Ramon, who had remained silent near the door. Ramon waved the door open and the two left.

He got up from the bed, strode over to the window, and tried to plow his fist through it. The rebound punched him in the forehead, which hurt worse than hitting the window. The clock provided the only thing he could throw and not risk serious injury. He yanked if off the nightstand and heaved it against the wall above the computer. It rebounded so hard it flew clear across the room and shattered against the opposite wall. At least he could break one thing on this damned planet. He got some minor satisfaction out of that.

The fury dissolved into a sick feeling in the pit of his stomach. He was alone and defenseless. They had all the unmitigated power. They could devise any scenario they wanted and there was nothing, no one, that could stop them. What was he against a powerful elite like the Kittrends? And Blaine wanted him to believe that he was above that? Believe that he cared more about some pathetic off-worlder than about a family that could buy out his pitiful little clinic with their spare change?

He collapsed in the middle of the floor. They didn't have a death penalty here. He would spend the rest of his life in another prison. A humane prison, maybe, but a prison all the same. He'd rather have the death penalty.

For some reason Tess's face came to mind. He closed his eyes and allowed himself to feel the touch of her hand on his chest, the scent of her hair. If only he could hold her one last time. Maybe he could send her a message. He'd give anything to hear her voice again, see her face, even if it wasn't live. He needed her. He got up and went over to the computer module.

Then he just stared at it. How would he explain to her that everything he'd told her was false had turned out to be true? How could he expect her to believe that he couldn't remember any of it before, that he'd forgotten a planet and a dead man? He leaned his head back and closed his eyes. He was so lost, so confused. Back to the window. Dark clouds had moved in, signaling a new winter storm. More snow, more cold, no hope. He turned and leaned against the wall. Despair made his mind a jumble of incoherent thought. He slid down and sat on the floor, burying his head between his bent knees.

Sometime later, a voice roused him from his stupor. "Dahv, it's Ramon, may I come in?"

Hours had passed. Without the clock, he wasn't sure how many, but the light through the window had grown steadily stronger, indicating the sun was well up in the sky. His stomach rumbled, reminding him he had missed sunfare, and now probably the midday meal as well. He hadn't moved from his spot on the floor.

"Dahv, are you okay?" A note of worry clouded the orderly's voice.

What would happen if they found he'd managed to get out the window, or was dead? But of course, none of that had happened.

"Dahv, you gotta be hungry by now. You want something to eat?" That did sound good, if only he could get the food without having to leave the room or let anyone in. That wasn't going to happen either.

"I'm hungry, but I don't want to go to the dining room. And I don't want to see Dr. Blaine."

"I can bring you a tray. I know what you like."

"That would be great."

A few minutes later Ramon was back at the door. This time Dahvin answered his call and told him to come in.

Ramon walked in, his soft-soled shoes making a bare whisper of footsteps. He handed the tray down and dropped to the floor next to him.

"Rough day yesterday, huh?"

"You could say that. Look, I really don't want to talk about it."

"I get that, but I have to tell you, I think you'll feel better if you do. You were pretty wiped out when they brought you in yesterday afternoon. I haven't seen more than a couple of other people in a state like that, and it tells me whatever you saw had to be really traumatic. Also tells me you were on overload, not able to cope. Am I right?"

He crammed half a roll in his mouth so he wouldn't have to answer right away, but there was no denying Ramon had it figured out. He nodded and swallowed the last chunk of the roll.

"I'm so scared. Ramon, what's the deal here? I'm up against the most powerful people on your planet. Dr. Blaine's a good man, I get that, but he can't stand against them."

Ramon shook his head. "It doesn't work like that here, honest. This Center's independent status is protected by law. It gives Dr. Blaine the freedom to assess individuals charged with crimes and submit unbiased evaluations to the court. Even the Kittrends wouldn't dare to interfere. Let him help you, Dahv. It's your best option, not to mention the best thing for your own mental health."

He looked up and studied Ramon's face. The orderly looked him straight in the eye. There wasn't a hint of duplicity in the man. Ramon might be wrong, but he believed every word he said. He needed help, no denying that. He was confused. He remembered only bits and pieces of what had happened here on Gehren. Like it or not, Blaine was his best bet for piecing the puzzle together.

He nodded side to side. "Okay. Tell Dr. Blaine I'll be as cooperative as I can."

Ramon reached up and squeezed Dahvin's shoulder. "You won't regret that, I promise." He got up from the floor and with a wave of his hand disappeared through the door.

A short time later Ramon returned to take him to Blaine's office.

He sat in front of Blaine's desk without looking at the doctor, convinced he could feel the intensity of Blaine's gaze. He stared at the floor, trying to shield himself from scrutiny as best he could.

"You remembered the place?"

All Blaine got in response was a slight nod.

"You really hadn't remembered being there before?" Blaine was compassionate, not accusatory.

He shook his head no. He still couldn't bring himself to look up or to speak.

"What exactly do you remember?"

Taking a deep breath, he started to answer, but then froze. A familiar chill ran through his body.

"I can use a technique to help you remember, if you like."

Out of the corner of his eye, he saw Blaine lean forward and rest his elbows on his desk. "It doesn't involve any medications. It's a type of machine that creates a state of mind that helps you recall details."

He looked up but avoided Blaine's direct gaze. "No, I will tell you what I can." He shivered as the chilling, vivid, memories that had come flooding back to him when he had looked out of the cruiser near the alley assaulted him once again.

"The man I knew, that I met here when I escaped from the Pruzzians, called himself Max. I was only here for a few days. I didn't kill him, I found him already dead in the alley."

"How did you know he was dead?"

Dahvin struggled to remember clearly. Was he certain the man had been dead? Could he have triggered the murder weapon and not remember it?

"I'm fairly certain he was dead, I couldn't see lifelight around him." He tried to place himself mentally in that place and time.

"Lifelight?" Blaine's eyebrows arched in the center.

"Yes. You may have a different term for it here. You know, it's the light that surrounds living things. Inanimate things have it somewhat, but so faint it's nearly invisible. But people have a strong lifelight."

Blaine sat, frowning, for a moment and tapped his forefingers against his lips. "I think I know what you're referring to. Living things have a certain energy field. Are you telling me you can see that field?"

"Yes, of course. You don't see it?"

"No. Our vision doesn't include that wavelength. I've never known anyone who could. We have a small percentage of our population that claims to be able to see it psychically."

That set him back a little. "I don't quite know what to say. I'm not psychic, or telepathic, or anything like that. It's something I see, like a cloud or the glow from a dim light source. I assumed everyone could see it."

"So you are fairly certain then that he was already dead?"

"He either was dead or so nearly dead that I couldn't see any light around him. And the alley is shielded from the sun by the buildings, dark enough I should have been able to see it unless he was very near death. Even then, when a person dies, you can see the light leave them."

He had seen enough death aboard the Pruzzian ship. The brutal beasts made sure their captives saw the full result of their tortures. He'd watched the lifelight leave the bodies of an uncountable number of children. Unable to talk freely with the other children, he'd assumed they all saw the same thing.

Blaine's eyebrows arched again and he tilted his head to one side. "I've heard psychics claim that they could see the aura around a person, even heard claims that they could see the life-energy depart the body, but I've never really taken the claims very seriously."

For long seconds, Blaine sat silent, tapping his fingers against his chin.

"And how did you meet Dom Kittrend, the man in whose murder you are a suspect?"

"I never heard that name. The man I knew called himself Max."

"His name was Maxillian Kittrend. 'Dom' is a courtesy, a title, used for Firstcaste, the wealthy class, in our society. Until recently, no one would have used a Firstcaste individual's personal, or first name, outside of their family and very close friends. That's why you probably hadn't heard it before."

His stomach flipped. Kittrend's real first name was Maxillian? That was too much of a coincidence. He still didn't know how Kittrend figured into things, but the man he knew couldn't have been the patriarch. "I don't see how the man I met could have been wealthy. The Max that I knew was a crazy old bum. If he hadn't taught me to hunt for food in the trash bins, I probably wouldn't have lived long enough to get off this planet. I had no reason to kill him."

"You were eating out of the trash bins?"

"Yes."

"Why didn't you ask someone for help?"

"I was too scared. I didn't know anyone. I couldn't speak the language. Even Max and I had trouble communicating. I would just follow him around and do what he did. I didn't trust anyone. I stayed in the shadowed areas of the alleys. I learned how to catch things from the waste chutes before they hit the disintegrator beam. Of course, I didn't know what all that was at the time."

He could almost see thoughts whirling in Blaine's head. "As you know by now, Dom Kittrend was the patriarch of the wealthiest and most influential family here in Durrand. I find it hard to believe he was wandering the back alleys digging around in trash bins."

"Hard to believe or not, that's what Max was doing. It's a good thing. I don't think I could have approached anyone else. I probably would have just given up and died. That's why I don't believe the man I knew was Kittrend. I don't know how your people managed to get his name mixed into this."

"Perhaps we'll come back to that in a bit. Do you remember the weapon?" Blaine asked.

He shook his head. That didn't ring a bell at all.

Blaine showed him a small square black box. A vague memory flashed into his mind of the man's body. He'd been lying on his back, with his hands folded over his chest and the little black box clutched in his hands. He thought it had been some "treasure" the man had retrieved from a trash bin. He frequently collected bits of worthless junk that he guarded as though they were finds of great value.

"I think I remember Max holding a black box like that when I found him dead, but I didn't know what it was. I thought it was one of the pieces of junk he kept pulling out of the trash bins."

"It's a personal laser." Blaine turned the nondescript box in his hand. "They used to be used for self-defense, but are less common now that we have such a low crime rate. This is an antiquated one. It's very possible Dom Kittrend purchased it in one of the antique shops. Odd though, that it would have had a charge in it."

"That's what killed him?" The thing was no bigger than a hand-held computer unit.

Blaine nodded.

"Wasn't me. I never saw it except in his hands after he was dead."

"Did you touch it at any time?"

He took a deep breath. "I might have picked it up to look at it. I remember I did go through his pockets. He sometimes had a little money on him, and I found a few coins in one pocket."

"Could it have fired when you picked it up?"

"Not unless it emitted some sort of invisible energy pulse. When I saw it, as I said, he was already dead, holding a little black box. It didn't do anything, no sound, no light, nothing."

But to be honest, he wasn't so sure. He really hadn't known what the thing was. Hadn't had any idea. Could he have fired it without realizing it? Would he remember that now if he had?

"Dahv, tell me more about Dom Kittrend, or Max as you knew him. Was he there in the alley all the time, or did he leave during the days and come back at night?"

"He was kind of crazy. I didn't have much to judge him by at the time, but he just seemed strange. He always hung around the waste bins. He caught all kinds of stuff as it came out of the chutes, broken bottles, pieces of junk, and acted like they were precious treasures. He wouldn't let me touch them. He had a big pile of them."

"Were you around him most of the time?"

"Pretty much, I think. Of course there were times when I slept, and sometimes when I woke up he would be gone. I tried to keep track of him because he was my food source."

"How was he dressed? Did he seem to you to be healthy?"

"He was pretty ragged and dirty, like me. He was thin, not to the point of starving, but you wouldn't say he looked well-fed either."

Blaine seemed lost in thought for a moment.

"I may need to ask Master Stohne about the autopsy. I wonder if it included any of that type of information. Certainly the physical condition of his body should have been noted."

"Could they tell from an autopsy if he had mental problems?"

"There is a rare illness on this planet that causes a progressive loss of mental capabilities. If he suffered from that, there would be identifiable changes in the brain. But I don't know if the postmortem examiner would have included such an examination in his autopsy. Since the cause of death seemed to be apparent, they might not have looked at other areas."

Blaine scribbled a few notes.

"Dahv, perhaps we need to go back to the beginning, talk about how you arrived here, and what happened during those few days that you say you were here. How much of that do you remember?"

He remembered, but not willingly. Severe pain and starvation had been his constant companion in those days.

"I really don't want to deal with those memories if I don't have to," he said, fighting the tightness in his throat. "It's not really relevant to whether or not I killed him, which I didn't."

Maybe if he just kept repeating it enough times.

"It will help establish the background of the event and what happened with Dom Kittrend, since his behavior as you describe it would have been totally out of character. Besides, Dahv, you need to talk about these things. I know they are painful, but if you continue to suppress them, they will continue to haunt you and cause emotional problems."

Yeah, he knew about those all right—flashbacks in which he relived the horrific events of his past and frequent nightmares in which he was hunted down and recaptured by the Pruzzians. All those things conditioned him to distrust anyone.

He shifted in his chair, trying without success to get comfortable. "I doubt talking is going to have much impact on my emotional state."

"You'd be surprised, and there are therapeutic techniques I can use that will help considerably."

Just what he needed—someone messing with his head. Even though he wasn't guilty, they could make him think he was. Make him beg to be punished. Creation, this kept getting worse all the time.

"I don't have any currency to pay for therapy. Even if I manage to get out of this murder charge, I'll be homeless and penniless when the whole thing is over with."

"If you are proven innocent, the Gehren government will likely offer some compensation for your arrest and the loss of your livelihood."

Well, that was the first time anyone had said anything about compensation. But he still didn't hold out much hope for this situation to end any way but with him in prison. Escape eluded him. As far as he could see, the chances of them finding him innocent were slim.

He couldn't reconcile the dirty, ragged, nut-case that he'd known and found dead with anybody of wealth. Could he and Blaine be talking about different people?

Blaine leaned back in his chair and clasped his hands over his roundish stomach. "In addition, as I mentioned before, I can use the Alpha Wave enhancer to help you remember. If you prefer, I can structure the sessions so that you don't have to remember what we discuss during the session. The procedure itself helps you feel rested and relaxed when you wake from that state. It's a lot like having a good night's sleep."

He could really use that. Good nights were few and far between. But he didn't like the idea of anyone questioning him when he wasn't in control of the answers. Not to mention having his brain hooked up to some machine that might mess with his brainwaves.

"I'll go ahead and schedule a session for tomorrow. I have an opening. It will take a couple of hours the first time, but I can do it in the morning."

He opened his mouth to protest, but Blaine raised his hand to cut him off.

"We need to do this. You don't have to do more than you want the first time. And if you want to remember what we've discussed when you wake up, we can do it that way."

He didn't like being forced into it, but couldn't see a way out of it. He would have to wing it tomorrow. Maybe he could fake the sleep-state.

Blaine pushed a button on his desk and an orderly appeared to escort him back to his room.

Alone again at last, he sat on his bed, trying to figure out a way to avoid tomorrow's Alpha Wave session. There was no doubt in his mind that Blaine would use it to twist his memories. While many details still eluded him, he was certain about the man he had known as "Max." No way the crazy man he'd known had been some wealthy patriarch. But what would he remember after the Alpha Wave session? Would "Max" be transformed in his mind to a well-dressed aristocrat?

He'd begun to trust Blaine. What a fool! He knew better. Even if Ramon had no reason to lie to him and believed in Blaine, *he* knew what was at stake. A worthless low-life like himself meant nothing to people like the Kittrends, and Blaine would have no choice but to acquiesce if pressured by them. What better way than forcing their scapegoat to believe that the crazy old bum was really Maxillian Kittrend.

Try as he had, he'd found no way out of the building. He'd even considered tackling one of the orderlies and trying to find one of the instruments that had opened the outer door, but he wasn't sure the orderlies carried them. Blaine was the only one he'd seen with one. If he tackled Blaine, he probably wouldn't even make it out of the office.

There was no escape. And by this time tomorrow, he would believe that he had murdered Dom Kittrend, and would complacently allow himself to be convicted. Would he ever remember the truth after that? Would he spend the rest of his life content to be in prison?

If his life was going to end tomorrow, he wanted one last chance to communicate with Tess. He could justify that. He owed it to her to let her know what was coming. She couldn't do anything about it either, but perhaps it would allow her to let go.

He trudged over to the computer. "Computer on. Message to EN238DT15732PV.

"Tess, I hope everything is okay at your end. Things have changed for me here. I hope you will know that what I am about to tell you is the truth. I found out that I was here on Gehren when Maxillian Kittrend was murdered, not long after I escaped from the Pruzzians. I didn't remember it because I didn't know where I was at the time. Yesterday, the ombudsman took me to a place in Durrand, and the memories came flooding back.

"I'm still not sure how long I was here, maybe a tennight or a little more. I met an old man named Max, a crazy old bum who lived in the alleys and scrounged for food from the trash bins. There's no way he could have been Dom Kittrend, but the authorities here are determined to make me responsible for Dom Kittrend's death."

He hit the pause button and stopped to take a breath. He was throwing a lot at her. Hope it's making sense.

"Dr. Blaine showed me logs that he said were from my ship. The entry I heard sounded like Marlon Tave's voice, and the date and time stamps were for Gehren on the day they claim Dom Kittrend died. I don't know whether they could have tampered with them. It's probably irrelevant, since it's clear to me now that I was here at least at some point. A lot of the details are still very fuzzy for me. I can only remember bits and pieces of what happened here. I do remember finding Max dead the last day I was here, but I am certain that he couldn't have been Kittrend. They did tell me that Kittrend's first name was Maxillian, though.

"Tomorrow, Dr. Blaine is going to use something called Alpha Wave enhancement, supposedly to help me 'remember' details about my time here."

He hit pause again. He needed to build up the nerve to tell her goodbye. He stared at the display. In his reflection he tried to conjure up an expression that would be serious but not depressed.

"Tess, I don't believe for an instant that they intend to help me remember what really happened. I am sure they will use the procedure to alter my memories so I end up confessing to the murder. No matter what happens, please believe me. I told you everything I could remember, and I am telling the truth now. I never killed anyone. I found Max already dead. I still don't believe the crazy old bum that I knew was Kittrend. That's just not possible.

"I can't know after tomorrow if I will even remember you. Try to remember me as you knew me on the ship, not as whatever they turn me into. I could have loved you if we'd only had the chance."

He gave her a little smile and pressed the send key quickly so he wouldn't have time to think better of it. The light outside was beginning to wane, and snow was falling again. The ice had melted off the trees a couple of days previously when the sun had come out for a while. The snow piled up on the branches and covered the last standing plants that had remained above the previous layers. It looked like everything would be buried this time. At least they could look forward to the hope of spring.

The buzzer at his door sounded. "Come in," Dahvin answered. There was no point in resisting. Ramon stood outside, waiting to take him to the dining room.

He stepped into the hall and started off without a word.

"You doing okay?"

"No."

"It will get better, Dahv. Just try to hold on."

"No, it won't. Forget it, okay."

Ramon didn't try to press the issue. They fell in step side by side, and didn't say another word.

The cafeteria was serving some of his favorite fruits and bread, but the smells still turned his stomach. The food seemed devoid of flavor, and he munched his way through like a robot disposing of refuse.

CONNECTED
RECIEVING....
CHAPTER 20

It had been a tennight since Dahvin had been delivered to the authorities on Gehren, but the way the arrest had been handled still troubled Tess. She'd talked with the counselor, but what she really wanted were straight-up answers from the captain.

She punched up his office on the com.

"Captain Djanou, Enforcer d'Tieri requesting a conference with you."

"I am available Officer, if you wish to come to my office now."

That startled her. She'd expected to have to set an appointment for another day. She'd never considered him to be particularly accessible to the crew. Maybe she'd been wrong.

"Thank you, Captain, I'm on my way."

When she reached the door to his office, she tugged at her uniform, and polished her boots against her pant legs. He still intimidated her.

She pressed the buzzer.

"Enter."

She stepped inside and crossed her right hand over her chest in a salute.

Djanou was seated this time, a holo display wavering in front of him. He closed it down as she entered. "At ease, Officer."

As Captain, he did not return salutes to subordinate officers. She dropped her right arm and folded both arms behind her in the "at ease" stance.

"Have a seat, Officer D'tieri." Djanou pointed to the chair in front of his desk. "What can I do for you?"

She'd never expected to be asked to sit in the Captain's office. She stepped over to the chair and sat straight, still uncomfortable with the idea of a relaxed posture. "Captain, I'm sorry to take up your time, but I am still troubled by the events on Mira. I have met with the ship's counselor. There are some questions I was hoping you would be willing to answer."

"I will answer what I can. What are your questions?" He leaned back in his chair and folded his hands in his lap. He seemed more relaxed than she'd ever seen him before. It gave her courage to forge ahead.

"I really would like to know your opinion of how the incident on Mira was handled. We caused a lot of chaos in the marketplace. Did that cause any repercussions for the Alliance? Will we be prohibited from going back there?"

"That is well above my position, fortunately. Such issues will be handled by the diplomatic corps. Gods deliver me from ever having that job." He actually grinned a little. She'd never seen him smile.

"I guess I've been a little worried that our team might have caused problems for you."

"That's my responsibility, not something for an EN-2 to worry about."

"Yes, sir. But I still would like to know, from you, if we should have handled things differently than we did."

"Have you discussed your concerns with your team leader?"

"Not exactly. Canton Treiner made it quite clear immediately after the incident that he felt it was a legal firing. That seemed to be all he was willing to say about it."

"So why are you questioning it?"

"Because we caused a lot of trouble. I wonder if it couldn't have been handled better."

The Captain paused, looking her straight in the eye. "Is it someone else's actions, or your own, that you question?"

She had to stop to think about that. Actually, it was both. Moag had shot Dahvin in the back, in her opinion, without provocation. Except that he was running away from them. Was that reason enough to shoot him? Djanou waited, more patient than she would have expected.

"I think the entire situation, from start to finish, troubles me. I wasn't present when Treiner and the others first identified Dahvin Tave as a target, so I can only assume that they identified themselves and then told him he was under arrest. Apparently he ran from them. Is that what they reported to you?"

"I can not discuss that with you. You know that."

She grimaced and nodded. She did know. She was just fishing. "If the target runs, is that reason enough to shoot him?"

Djanou cocked his head to one side. "It can be. Our mission is to bring the target in. If disabling him is the only way to accomplish that, then it is a legal firing, just as Canton Treiner told you. So he did run, is that correct?"

Tess shrugged. "He was running when I first saw him. He came around the corner of a stall and stopped when he saw me."

"Why did he stop? Did you two know each other previously?"

"No. I don't know why he stopped. I think it startled him because he ran into another enforcer. Then Canton Treiner, Officer Moag, and Officer Krugg came up behind him and Officer Moag shot him."

"Do you believe that Tave would have stopped and surrendered peacefully at that point, and therefore the firing was unnecessary?"

Probably not, she had to admit. If Dahvin had realized the others were behind him, he surely would have taken off again. Could she have talked him into surrendering at that point? Also not likely, especially given what she now knew about his past. He would have attempted to escape no matter what.

"No. He would have run again if he'd realized they were there."

"Undoubtedly Canton Treiner assumed that as well. You are worrying about issues that are not relevant to your position on the team. It is the responsibility of the team leader to assess the situation and determine the correct course of action for the team members. Do you believe Canton Treiner failed in his duties, or committed any errors, in his duties on Mira?"

That was a loaded question. If she said yes, it would trigger a formal complaint and an investigation. On one hand, she felt it deserved an investigation. But the way Djanou had presented it, he seemed satisfied with how things had happened. If he hadn't been, he surely would have heard from his own superiors by now, and Treiner in turn would have been reprimanded. She might not know if Treiner had been reprimanded, but as Djanou pointed out, that wasn't her business either. She didn't really want to get Treiner in trouble. She just wanted answers to satisfy her own sense of unease.

"No. I can't say he did anything wrong. I guess that's what I really want to know, is whether our team did anything wrong."

"Again, something for you to discuss with your team leader."

"I know what his opinion is. I guess I wanted to know what your opinion was."

Djanou studied her, seemingly debating what to say next. Or was he waiting for her next move?

"My opinion of your team leader's actions are for me to discuss with him. If your leader had concerns about the actions of the other members of his team, then he would have discussed them with those individuals. Has Canton Treiner expressed any concerns about your actions on Mira?"

"No. He seems satisfied with everything that happened. It just seemed like a big mess to me."

"Firing on a target, even a legal firing, is not a neat and tidy thing."

No argument with that statement.

"Do you have concerns about your own actions?"

There it was, that big, black, scary, thing that kept eating at her. Did she dare admit it? Could she live with herself if she didn't? She tried to look Djanou in the eye, but failed, and looked at her hands in her lap.

"Yes. It was unnecessary for me to fire on him a second time."

"I agree. However, Canton Treiner has seen fit not to file a reprimand."

She gulped. Tears stung her eyes, but she fought them back. It was true. If anyone in the group could have been criticized for their actions, it was she. And Treiner had held back, protected her. She looked up and met the Captain's eyes.

"Why did you fire?"

"When Officer Moag shot him from behind, it knocked him forward a step, and I fired. I had my weapon out because Canton Treiner had issued an alert that they were pursuing a suspect."

"So you were aware he'd been identified and that he was fleeing, correct?"

"I didn't know he was the target until Officer Moag fired on him. But I admit, it wasn't necessary for me to fire on him a second time. The first shot should have incapacitated him enough to be apprehended."

"Do you believe you require additional situational training?"

"No. I don't think I will ever make that mistake again."

"No doubt, that is Canton Treiner's assessment as well, and the reason he did not feel a reprimand, or additional training, was necessary."

She had to give Djanou credit, he seemed to be able to take a very complex problem and lay it out in a precise and logical manner. He made the Standard protocols seem perfectly reasonable, even made Treiner seem like a good team leader. Maybe he was better than she'd been willing to give him credit for. She was glad she'd gotten up the nerve to talk to the Captain.

"Thank you, sir. You've given me a much clearer picture of the whole situation. I guess I really knew all of that, I just couldn't come to grips with it."

"I understand that it can be difficult to justify firing on a live person, Officer d'Tieri. Especially the first time. Which is why I recommended that you see the counselor. However, in this case, you need to realize that you compounded the situation, and your own difficulties, by becoming personally involved with the suspect. There are important, valid reasons why it is forbidden. I trust you also will not fall into that trap again?"

She took a deep breath. How would he react if he knew that she had contacted Dahvin on Gehren and given him a code to allow him to respond? She was looking for big trouble. But there wasn't going to be another suspect like Dahvin. She was sure of that.

"No, sir, that won't happen again, either."

"Then, have we adequately addressed the issues that you wished to bring to my attention?"

"Yes, sir. Thank you."

"Officer d'Tieri, trust your team leader. If you feel you can't trust him, request reassignment. Understand?"

"Yes, sir." She did trust him in the field. More now than she had before.

"One last thing," Djanou said, standing up to signal she was about to be dismissed. "I do want my crew to feel they can come to me when they have a problem. Do you feel that I have addressed your concerns fairly and openly?"

She stood up, smiled at him, and saluted. "Yes, sir, you have. Thank you, sir."

"Good. Dismissed."

She executed a military about-face and walked out. She drifted down the corridor, head down, mulling over the conversation. Although the captain had eased her concerns about the legalities of the incident on Mira, she still worried about Dahvin. She hadn't heard from him in days. The case hadn't progressed far enough for her to get any updates from the Enforcer database. She wondered whether he'd had any therapy sessions with the doctor at the center where they were holding him.

How was he sleeping?

She knew he probably was avoiding communicating with her because he thought he was protecting her. Maybe she should go ahead and send him another message, let him know she wouldn't give up on him so easily.

Engrossed in her thoughts, she didn't see Treiner until she plowed straight into him.

"Whoa, Tess. Watch out, there. What's eating you? Can't still be mooning over that murderer could you?"

"Not that it's any of your business if I'm mooning over anybody."

Treiner moved closer, forcing her to back up a step. "How about dinner?"

"No thanks."

Treiner stepped back as though to let her pass, but when she moved past him, he stepped in, forcing her to step toward the corridor wall.

"What are you doing? Back off a little, okay?"

Instead, he stepped in closer, his body touching hers. He placed both hands against the wall on either side of her shoulders, leaving her precious little room to wiggle out.

"Treiner, I'm not kidding. We've talked about this. I'm not interested in becoming one of your shipboard conquests."

Treiner pressed even closer. Tess had to turn her head a little to keep her face from pressing into his chest.

"C'mon Tess. You don't know what you're missing. I don't think I've ever had a complaint, at least not while I was romancing a girl. Give a guy a chance. I can make you feel good."

She managed to get her arms up to her sides, swung her palms in against his ribs and shoved with everything she had. She took him by surprise and managed to push him back a couple of steps.

"I am not kidding! Get this through your thick skull. Keep your hands to yourself. If you so much as lay another finger on me, I promise you I will file a harassment complaint against you. We have a good team, and I don't want to break it up, but if you don't leave me alone, I will do what I have to do. Got that?"

Treiner glared at her for a moment. Then without a word he stomped down the corridor headed away from her cabin. She wasn't sure if that was a win or if there'd be payback later on. She'd have to watch every move she made, because she had no doubt if she made even the slightest mistake, she'd be on report instead of him.

She heaved a deep sigh and went on to her cabin. She'd figured this was coming. She'd just kept hoping he'd take her earlier remarks to heart and leave things be. But she'd known better.

After a quick shower, she slipped into a casual shirt and pants. On her way back out the door to grab something to eat, she noticed the blinking private message icon on her computer. Dahvin! At last.

A quick swipe of her finger loaded the message. One line punched her hard. "I found out that I was here on Gehren when Maxillian Kittrend was murdered." He had been to Gehren after all. But his explanation of why he hadn't remembered it made sense. He hadn't lied to her. He truly didn't know he'd been there. She couldn't blame him for fearing that they would pin the murder on him, even if he wasn't guilty. Could there be another explanation for Kittrend's death?

Hopefully he would trust Dr. Blaine. Over the last few days she'd researched the Blaine Mental Health and Evaluation Center, and the doctor himself. It had an outstanding reputation planet-wide, and he'd even handled a number of patients from other planets.

Those convicted of crimes on Gehren were sent to the Blaine Center for evaluation prior to trial. If found guilty, most of them were provided with psychiatric treatment and "reconditioning" rather than incarceration. The ones incarcerated seemed to be those that had to be confined during treatment to protect themselves or others, so maybe Dahvin wouldn't be confined for treatment even if they declared him guilty. For Dahvin, though, there wasn't much difference between incarceration and confinement to a treatment center if he was controlled by others and not free to live his life.

Of course, she still didn't think he had murdered the man, but something had happened.

Blaine's reputation hinted that he would do everything possible to help Dahvin. He needed it. She'd never heard of the Alpha Wave being used the way Dahvin described it. Poor guy, he couldn't ever believe anyone was on his side.

The last line really set her back, though. "I could have loved you if we'd only had the chance."

He'd never said anything like that before. And a kiss. Whoo-hoo! Just hang in there sweetheart, we'll have a chance, one way or another. I'll make it happen.

Lingering for a moment on the image of his face, she closed his com. "Open new message."

—

When he got back to his room, Dahvin discovered a message waiting for him on the computer. His stomach flipped in anticipation, then a chill ran down his back. How had she reacted to what he'd told her? Good or bad, he needed to hear her voice. He knew she would try to lift his spirits.

"Computer, play message."

Tess's face filled the display. Her hair fell loose around her shoulders, the way he loved it. Had she taken it down especially for him? He could pretend, anyway. He hit pause, taking a moment just to study her face. Her eyes were soft, almost a little teary. He traced her outline with his fingertips. It was the closest he would ever come to touching her again. Pain knifed straight through his heart.

"Computer, resume."

Tess's image looked him right in the eye. *"Dahv, I love you. Don't give up! I don't think things are as bleak as you think. I've heard of the Alpha Wave enhancement procedure. It's just a memory enhancement technique, although it's also used to help people calm down, reduce stress, and improve sleep. It's not a brainwashing machine, trust me.*

"I have done a lot of research about Gehren over the last week. It has a reputation throughout the Alliance as a very stable, compassionate society. They value justice and take great pride in their legal system. I can't see them manipulating you into believing something that didn't happen."

She leaned even closer. He could almost feel her breath across the void of space.

"Dahv, we didn't have much time together, but I know you at least a little. When you are scared you close down. Don't do that. Open up to Dr. Blaine. I also researched his center, and he has an excellent reputation for helping people that other doctors have thought were beyond help. I think he will do everything he can to help you, but you have to work with him, not hold back and let fear get the better of you.

"I know it's hard for you to trust people. I get it. But you know I would never lead you astray. I love you. Believe in that.

"Message me back tomorrow after the Alpha Wave session. I know you'll feel better then."

The *End Message* symbol popped up on the display. He paused the message just as it finished so her image froze in front of him and studied her eyes again. He could see the love. He could only hope she knew what she was talking about, and that he was just being paranoid. That was possible. Either way, he would know tomorrow.

Or would he?

He spent some time researching the Alpha Wave technique himself. The computer seemed to allow free access to any questions he put to it about the procedure. His own studies confirmed what Tess had said. He couldn't find any indication that the machine had ever been used for any purpose other than to improve memory, relieve extreme stress, and improve sleep. In fact it seemed that improved sleep was a consistent "side effect" of the machine's use in almost every case.

The information reassured him somewhat, but his natural distrust refused to be laid to rest. The one question that still plagued him was how the old man he had known could possibly be Maxillian Kittrend. He couldn't deny that the names were a startling coincidence. But the man he'd known was dirty, ragged, nothing like a rich man. Maybe he would get some answers tomorrow. He hoped so. He just didn't believe so.

Two hours later by the computer's clock, he gave up on his research and drifted over to the window. The last daylight had waned long ago, and the big moon shone well up in the sky. The clouds had cleared out, allowing the moonlight to shine on the new fallen snow. Crystals of snow glistened like gems, which made him think of Tess. He shook his head. Better quit feeling sorry for himself and start thinking strategically.

He laid down on the bed, calling to mind his last evening with Tess and that all-too-brief kiss.

He awoke in a sweat in the middle of the night, panting from nightmares in which he ran from unseen terrors relentlessly pursuing him. He got up and went to the computer. Maybe replaying Tess's message would help calm him.

He ran the message twice more. At the end of the second run he froze the image and ran his fingers over her face again. Maybe she was right. He couldn't argue that he was paranoid. With good reason, maybe, but as Marlon had always warned him, fear posed a danger in itself, more apt to make a man do something stupid than to save him.

CHAPTER 21

CONNECTED

RECIEVING....

Dahvin was just finishing the morning meal when an orderly approached his table and told him Dr. Blaine wanted to see him as soon as he finished. In spite of his research and Tess's assurances, it still unnerved him that Blaine would be able to control the interrogation process. He would have little chance to do anything but respond to the doctor's questions.

He tried to eat his last few bites as slowly as possible while he mulled over the situation. Would he be able to control his own mental state in spite of the use of the machine? Doubtful. When he could not prolong the meal any longer, he nodded to the orderly, and took his tray to the cleanup window. The two walked silently to Blaine's office.

"Good morning, Dahv." Blaine smiled, his eyes and mouth crinkling. "How did you sleep last night?"

"Okay." Honestly, he'd slept very little for worrying about what was to come the next day, and when he did it had been plagued by nightmares.

"Come over here and stretch out on the couch. We'll just talk a little bit first. I want you to be completely comfortable and relaxed."

He did as instructed, but for some reason lying down jumped his heart rate even more.

"Dahv, do you trust me?"

Blaine had a very direct and honest approach with his patients, but that was a little more direct than he was expecting. He had to think for a moment. He trusted Blaine as much as he had ever trusted anyone except Marlon. And Tess, of course. But did he trust Blaine enough to do what the doctor expected of him? He wasn't sure he could trust anyone that much.

Blaine watched him. Dahvin had to look away. No doubt the doctor had accurately interpreted his moment of hesitation. "I guess so."

"Dahv, I understand how difficult it is for you to trust anyone, so I will ask you to think about these things. One, I have never lied to you or put you in a position where you would be compromised or hurt, and I will never do that. My professional ethics, as well as the fact that I honestly care about your well-being, would prevent that. Two, this procedure is important for your own healing, as well as possibly being an avenue to uncover the truth about the events that occurred while you were here three years ago.

"For all of us, memories fade over time, or we misinterpret things we do not fully understand. Under hypnosis, I will be able to see through your eyes what you saw and hear what you heard during past events. You may even be able to describe sounds and smells that you would not consciously remember.

"For the procedure to be successful, you must allow me to control the session. It *will* benefit you. You will feel relaxed and comfortable about what we did when it is over."

"You seem pretty sure of yourself." He studied the doctor's face, searching for any sign of dishonesty. Nothing in Blaine's face, voice, or body language hinted at anything but honest caring.

"I am sure. I have used this technique with over a hundred different patients, including non-Gehrens. It always benefits the patient—it has never failed to do that. You will come out of it feeling safe and relaxed. Can you do something that I guarantee you is in your own best interest?"

Feeling safe and relaxed maybe, but how much of it could be planted suggestion? "How can it be in my best interest if I end up looking like I'm guilty?"

"Do you believe you are guilty?"

"No."

"I cannot plant an image in your mind that is not there. Do you believe that you did anything three years ago that would make you appear guilty?"

"No." He tried to say it with a conviction that he didn't feel. Could he have fired the laser without knowing or remembering it? Could he have killed Max, even if only accidentally?

"Let me reassure you. This will be a very positive experience for you. Let yourself relax. Follow my instructions and allow me to take you to where you can remember things exactly as they happened. You will come out of it relaxed and knowing that what we did was good for you.

"Raise your right arm and hold it in the air. Feel how heavy it becomes."

He raised his right arm as requested. It took only a moment before it felt like he had a barium weight tied to it.

"Now relax your arm down slowly, feeling how heavy it is. Your arms and legs are getting heavy. Your eyelids are getting heavy and it is hard to keep your eyes open."

As Blaine continued talking, Dahvin's fears subsided. His eyes closed and his whole body felt heavy and limp.

"Are you ready to proceed?"

"Yes." His voice sounded distant to his own ears. He heard a slight hum, like an insect buzzing outside a closed window.

—

"Dahv, can you hear my voice clearly?" A readout on the AWE machine told Blaine his patient had reached the desired mental level.

"Yes." The answer was firm, the tone slow and relaxed.

"You are completely at ease. Nothing can distract you. You do not hear anything in this room but my words. You will follow my instructions. We are going to go back to a time before you arrived on Gehren. It is the day before you escaped from the Pruzzians. Where are you?"

"I'm in my cage." Dahvin's body tensed, his muscles taut.

"Where is your cage?"

"In the belly of the ship, where the slaves are kept."

"What are you doing?"

"I'm hanging."

"Hanging? How are you hanging?"

"I'm face down with my hands chained behind me to the top of the cage, and my feet chained behind me to the bottom." Dahvin shifted, as if trying to relieve strained muscles.

"Dahv, you will view this situation as if you are looking at it from outside your body. You will not experience any of the physical or mental sensations that this body is feeling."

Dahvin relaxed slightly with the suggestion.

"I want you to move out of that situation and forward a little in time. You are out of your cage now. What are you doing?"

"We're loading crates onto a Rakshi ship. They trade with the Pruzzians. I can't move this crate—it's too heavy, and I'm too weak. The work master keeps whipping me, but I can't do it. I'm going to die soon. It's my time to die."

With the influence of the AWE, Dahvin still spoke in Alliance Standard, but his voice had a higher pitch, like that of a child, and his vocabulary was more simplistic.

"Why is it your time to die?"

"Because I'm too old. They don't keep us when we get older. They stopped feeding me a long time ago, and they beat me every time they take me out of the cage. I will die soon, maybe today."

"Do you know how old you are?"

"I don't know, maybe about fourteen. They usually kill the slaves when our bodies start to change."

From Dahvin's scars and medical history, Blaine had known the boy's past was brutal. But that knowledge had not prepared him for the depth of this reality. He was sweating, in spite of the comfortable temperature in the room, and his own heart rate had ramped up. He struggled to keep his voice calm and even.

"Okay, I want you to move forward in time just a little, and tell me what is happening now."

Dahvin's head turned as he studied his surroundings.

"I'm lying on the floor, behind some crates. Oh—there's some food here. Someone left it here."

"Do you eat the food?"

"Yes, of course, I'm starving! Oh, I don't know where I am. This isn't the Pruzzian loading bay. I think I'm on the Rakshi ship. Maybe they don't know I'm here. The ship is humming. I think it's moving. I think I'm going away!"

Dahvin's voice rose with elation and relief, and the machine registered a slight increase in his heart rate.

"Dahv, move ahead a day and tell me about where you are and what is happening around you."

"I am definitely on the Rakshi ship. One of the crewmen is in here checking the cargo, so I'm staying hidden behind this crate. I think he knows I'm here, but I don't think he's told anyone, because no one has come looking for me. He's leaving some more food where I can get to it without being seen, and some clothing. The Pruzzians never let us wear any clothing."

"So this Rakshi is trying to take care of you?"

"I think so. I don't know why. Maybe he would get in trouble if I died here and they found out I got left on board."

"Okay, let's move forward a little bit more. Tell me about what happens when this Rakshi ship lands. Where does it land?"

"I don't know where we are. They are starting to unload the crates from the Pruzzian ship. They will find me soon. I have to get off before anybody sees me. I'm hiding behind a big crate and following it out the door. The mover can't see me and no one else is paying attention. I'm off the ship! I'm free! I'm in a city of some kind, I think. I haven't been anywhere like this before, except maybe when I was a child, before I was taken by the Pruzzians."

"Are you on your home planet?"

"I don't know. This doesn't look like any place I remember. I don't know the words people are speaking. It's all very strange."

"Let's go to the next day. Where are you?"

Dahvin frowned and rubbed his eyes.

"I'm in a space between two buildings. It's kind of dark here. I don't think anyone will see me. I can see people passing by on the street, but they don't come in here."

"Have you found any food in the alley?"

"No, and I'm so hungry. My stomach hurts so bad. I think I'm going to die, even though I got away. I don't know where to get any food. I'm afraid to go out into the light. I'm afraid someone will see me."

Dahvin seemed to be having some trouble breathing during this memory. Readings on the AWE indicated his heart rate was elevated, and his hands clutched his stomach.

"Dahv, remember, you cannot feel anything this body feels. You are observing what is happening as though you are watching it happen to someone else. Move forward one more day and tell me where you are."

The monitor showed Dahvin's heart rate and breathing even out.

"I'm still in the alley. There is another man here. I've been watching him. He opens big metal boxes that are in this alley. Stuff comes down a tube and hits a blue beam. It makes a buzzing sound and disappears. But he catches some things before they hit the blue beam. He's leaving, so I'm going to try it. It's hard to reach the things without touching the blue beam. I think my hand will disappear if I touch it. Oh, I caught a piece of food."

Dahvin's hand reached up and his fingers closed around the invisible morsel. "I think this is where people throw stuff away."

"Yes, those are trash disintegrator bins. Did the other man see you?"

"No. He isn't here now."

"What does the other man look like?"

"He is very dirty and he has some short hair on his face. He has white hair and looks like an older man."

"Move ahead another day, and tell me what you are doing."

Dahvin hunched his shoulders. Blaine glanced at the readouts for signs of stress, but the monitor showed acceptable levels.

"The man found me while I was sleeping. He's yelling at me and pointing to the street. I can't understand him but I think he wants me to leave his alley. I'm too afraid. I just curled up on the ground in case he tries to beat me."

Could this be the answer? Did Maxillian Kittrend beat Dahvin, and did that instigate the fatal laser shot?

"Does the man beat you?"

"No. He's stopped yelling at me and he's just walking away. I'm following him to see where he goes to hunt for food. He's letting me follow him. He's showing me where some good food is and he lets me have some."

Blaine checked the readings on the AWE again. In spite of the trauma Dahvin was relating, his breathing had settled into a normal pattern and his heart rate had also dropped back to a normal level—normal for Dahvin, that is. Blaine took a deep breath and tried to calm his own racing heart.

"It is now a few days later. Are you still staying around this man?"

"Yes. He is showing me all the back ways behind and between the buildings. He gets all kinds of stuff out of the trash bins. Not all of it is food. I think some of it is just silly stuff. I think he is a little crazy. But he doesn't hurt me."

"Do you go anywhere else besides in the alley?"

"I'm going into one of the buildings that has a lot of food. There is a box of pretty fruit here. Oh! I have to run! The man from the store is chasing me!"

Dahvin's feet moved with the vision. "I'm safe now. I'm back here in the alley. He's not following me."

"The owner chased you away? Do you think he knows that you are hungry, that you need help?"

"I'm sure he knows. The clothes the Rakshi gave me are all dirty now, like the old man, and there is blood all over my clothes, from where I was bleeding when the Pruzzians whipped me. I don't have any shoes, like people here wear, and I cut my feet on some broken things in the alley, so my feet are all bloody too. I look terrible. I understand why they don't want me in there. All the people in the buildings and on the street look nice. I will try to stay away from them. But I'm so hungry. I couldn't find any food today. I can't find Max."

Blaine paused for a moment to wipe away tears he was powerless to suppress. Through Dahvin's eyes he could clearly envision the ragged, bloody, starving child. In Gehren's peaceful, socially and morally conscientious society, how could anyone be so cruel as to turn away a child so desperately in need of help. Why hadn't the shop owner called the social authorities? Dahvin couldn't answer that question, and it was time to move on to the critical period.

"Dahv, I want you to now move forward to the time when you found Max dead. Tell me what you see."

Dahvin's body tensed and he inhaled a sharp, deep breath.

"Oh, no, Max is lying on the ground like he's sleeping, but there's no lifelight left in him. He's dead. I'm going to die, too. I don't think I can find enough food without him."

"Tell me more about what you do when you find Max."

"I'm shaking him a little, just in case he isn't really dead. But he is. Oh, no, no, no."

"Dahv, do you know why he died?"

"No. I think he's just too old. He doesn't look injured. He's just lying there with his hands folded across his chest, like he lay down to sleep and didn't wake up. I'm going through his pockets. Sometimes he has little round things in his pockets that he uses to get things from the stores here. Maybe if I have some of those round things they won't chase me away."

"Those round things are antique coins. They can still be used for money. Does Max have anything else on him, or in his hands?"

"He has a little black box in his hands. I think it's one of the pieces of junk that he found in the trash bins."

"Do you touch it?

"Yes. I picked it up and I'm looking at it, but it's just a piece of junk. Just a black box. I don't think I can use it to get food. So I'm just laying it on the ground next to him."

"What do you do with the coins?"

"I'm going back to the store with the food. I put the coins on the counter where other people put them and I'm getting some food packages from a shelf. Oh-oh. The store man is yelling at me again. Maybe I don't have enough coins. I have to run. It's so hard. My feet hurt so bad."

That was confusing. Antique coins were an acceptable currency in the shops of Olde Towne. Even if Dahvin didn't have enough money, the shopkeeper should have shown him what he was allowed to purchase. Had he really driven the boy away because of his appearance? Blaine shook his head. He just couldn't believe that.

"Where are you now?"

"I don't know, I'm lost. I think I turned the wrong way when I ran out of the shop. I can't find my way back. Oh, I know, I'm back to the place where the Rakshi ship landed and unloaded. There's another ship right there with the ramp to the hold open. I can get in there and hide. Maybe the man from the store won't find me. Maybe I'll get away."

Blaine checked the AWE readout to be sure Dahvin continued to follow his suggestion to remain separate from the body he was observing. In spite of what had to have been a run of several city blocks, Dahvin's heart rate and breathing were steady.

"Are you on the ship now?"

"I just woke up. I'm on a ship, but I'm not in the cargo hold. Somehow, I think I must have passed out, and somebody moved me here. I have on some clean clothes, and I have bandages on my feet, and maybe on my back where the whip marks are. I'm a little hungry right now, but it's not so bad. There's a robot here taking care of me. This is very strange."

Without a suggestion, Dahvin had skipped ahead in time, indicating he had indeed been unconscious for a while. "Okay, Dahv, move ahead a few more days and tell me what you are doing."

Readings on the AWE indicated Dahvin's heart rate and breathing had both slowed even more, signaling a deep, relaxed state.

"I'm sitting at the control console with Marlon. He is showing me how to fly the ship. He's teaching me how to read and count and all kinds of things. He feeds me a lot. I'm never hungry any more. I remember my first name, Dahvin, but I don't know my last name, so he said I can be Dahvin Tave, and I can be his son, because he never had a son. He smiles a lot. I smile a lot now, too."

"Dahv, I'm very happy that you found someone who cares for you."

This seemed like a good point to end the session, with Dahvin in a happy place. Blaine adjusted the machine to begin a gradual wake-up cycle.

—

Dahvin opened his eyes to see Blaine sitting close to the couch.

"How are you feeling?"

"Great!" It was no lie—his body felt light, as though he could float right off the couch, and he was well rested, as though he had just awakened from one of the nights on the Enforcer ship after Dr. Bruin's sedative tea had put him to sleep. "I was just thinking about Marlon Tave. Was I talking about him?"

"Yes. I'm glad you finally found someone you could trust and rely on. How did he pass away?"

"He had a sudden heart attack about a year and a half ago, Standard time. It was really, really hard to lose him."

"I can imagine that would have been devastating for you. What did you do afterward?"

"Well, by then, he had taught me everything about flying the ship and managing the cargo business, so I just kept on doing what he taught me to do. I missed him, but I had a pretty good life, 'til the Alliance showed up and decided to haul me back here."

He sat up, swung his legs off the couch, and turned to face Blaine.

The doctor had pulled his desk chair close to the couch, and he leaned forward with his elbows on his knees. "Under hypnosis, your description of what happened when you found Kittrend, the man you call Max, was very much the same as what you had told me before. One thing I noted in particular, the personal laser was clearly dead when you found it. I will be sure that Master Stohne is advised of that."

"Will he believe it?" In spite of his relaxed state, old fears crept back.

"There's no reason not to believe. He would accept my professional opinion."

"Okay. Maybe at least it's a step in the right direction."

Blaine didn't take the discussion any further, and Dahvin couldn't remember everything they had covered. That fact still nagged at him. Blaine summoned one of the orderlies and let him go back to his room. The physical after-effects of the session were just as Blaine had promised. Hopefully he'd at least be able to sleep tonight with no nightmares.

CONNECTED
RECIEVING....
CHAPTER 22

Dahvin slept so well after his session with Blaine that he missed sunfare. He woke up with his stomach growling in complaint, but it wasn't quite time for the midday meal. With time to spare, he sauntered over to the computer console to do more research on the Kittrend family.

Five hundred years ago in Gehren time, after technology had reached the point where any one of the nations could have destroyed the entire planet, a single leader had captured the respect of people from both continents. No surprise that leader had been a Kittrend—Karrien Kittrend. The planetary government had been established in the Gehren year 2362, and members of the Kittrend family had held office almost continuously ever since. Male members, that is.

Social upheaval about a hundred years before the present had upset the caste system, but from the way the Kittrends were identified in the news and historical archives, it hadn't knocked them off their high place. Except for the individuals who were at least a couple of generations removed, none of the articles he found mentioned first names, which explained why he'd never heard Maxillian's name before he arrived here. All his research on the ship had called him either Dom Kittrend or Dom-el Kittrend, and he'd never realized that "Dom" was a title. Two articles from today's Durrand news leads speculated that "Dom Kittrend" had been earmarked to run for Samir, the head of the Executive Council, and showed a picture of a young man. Must be Maxillian Kittrend's son.

He was way out of his league in this battle. He buried his face in his hands. No matter what direction he turned, it seemed he couldn't find a way out of this predicament. Such an easy scapegoat. Maybe Maxillian's behavior had embarrassed the family, and his own son was the one who wanted him dead. Dahvin's DNA had given them the perfect opportunity.

So alone—he desperately needed someone, a friend. He needed Marlon. But Marlon was dead. There was no one else—except Tess.

Dom Kittrend's image froze in view on the holo display. He had a gut instinct to punch him. Instead, he closed out the article and sat staring at the blank module for a while longer. Closing his eyes, he pictured Tess, but he didn't know yet what effect yesterday's Alpha Wave would have on his predicament. No sense in risking trouble for her just yet.

More time had passed than he realized, but his rumbling stomach reminded him it was time for midfare. A buzz sounded at his door. Sometimes he wondered if the staff was telepathic.

His favorite orderly opened his door. Ramon's permanently cheerful demeanor eased his dark mood somewhat.

As soon as he entered the hallway he could smell the enticing aromas of the dining hall. They usually served two choices of meats, for which he had no taste. At least he'd learned to tolerate the smell of cooked meat. Fortunately, the kitchen also offered a variety of very tasty vegetables and fruits, and his favorite pastry, a type of round bread, crusty on the outside and soft inside.

The aroma of the bread called to him from the dining room.

"Hey, Dahv, they've got your favorite rolls today, lucky you. And my favorite dish, the kucko."

Dahvin wrinkled his nose. The kucko was a type of local poultry.

"What else do they have? You know kucko is not my style."

"Oranges and pinks, and those steamed squash that you like."

"Good, because I'm really hungry."

"Yeah, I noticed you missed sunfare. That's not like you."

"No. I slept like I was out in space."

Ramon laughed out loud. "Guess you're just not a ground person."

A blinding flash of light flared through the stairway door, followed by a deafening explosion. Dahvin dove for cover against the nearest wall, curling into a tight ball.

"Whooeee. That one was right on top of us. Hey, Dahv, it's okay, it's only a thunderstorm." Ramon reached out a hand to help him up.

That had looked and sounded like a bomb going off—he'd even felt a vibration in the floor. He uncurled and reached for the offered hand.

"Don't they have thunderstorms where you come from?" Ramon had a good-natured grin.

"I come from space, and no, we don't have thunderstorms. Meteor storms, maybe. I've never been planetside when one struck. Heard of them. Are they always that loud? And what was that flash? Looked like a phosphor bomb."

"The flash was lightning."

"Oh, yeah, of course. Man, it was bright!"

"Yeah, that one was right over us. I suspect that lightning bolt hit the ground somewhere."

Another flash and a boom, only slightly less frightening than the first, interrupted their discussion. "Are we in any danger?"

"No, not inside. I don't recommend you be outdoors in one this close, though. People don't get struck by lightning often, but it does happen. It can be fatal, and at the very least, do serious injury."

"Good to know. I'll watch the weather with a little more respect from here on."

Ramon chuckled. Another boom cut off the end of his chortle.

Though he couldn't help flinching with each blast, he noticed that the last one had come a second or two after the flash. "Is it moving away? The boom was later this time."

"Very astute. Yeah, the speed of sound being slower than the speed of light, and all that. In fact, you can kind of figure out how far away the center of the storm is by counting the seconds between the flash and the boom."

"So long as it's getting longer and not shorter. Now, how about that midfare?"

The meal was everything he'd come to expect, and he left the dining room a little overstuffed. On his way back to his room he spotted Stohne in the hall on his way to Dr. Blaine's office. Stohne caught sight of him out of the corner of his eye, and motioned for Dahvin to join him.

"I understand Dr. Blaine had a very productive session with you yesterday." Stohne looked him in the eye, studying him. "He may have some new information for me."

"I don't think he really got anything new. He seemed to think my description of the black box—what you call a personal laser—was more detailed under the Alpha Wave Enhancer. Did he tell you he used it?"

"Yes, he did. Frankly, I'm a little surprised he could get you into alpha-sleep. Even with the enhancer, that usually requires a certain level of trust."

"Yeah. He was kind of tricky, I think. I don't really remember going under."

"I've dealt with him before. He is very good at what he does."

The question was—did Stohne trust the doctor? And to what degree did he trust Dahvin himself? He touched Stohne on the arm, halting him in the hallway.

"I need to know where you stand, what your role is. Would you present evidence if it showed I'm innocent, or do you have to find a non-Gehren to take the fall for the murder of your most influential citizen?"

The other man's face didn't register any emotion at all.

"That's a fair question, under the circumstances. My responsibility is to present all the evidence, regardless of the direction it leads. I'm sure the Kittrend family would be happy to have an off-worlder convicted of the murder, but I am not obligated to them. My purpose is to find the truth, whatever that may be."

He watched Stohne's eyes and thought he saw a flicker of hesitation. He studied the man's body language. There was a certain caution, a reservation in the ombudsman's manner. What was Stohne not saying? Stohne made no attempt to move on until Dahvin nodded and waved toward Blaine's office.

At the door, Stohne announced their presence, then stood back and allowed Dahvin to enter first. Blaine looked up and smiled at the two of them.

"Ah, you're both here. Good timing. Dahv, I'd like for Master Stohne to review the recording of your session yesterday, if that would be all right with you."

"I don't remember any of it except at the end. You tell me, is there any reason I should not want him to review it?"

"No. As I told you, it's pretty much the same as you told me the previous day, only in more detail."

"I guess it's all right." In spite of all Blaine's reassurances, he still had that slight uneasy quiver in his stomach. Blaine seemed so straightforward, but had he missed something?

"If you don't mind, it will take Master Stohne a couple of hours to go through the recording. When he's done, I will call you back in. All right?"

"Yeah, fine. Is it all right if I just stay in the lounge?"

"Of course. You don't need an escort to the lounge. You'll just need to let one of the orderlies know when you want to go to your room so they can open the door for you."

He'd never taken much advantage of the lounge. It provided a good location for observing the behavior of others, and he could watch a movie on one of the recreational consoles while he watched people enter or leave the center. He still hoped to devise an escape plan.

As promised, a couple of hours later Dr. Blaine sent an orderly for him. No one else had entered or left the Center during that time, and the residents in the lounge were doing nothing more interesting than playing a couple of local card games.

He studied the ombudsman and doctor as he entered. Blaine seemed relaxed, Stohne lost in thought.

"Well, what did you think?" He searched Stohne's face for clues.

"Your account raises a lot more questions that it gives answers. I can't understand what a man like Dom-el Kittrend was doing raiding trash cans in the back alley. And Dr. Blaine has brought up a good point about why other people in the vicinity were aware you were there and in trouble, yet no one offered help. That is very unusual in our society.

"Actually, everything about this case is strange for our society. It seems I have quite a mystery to unravel."

"What will you do next?"

"I plan to interview some of the members of the Kittrend family again tomorrow. I spoke with Dom Kittrend and his sister before you arrived, but I think I need to dig a little deeper. Neither one of them elected to mention that their father had been missing. The way you described his condition under alpha-sleep sounds like he was somewhat malnourished, which would have meant he hadn't been home for quite some time before his death.

"I'd also like to have another talk with the coroner who performed the autopsy. He didn't mention that Dom-el Kittrend was in anything but normal health at the time of his death. Things just don't add up. I may question some of the business owners on Northport street."

"Is there anything I need to do?"

"No. You'll just have to sit tight. The trial is scheduled in ten days. I'll have to hustle to get the evidence I need to wrap this up."

Ten days? He'd had no idea the trial was that close. No matter how much evidence Stohne gathered, he still dreaded the prospect of the trial itself. Time was running out, and he still wasn't hearing the definitive "I can prove you're innocent" that he needed to hear.

"Oh, by the way..." Stohne stood to go out the door. *EN238*, the ship that apprehended you and brought you here, will be summoned back to testify regarding your arrest. I am certain I can make a strong case that you had no reason to suspect you were wanted by the Alliance, and therefore were not resisting arrest when they approached you on Mira. Under those circumstances, the fact that they fired on you would be considered inappropriate use of force, and you should be compensated for the loss of your ship."

Dahvin's thoughts immediately went to Tess. While he wouldn't mind seeing Moag reprimanded, he wouldn't want Tess to lose her position or face sanction.

"Will charges be filed against the Enforcer crew because they fired at me?"

"That's really up to the commander of the Enforcer League and the captain of their own ship. There's no way to know that."

"You're going to think this is crazy, but I really don't want to cause them to lose rank, or worse, lose their positions. I do want to be compensated for the loss of my ship. I need that money to get re-established if I'm released. But, especially Tess, I just don't want to cause her any trouble. I realize they were just doing what they thought they were supposed to do."

Stohne looked at him somewhat quizzically. "Like I said, I don't have any control over that. Is there something I should know about here?"

"No, not really, I just, I guess I kind of got to where I liked Tess. Moag, on the other hand, I wouldn't mind seeing knocked down a few pegs."

Stohne grinned. "I can understand that. I met him after they first brought you in. He is a sort of brutish fellow. We'll see how it goes, but the evidence regarding your arrest will have to be presented. Of course, Tess and Moag will have a chance to testify on their own behalf, and probably their captain as well."

Dahvin nodded. There didn't seem to be much he could do to help Tess or himself. The door appeared before them, triggered by Blaine from his desk. Dahvin stepped back to allow Stohne to go first, as the ombudsman had done for him earlier. He still wouldn't bow to anyone, but he could at least offer that courtesy.

"Thanks, but I have a little more to discuss with Dr. Blaine. I'll just be a few minutes more."

Dahvin stepped outside, staying close to the door, which disappeared behind him. Two orderlies stood several paces away engrossed in a conversation of their own, and didn't seem to notice him.

He leaned against the wall, trying to look casual, keeping his right ear to the space where the door appeared and one eye on the orderlies down the hall. From within Blaine's office, he could hear the conversation between the two men.

"Marken, what is your honest assessment of the effectiveness of the Alpha Wave session with Dahv?"

"It went very well, I thought. Why?"

"His story about Kittrend being in the back alleys in Olde Towne for a prolonged period—you know that doesn't ring true. If the patriarch of Firstcaste had gone missing, the whole city would have been out looking for him. I can't say his account of the situation at the time of Dom-el Kittrend's death necessarily absolves him of guilt."

"But he found Dom-el Kittrend already dead."

"So he says, but he admits to handling the laser, even admits stealing money from his body. We're talking about someone who was struggling to survive, and someone he figured had money on him. To a non-Gehren, that might be a reasonable motive for murder."

"He handled it, but he didn't see it fire. He would have seen it if it had fired when he handled it. If that happened, it should have come out in the Alpha Wave session."

"How much do you know about his physiology? Are you certain he couldn't have manipulated the session in some way? Are you certain he was completely under and answering honestly? We don't even know what race he is. How can you be sure the technique was foolproof?"

"I suppose there's no way to be one hundred percent sure." Blaine's voice dropped so low Dahvin could barely hear it through the door. "But I know my gut feelings, what I have come to believe about Dahvin and what he's been through. His account under alpha-sleep was sufficiently detailed that he would have had to deliberately manufacture details. And I didn't tell him about the Alpha Wave Enhancer until just the day before I used it."

"Perhaps, but I can't risk basing this case on gut feelings, especially not with the Kittrends' financial future at stake. The evidence I have from other sources so far does not support any of what Dahvin claimed."

So, Stohne was determined to convict him after all. Would the ombudsman be able to swing Blaine around to his way of thinking?

"I'm not saying I'm giving up," Stohne continued. "As I told Dahvin, I've still got some additional interviews to conduct. Perhaps I'll find out something else, or someone will get nervous and say more than they have in the past. I just wanted you to know where I think things stand at the moment."

"I appreciate your candor," Blaine answered. He sounded deflated.

Dahvin quickly stepped a few paces away from the door and turned as though he was just coming back from the dining hall.

"Oh, Dahv, thought you'd be in your room by now," Stohne said as he came out of Blaine's office.

"Yeah, I decided I'd swing back by the dining hall for a snack. They usually have a fruit out that I've become particularly fond of. I think it's called a dactil." He kept his voice open and friendly.

"I like those, too. I have a dactil tree near my house, but I don't have time to tend it properly, and the fruit isn't as sweet as it should be."

"The ones here are very good."

Blaine exited the office a few steps behind Stohne. He waved a small cylindrical device over a circle next to the stairway door. With a slight buzz, the lock on the door released and the door popped slightly open. Dahvin stepped over and held the door open. The ombudsman nodded, acknowledging the gesture.

"Thanks, Dahvin. I'll see you again before the trial. Just try to sit tight and be patient. I know that's difficult at this point."

"Very difficult." He glanced down the hall at the orderlies, who were still chatting and laughing, paying no attention to the three men at the door. Stohne stepped into the stairway, and Dahvin let the door close behind him, but kept it from latching securely.

"Are you headed back to your room? I'll call one of the orderlies for you," Blaine offered.

An escort—just what he didn't need. "No, if it's all right, I think I'll go back to the lounge for a while."

"That's fine. I think a little relaxation would do you good."

Dahvin grinned. Something else would do him more good, and that door was unlocked.

Blaine returned to his office. Dahvin took a few steps, keeping an eye on the orderlies, who headed into the dining room. He paused, allowing enough time for Stohne to have reached his vehicle. Then he turned back toward the stairway door. The hallway was empty. It was now or never. He couldn't trust Stohne.

He slipped through the stairway door, reached the door at the bottom of the stairs, and looked about. Through the transparent doors and the windows above and around it, he had a clear view of the street outside. Stohne had left, and there was no one else in sight in either direction on the walkway. Cruisers glided past on the busy street, but they had no reason to notice him.

He tested the outer door. Unlocked. He slipped out, jumped the small bushes next to the front walkway, and snuck around the corner, using the building to shield him from the sight of anyone coming to the front door. Once around the corner, he broke into a full run, crossing the small side street diagonally and cutting behind the building on the other side. He stopped just long enough to peer back and see if anyone seemed to be looking for him.

There was no one.

CONNECTED
RECIEVING....
CHAPTER 23

Dahvin estimated he had about three hours of daylight. Stohne had made the drive to the old part of town in about half an hour, so if he headed in the right direction, he should be able to make the spaceport before dark. Pitfire and damnation! He should have paid more attention to the route while they were driving.

He had a map of the city between the Evaluation Center and the spaceport in his head. Close to the spaceport many streets dead-ended, and he couldn't read the street names in the native language. Couldn't risk asking someone. His loose, collarless shirt and baggy pants were not the norm of dress for business people in this part of town. The less contact he had with people, the less likely he was to be identified by authorities and recaptured.

On the other hand, he was not dressed for the weather. The daytime temperature was below the freezing point of water, and the nighttime temperature would be much lower. With a high natural basal body temperature, he would be suffering from hypothermia in a short time. He had three local hours before dark. He had to move fast.

He started in the direction they had initially driven. Trying to stay out of sight wasn't easy. There was a lot of cruiser traffic, and pedestrians moving between buildings as well. This part of the city didn't have a convenient network of shadowy back alleys, like in Olde Towne. The multi-story glistening buildings were built in unbroken rows, the only differences between one and the next being variations in the colors of their exteriors. Up close he could see the glistening surface of the living protiki that Stohne had described. When he touched a wall, it had a soft, spongy, feel, though not slimy as he had expected.

He clung to doorways as people passed, or turned his back and pretended to look into windows, but the constant dodging slowed his progress tremendously. He wasn't wrong about his appearance, however. Those who did spot him seemed to look twice, or was it just his paranoid imagination? Several times he thought they activated their personal com devices after looking him over. He fought to remain calm and prevent panic from clouding his judgment. He scanned each cruiser, watching for the police insignia on the side.

All he could see above the buildings was the turquoise sky, so he couldn't get a fix on the position of the sun. Between trying to look up, looking over his shoulder, and trying to move forward, he began to feel dizzy. By the end of the next block, he was feeling nauseous and had a headache. He finally found a niche where one building jutted out slightly farther than its neighbor, and stopped to rest.

He struggled to remember the sequence and direction of turns Stohne had made. He'd started out in the same general direction as the cruiser had when it left the Evaluation Center. They had made one right turn fairly soon afterwards, and he had turned right once as well. But none of these buildings looked familiar. He tried to remember names or numbers or colors on buildings, but nothing seemed to click. He'd been too upset after reading Marlon Tave's logs. Distraught by the vague memories of his own pain and suffering, and jolted hard by the realization that he had in fact been here on Gehren at the time of Kittrend's murder, he'd been completely distracted during the drive with Stohne.

The light was fading and the temperature was falling fast. He didn't know how long he'd been wandering, and he now was hopelessly lost. Worse, large wet flakes of snow drifted down. He reached to catch a flake, only to have it disappear in his hand, cold and wet. He'd never felt it before, hadn't thought about how it would melt against the warmth of his skin. It started falling faster, until he could only see about half a block ahead of him. The shoulders and back of his shirt, soaked from the flakes as they melted, sapped the last of his body heat. He shivered so hard his teeth chattered.

Traffic on the streets and sidewalks diminished as the sun went down, allowing him to move a little faster. But if he didn't get a fix on his direction soon, it wouldn't matter. At the moment, however, there was no one around to ask for directions.

He moved straight forward another block, and finally spotted a man stepping out of one of the buildings a few paces ahead of him. He'd have to risk asking for help.

"Excuse me, sir, do you speak Alliance?"

"Yes, of course. How may I help you?" The man looked him over, but responded with typical Gehren politeness.

"I seem to have gotten lost. Can you tell me how to get back to the spaceport?"

"Oh, that's quite a distance from here. It's about ten mets in that general direction." The man pointed on a diagonal across the city. Perhaps you'd better summon a transport to take you there."

"Thank you very much. I will try that."

Of course, he had no intention of trying to flag down a taxi, even if he could spot one. In fact, he wasn't sure what emblem identified Durrand's hired transports, so he didn't know a taxi from any other vehicle. Not to mention the fact that he had no way to pay a fare. And how far was a "met?"

At least he had a sort of angular fix on the spaceport's direction. He'd been moving in the right general direction, but he'd seriously misjudged the distance. The sun was setting fast and the temperature was dropping even faster. Maybe if he jogged it would help keep him warmer. He struck out in a general diagonal direction, trying to turn left and right on even-numbered blocks to maintain a relatively straight line. He kept hoping he would spot that big circular intersection, but he never did. In the dim twilight, the buildings all merged into a nondescript gray, and the ground cover of the streets a deeper shade of gray.

He jogged off and on for what he guessed was the equivalent of a Standard ken, then stopped to catch his breath. His legs were beginning to cramp. He had exercised on his ship regularly, but he wasn't used to this kind of exercise under real gravity. And he hadn't been able to work out much since his capture, which he estimated was probably five tennights ago.

Where the pitfire was he? If a "met" was anything close to a Standard ken, he had a long ways to go. His muscles screamed, tightening like hard bands. He leaned against a building and stretched his legs, then pushed on. It wasn't much farther before his legs simply refused to go on. He had to stop.

As the darkness deepened, he tried to use the stars overhead, but saw no recognizable patterns. The streets were empty now. He wasn't afraid of the dark, but being alone in the dark and in danger aroused old fears. The jogging had warmed him up some, but now sweat cooled in the sub-freezing night air, and he began to shiver again. At last he found a space between two buildings, not quite a street. He moved toward the back of the alley, only to discover it was nothing more than a storage area between two parts of the same building.

A platform, head high, filled the space at the back of the alley, and storage units lined both walls. The only door he could find was at the top of the platform, which had stairs on one side and a long sloped ramp on the other. He climbed up to the door, but found it locked. At least the wind was somewhat blocked back here.

That wasn't going to make much difference. His body shook violently, his legs so shaky he had to concentrate on taking a step. It didn't matter—he was too exhausted to try to move on. He could only hope he could survive long enough to rest some and then try again.

Two people could have fit into each storage unit, but they were locked up. He finally huddled in the small space between the bottom of the loading dock stairs and the storage unit closest to them. Tess's image popped into his mind, and the memory of her touch warmed him a little. He lost himself in the memory of his last time with her.

He stopped shivering. Dream images mixed with the reality of a lonely alley. The dreams won out as he drifted off in the warmth and comfort of Tess's arms.

CONNECTED
RECIEVING....
CHAPTER 24

Stohne hadn't even made it through the front door of his home when he received a call from the evaluation center. Blaine apologized and explained he hadn't known Dahvin was missing until time for the evening meal. The orderly sent to escort him to evenfare had found the room empty, and a search of the building had proved Dahvin was nowhere to be found. How he'd escaped, no one knew.

Minutes later he charged through the door of the evaluation center and found Blaine waiting for him in the corridor. "I've asked the spaceport authorities to hold all outgoing flights until further notice."

"He isn't dressed for this weather. He won't make it through the night if he doesn't find shelter." Blaine shook his head, worry clouding his face. "We've got to find him quickly, for his sake as well as to get space traffic moving again."

"The police are on high alert. Every available man is searching for him. I'm a little surprised he pulled something like this. Surely he understands this will work against him."

"From a psychological standpoint it's not at all surprising. Think of how terrified he must be of facing any kind of imprisonment. Being confined here has to have been difficult for him. And with what we've uncovered in the last few days, making it look more and more like he was connected with Dom-el Kittrend, I don't think he saw any other way out."

"You still think he's innocent of murder?"

"Yes, absolutely. I'm not saying he couldn't have triggered the device accidentally, but I am convinced he did not harm Kittrend deliberately. He was dependent on the man for food. Why kill him?"

"Unfortunately, that doesn't tie in at all with what Dom-el Kittrend's family told me. Why would the Kittrend patriarch have been living in the alleys, going hungry himself and getting food out of garbage bins, and no one noticing he was missing? You know that doesn't make any sense."

"No, I realize that it doesn't. There are a lot of details about this case that just don't seem to add up." Blaine hung his head and looked at the floor.

"I understand how you feel about Dahvin." Stohne softened his tone. "But to be honest, they add up pretty well if you allow yourself to admit that he fired the laser, even if that didn't come out under alpha enhancement."

Blaine heaved a deep sigh. "But why would Dahvin have lied about Dom-el Kittrend living in the alleys? And that came out under alpha enhancement, too."

"Maybe he was confused. Maybe he thought that would make a good cover story. I don't know. I'd like to have every single detail answered, but it doesn't look like that's going to happen."

"First we've got to find him, and it's already getting dark. What about contacting the *EN238* crew? I understand they've returned in preparation for the trial."

"That probably wouldn't hurt. Just as long as they don't get trigger happy. I want him tried, not executed. I'll contact their commander and speak with him myself."

He stepped into Blaine's conference room to gain a little privacy and tapped the single key on his com that connected him to the Superior's direct link.

"Art, what can I do for you?"

"I need to contact the Enforcer ship, *EN238*. I would like to speak directly to its captain. I could use their help in the search for Misyer Tave, but I want it handled carefully. I don't want any bloodshed."

"Agreed. Give me a moment, I'll have Madra connect you."

His com fell silent for several seconds, then he heard an unfamiliar, deep male voice. *"Master Stohne, this is EN238, Captain Djanou. How may we assist you?"*

"Dahvin Tave, who is accused of murder here on Gehren, and whom you transported on our behalf, has escaped our custody. We could use some additional manpower in searching for him. Could you spare a few officers?"

"Of course. It is our duty to serve all our member planets in any enforcement capacity possible. How many officers do you need?"

"One additional team should suffice. But in particular, I believe you have some advanced DNA tracking technology that has a broader range than our own. Could you provide that as well?"

"We'll be happy to do so as long as the apparatus remains in the hands of our own officers."

"Agreed. One other thing, Captain, please make it clear to your officers that Misyer Tave is not to be fired upon. By our laws, he is innocent until convicted, and entitled to all the legal protections of any of our own citizens. Please be sure that the officers you send will comply with that instruction."

"They will follow your instructions as if they were my own, Master Stohne. You have my word."

"Thank you Captain. How soon can you get them to the planet? I will assign one of my officers to meet them and share what information we already have."

"I have already summoned a team. They will launch from our ship within minutes, and should land there in less than a Standard half-hour."

"Thank you, Captain. Your rapid response is very much appreciated."

"Our pleasure, Master Stohne."

He stepped back into Blaine's office, just as the doctor closed a comlink on his own desk. "Have you gotten any additional information?"

"No, I'm afraid not yet. I just spoke with a dispatch officer at MSAPA. Their search teams are reporting every quarter of an hour, but they've had no luck finding him."

"*EN238* will have enforcers on the ground within the hour. They have some additional DNA tracking technology that might speed up the search."

"Good. You did remind them they're not to fire on him, right?"

"Absolutely. Marken, you know I don't want any harm to come to him."

"I'm already concerned about his condition in this cold. I just hope we can find him in time."

Blaine was right, time was quickly running out. Stohne punched his com twice and connected with the duty officer. "This is Master Stohne. I've asked the Enforcer ship to send a team to help with the search for Dahvin Tave. Please send Officer Destry to meet them at the spaceport. Advise him he is to convey all information we have or receive regarding the search. Tell him, he's also supposed to be sure no one gets trigger happy and shoots Tave. Understood?"

"Understood. He's on his way."

—

Tess got the Priority One page in her quarters and headed for the team assembly room. Treiner met her in the corridor outside the door.

"Tess, I need you on the team we're assembling to assist in a search requested by the police on Gehren."

Tess nodded at Treiner. Krugg and Moag stood next to him. "Okay. Who are we looking for?" She prayed it wouldn't it be Dahv.

"Who do you think? It's Tave."

Tess closed her eyes and shook her head. "I was hoping he wouldn't do anything stupid."

"Guess he's just not that smart."

She shot him a dirty look.

"Keep your head on straight, Tess. I'm asking you to assist for his sake. You probably know him better than anybody. If you have any hunches, let me know."

"He'll head for the spaceport most likely."

"Yeah, apparently they already figured that much out. They've locked down everything scheduled to fly out."

"What about Dr. Bruin? She had a good rapport with him," Tess suggested.

Treiner cocked his head with a cynical expression. "I'd rather not add her.

We have orders not to kill him, that doesn't mean we won't necessarily have to shoot. She's trained to shoot, but—"

"You son-of-a—you'd just love to have the chance at that, wouldn't you."

Treiner grinned. "Hey, it's the job, you know."

"Son-of-a—" under her breath this time, but he heard. He shrugged and chuckled. Ordinarily, a junior officer wouldn't be allowed to cuss at her superior, but it was obvious he was enjoying irritating her. She was a fool to let him bait her.

The Enforcer search party reached the planet half an hour later, shuttling through the atmosphere at top speed. Once at the spaceport, they locked the ship down to make sure no one could enter without proper authorization.

Tess cringed in the biting cold as soon as they stepped off their ship, shivering slightly, in spite of having come prepared with an insulated coversuit. "Treiner, does anyone know how Dahv's dressed, or how long he's been missing?"

"I know they said he's been missing since sometime this afternoon. They think they discovered his absence in time to get the spaceport locked down before he could get to it, but even that's not certain. This could be a totally useless chase."

"He certainly would have headed there as fast as possible. But if he didn't make it, and if he's not heavily dressed, he's in serious trouble."

"How's that?"

"Dahvin's normal body temperature is several degrees above average for humans. He has a very low tolerance for cold temperatures." She watched her breath form a thick white vapor in the freezing air. "And this temperature is definitely way below his tolerance level. It's been dark for a couple of hours. He may already be suffering from hypothermia."

"Then we'd better be fast and diligent. Tess, I'll admit to hassling you a little over Dahvin. You got closer to him than you should have. But I just want you to know, I don't really wish him any harm. We'll find him, or we'll prove that he isn't here."

She eyed Treiner, not quite believing him. "Thanks, but I really thought you kind of had it in for him. Especially because of what happened with Grippa."

"I'll admit, I was furious over that at first. But she and I had several conversations about it. She made me realize it wasn't his fault. And, I guess, she also made me feel kind of sorry for the guy. Anyway, I know you two got to be pretty close. I'll do what I can to bring him in safe."

"Thank you. You had me a little worried with that crack about shooting him."

"Yeah, I know." Treiner's smug grin ran from ear to ear. "I was just firing your jets. Truth is, we have orders not to fire on him and I'm only issuing defensive weapons."

She shot him another dirty look as he handed each of the team members a stunner. "Son-of a runtboor. C'mon, we're wasting time."

She and Treiner joined up with a uniformed officer from the Durrand police force, who introduced himself as Officer Destry, while Krugg and Moag joined another officer. Treiner started to conduct a wide-range genetic scan of the landing area, but the Durrand officer interrupted him.

"We've already completed detailed scans of every inch of the spaceport, and officers have searched about ten square blocks surrounding the port. He either escaped before we were alerted, or he didn't make it this far."

"Why don't you show us a detailed map of the area between here and the Blaine Evaluation Center," Treiner suggested.

"My cruiser has a real-time mapping and positioning system. We can drive while we review possible routes."

Tess grabbed the front passenger seat next to the officer so she had the best view of the map. Treiner smacked his lips in annoyance, but tossed a small black bag in the back seat of the cruiser and climbed in after it with no verbal protest.

She studied the map the officer had pulled up on a screen on the dashboard. "It looks like the shortest route would be a sort of zig-zag through the city on a diagonal from the Evaluation Center to the spaceport. Has anyone followed that route in the search?"

"Yes, two of our units were working their way this direction from the Evaluation Center," Destry said. "But the Center is near the northern edge of the city, and the Spaceport is near the bay at the south end, and there's no direct route. He's very likely gotten lost somewhere in between."

"Then let's start at the spaceport and work back that way. Is your cruiser equipped with an external DNA scanner?"

"No, not this one."

"Tess, use this sensor lead." Treiner pulled a cable out of his bag. "You can put the sensor just outside the window and view the scanner inside. It should give you about a half-ken range."

She attached the cord Treiner handed her, cracked the window a bit, and threaded the sensor end of the lead out the window. Even the small crack brought a gust of frigid air into the cruiser, and she shivered in spite of her thermal suit. She slipped a chip into the scanner mounted in the front control panel of the cruiser, and downloaded Dahvin's DNA, then pressed *search*.

The threesome drove in silence for almost an hour, twisting their way through Durrand's deserted streets. Tess started slightly when the scanner emitted a soft beep. A blip showed on the display just about three blocks from their position.

"I think we've located him." She pointed out the route to Officer Destry.

The cruiser glided to a silent stop at a narrow space between two buildings. "He should be in there." Tess peered into the eerie darkness. Although there were lights along the street, no light penetrated the depths of the alley.

Destry got out first, pulled his hand weapon from its holster, and crouched down behind his side of the cruiser.

Tess looked at him with her hands on her hips. "I don't think there will be a need for that. Treiner, I want to go in first, alone, see if I can talk him out."

"Are you sure that's a good idea?" Destry asked.

The officer's attitude annoyed her more than she allowed herself to let on. The enforcer crew had been told to apprehend without firing. What about the Durrand police? "Please. I can handle myself."

"Do you want me to follow you in?" The officer was still crouched behind his cruiser, and he sounded like he hoped she'd say no.

She hesitated. To be honest, she wasn't as certain as she wanted Treiner to think. She could best Dahvin physically if she had to, if he was in a weakened state from hypothermia. But if he managed to grab Destry's weapon, even if he wouldn't fire on her, he might try to shoot his way past Treiner and Destry. All in all, she felt safer with no weapon in the mix.

"No. Let me try it my way first. I'll yell if I need backup."

CONNECTED
RECIEVING....
CHAPTER 25

"Dahv? Dahv!"

Somewhere in the depths of his darkness, Dahvin heard Tess's voice calling to him. His mind turned slowly, searching for a light in the dark tunnel. There was no light, only a far distant voice calling his name. Her voice. How he wanted to go to that sweet, tender voice.

The darkness offered no direction. He tried to make his feet move, but he could not feel his body, any part of it. A mind without a body. He drifted in the void without direction. Was he dead?

"Dahv, where are you? Come out. Please."

Her sweet voice called to him. He could feel his heart now, still beating in his chest. Lungs expanded a little, and burned like they were on fire. But where was the rest of his body? He couldn't see, couldn't move—a beating, breathing corpse.

"Dahv, it's me, Tess. Please come out. I won't hurt you. Please let me help you."

Such a sweet, sweet voice. Where was it coming from? He needed it, would move planet and moon to find it, but couldn't move his body. Dahvin sucked in a deeper breath. Frigid air burned into his lungs. Cold. So cold. Why was it so cold? He would move. By the stars, no matter what it took, he would move for *her*.

"Tess." He managed only a whisper. His throat was so dry. He struggled for another breath. "Tess."

By sheer force of will he uncurled the upper part of his body. He still couldn't see, but awareness of a hard cold wall penetrated the darkness of his mind. He pushed against it, willing his numbed legs to move. He could sense some movement in his lower body. Push! Push *hard!*

One knee pressed against his chest and he commanded the leg to straighten upward. He couldn't feel the ground, but his body heaved upward, sliding along the wall. Finally, he stood.

A light pierced the darkness, a beam that originated nowhere and landed on his chest.

"Dahv, is that you?"

Ah, her sweet voice again. Not a dream—real—here in this frigid darkness.

"Tess. *Tess!* Are you really here?" His voice still sounded dry and hoarse.

"I'm here Dahv. I'm here. Step out of the corner."

"I can't. I can't move. I'm…."

"You're hypothermic. I'm going to try to help you out of here."

The light moved closer, and finally he could make out Tess's outline behind it. He needed her warm touch. His mind flashed back to that evening on the ship when he'd held her in his arms. His frozen body cried out for the warmth of hers.

"Tess, please, touch me the way you did that night on the ship." He reached out toward her, reaching toward the light for her hands. He found them, pulled them to him, placed her hands on his chest. The heat of her palms burned through his skin deep into his chest. It touched his heart, and spread. He shivered violently.

"Come on. We have to get you out of here."

"I can't. They'll kill me. Creation, Tess, I love you. But I can't go. You have to leave me. Let me die."

"No one is going to kill you, and I am not going to leave you to die."

He never could resist her.

"Treiner, Destry, we're coming out," Tess yelled.

He allowed himself to be led toward the end of the alley—managing only a meager shuffle, still unable to feel his feet. It was a slow trip out. The effort raised his body temperature just enough to cause him to shake even harder, making it difficult to maintain his balance. He tried to speak again to Tess, but only managed to make his teeth chatter.

"Just take it easy. We're almost there." Her voice was his lifeline, soft, encouraging. "Keep moving."

They finally reached the end of the alley. The Gehren officer had his weapon drawn and aimed at him.

"Put that away!" Tess ordered. "He's unarmed, and too weak to be any danger."

Destry pulled out wrist restraints and started toward him.

"We don't need those either, do we Dahvin?" Treiner asked.

Dahvin shook his head no.

Treiner opened a black bag he held in his hand, pulled a blanket out of a warming compartment, and wrapped it around his shivering shoulders. Treiner's gesture startled him. This was not the way he remembered the man.

"Th—th—th—anks," he managed to stutter. His legs failed him and he sank to the ground.

"What are you doing?" Destry asked. "He's supposed to be under arrest. Thought you guys were supposed to be real brick-butts. Do you always treat your criminals with such delicacy?"

"No. Just this one." Treiner chucked Tess on the shoulder.

Treiner and Tess each took one arm and half-guided, half-dragged Dahvin to the cruiser.

—

Back at the Evaluation Center Dr. Blaine ordered Dahvin into a whirlpool bath filled with glowing, pale blue fluid, and started an intravenous solution. The tub felt uncomfortably hot at first, but as his body gradually warmed, he relaxed to the point where he couldn't even sense the liquid. Tess stayed by his side for nearly an hour.

"Dahv, I have to go. I'm really not supposed to be here with you."

"Why not?"

"Because I have to testify at your trial. We're not supposed to communicate prior to the trial, not one-on-one, anyway. The team will be waiting for me. We have to get back to the ship."

He leaned his head against the edge of the tub and closed his eyes. "The ombudsman warned me your crew would have to testify. Will you testify against me?"

"No, not against you. I'll just have to testify to what happened when we arrested you on Mira."

"What about what happened between us on the ship? And what happened with Grippa?"

"I don't know. I'm hoping they don't know about that. And I can't tell them much about that, anyway. All I know would be hearsay from somebody else. Same with Treiner. And as far as I know, they haven't requested that Grippa testify. So I don't think that will come out. Besides, that wasn't something you did deliberately. I doubt it would be relevant."

"But what about us?"

Tess hesitated. "I don't know. I mean, we didn't really do anything wrong, but I shouldn't have gotten so involved with you. It wasn't professional. I just…."

She didn't really have to finish the sentence. He hoped he knew the ending. He opened his eyes and sat up.

"Tess, I couldn't have made it this far without you. And I don't mean just rescuing me from the cold. Even before that, on the ship. If you hadn't reached out to me, I don't know what would have happened to me. I think I would have ended up mentally back on that slave ship. You know that's what happened with Grippa as it was. Without you, I might have slipped back and just stayed there. You don't know how scared I was. How scared I still am."

"I do know. You wouldn't have run otherwise. And you wouldn't have asked me to let you die."

He didn't remember asking her that. But he did remember that as he was losing consciousness he had decided he'd rather die than seek help and end up back here. Yet here he was—because of her. And now she was leaving again.

"Dahv, why are you so afraid someone will try to kill you? This isn't The Fringe. They don't just go around killing people."

"It's more like The Fringe than you think. After that Alpha Wave session with Dr. Blaine, I remembered the last day with Max. I did not fire that laser and kill him. But somebody killed Kittrend. They need a scapegoat that's not one of their own, and I'm it. I don't think they can afford to let me live. Even if they just imprison me, there would always be the chance that the truth would come out. Think about it. The old man I knew in the alley, the one from whom they got my DNA, couldn't have been Kittrend. Somebody went to a lot of trouble to set this up. Kittrend must have been killed by a powerful opponent."

Tess sat in stunned silence for several seconds. "Dahv, they don't even have a death penalty here. I just don't think that will happen. But I can see why you're worried about being convicted. I will keep an eye on the investigation as well as I can from the ship. If there's anything I can do to help, you know I will."

Gehren might not have a death penalty under law, but that didn't mean he couldn't be assassinated. If they could get to someone as powerful as Kittrend, he would be an easy mark. Surprising that they hadn't eliminated him already.

Maybe the risk of another body was too high. If they could discredit him and keep him under control, locked away for the rest of his life in a psychiatric institution, that might serve their needs. He'd read about that somewhere—"rehabilitation and reconditioning" they called it.

Great. Just great. He'd rather be assassinated.

"Tess, is there any way you can stay? Please." It was hard to bring himself to beg. But not as hard as seeing her go.

"Dahv, I'm afraid I'll only make things worse for you. We'd better play by the rules. You've already caused yourself a lot of problems."

"I know. Try to com me when you think nobody's looking."

"I'll have to be careful about using a direct comlink. I don't know if they're recording incoming signals to you. But I'll still use the particle-beam link we've been using secretly. At this range, it will be almost instantaneous."

He nodded. She had his trust. More than anyone else he'd ever known. Tess bent down and kissed his forehead.

Then without looking back, she strode out the door.

—

Treiner didn't say a word when Tess commed him to tell him she was ready to return to the ship. She'd expected a rude comment at the very least. Dr. Blaine had called a transport for her, and it was waiting when she stepped outside the Blaine Center.

During the ride to the spaceport, she tried to imagine a conversation with him. He knew where she'd been for the last hour. She'd shattered any doubt of her involvement with Dahvin. She'd have to beg him not to inform the captain. Even if he agreed, one of the other crew mates might inform on her.

She stepped out of the transport at the spaceport and saw Treiner leaning against the station wall, waiting for her. The rest of the team must have already boarded the shuttle.

"Ready?" he asked.

She nodded. Was that all he was going to say?

"Dirk," she touched his arm. "We need to talk."

"No, we don't." He started away, then turned back.

"Look, I know you realize you're treading on very dangerous ground. Still, you seem determined to do it. I'm not going to try to stop you. I won't report you, if that's what you're worried about. Just watch your step, okay?"

Tess heaved a sigh of relief. "I will. And Dirk, try to understand, this isn't some sort of dumb guilt-ridden infatuation. I can't explain it, but there is something special between Dahvin and me. Something I can't just ignore."

"I get that, which is why I'm letting it go." Treiner grabbed her hand. "Like I said, be careful. It could cost you everything."

She understood all too well. Her thoughts turned back to Dahvin and the things he'd said while in recovery at the center. Did he really believe his life was in danger? Was she being naive, or was he being paranoid? All of a sudden she wasn't so sure she was right.

CHAPTER 26

Stohne was running out of time.

With all the furor over the past couple of days caused by Dahvin's escape and recapture, he hadn't had time to conduct the follow-up investigation critical to the case. He needed to find out if there was any chance that Maxillian Kittrend could have been away from his estate for a prolonged period, as Dahvin had indicated.

He called the Kittrend estate, and asked the receptionist if he could meet with Dom Kittrend that day. After a short pause, the receptionist informed him that Dom Kittrend had a full schedule, but would make time to see him if he could make it brief. Brief was better than nothing. He told the receptionist he was on his way.

He had to wait for about half an hour in a reception area adjoining the business offices before Daks Kittrend came out to greet him and led him into his office. Two or three of the MSAPA offices could have fit into the room. At the far end opposite the door sat a large, ornately carved, antique bluewood desk. Between the door and the desk, comfortable, antique-looking but modern flexer chairs circled a hand-woven carpet, a style that the indigenous population of the southern continent were once famous for. Each chair had panels in the arms to activate a holographic display or extend a table top for a personal pad. The intricate patterns of deep blues and greens in the furnishings, accented with glittering gold threads, complemented the muted tones of Kittrend's desk. The walls held paintings from several of Gehren's great masters. Stohne felt a pang of jealousy, mixed with bitterness, that a few families could amass so much wealth at the expense of others.

Kittrend led him to one of the center chairs and sat down facing him.

Stohne activated the recording chip embedded in his palm. "I will be as brief as I can, and therefore, if you will forgive me, I will need to be direct."

"Not a problem. As I told you before, I will do whatever I can to assist you."

"Dom Kittrend, I must know, was there a period prior to your father's death when he left the estate for a prolonged time?"

"No. Not that I can think of."

"The records from the entry gate that I reviewed earlier did not show your father entering the estate for several months prior to his death."

"Did they show that he left the estate?"

Kittrend was shrewder than Stohne had hoped. "No. They did not."

"Then, that would explain why they didn't show him entering, would it not?"

"Are you telling me that your father never once left the estate for months prior to his death?"

"I told you before that I did not keep track of his daily activities."

"Was he ill prior to his death?"

"His health is confidential information. I don't see how it is in *any* way pertinent to your investigation."

"Dom Kittrend, how often did you see your father prior to his death? Was it on a daily basis?"

Kittrend hesitated, a bit too long in Stohne's estimation. He studied Kittrend's body language, formal, but at ease. On the other hand, the man was an exceedingly skilled business negotiator. If he lied, Stohne would likely never be able to detect it without appropriate equipment.

"My father was not in the best of health, it's true. There were days when I did not see him at all, and he missed meetings that I handled in his stead.

None of that is surprising considering his age. As I told you before, I was being trained to take over as head of the business."

"Do you think it's plausible he would not have left the estate at all for those months?"

"That's quite possible. We have everything we need here. Anything he wanted that we didn't have, he certainly could have sent an associate after. There really is no need to leave the estate."

"He was off the estate when he died, yet there is no record of him leaving that day or several days prior to that. Forgive me, Dom Kittrend, but is it possible he was staying with a mistress?"

"*Ombudsman!* Enough!"

Kittrend had asserted his social superiority. Addressing Stohne by job title only was a deliberate breach of professional courtesy. Stohne hadn't really expected an answer to the latter question, though he had hoped.

"Forgive me, Dom Kittrend. It is critical to my investigation that I determine where your father was during the two weeks prior to his death."

Kittrend had started for the door to show him out, but paused with his hand on the carved lever, his back to Stohne. "If my father had a mistress, I was not aware of it. He protected his privacy with a vengeance, even from me. I saw him when he wanted to see me. I truly don't know everything he might have been doing at that time. I doubt anyone does."

Kittrend's shoulders had drooped noticeably. He had revealed far more of his relationship with his father than he would have wished. At any rate, nothing seemed to support Dahvin's account of the two weeks prior to the elder's death. But there was still Dom-el Kittrend's personal assistant Lane Coutier, if he could find him.

Stohne left the Kittrend estate and headed for the Division of Security and Public Assistance. He called ahead and asked one of the juniors to locate Lane Courtier. Tal Quint was waiting in Stohne's office when he arrived.

"I have Lane Coutier's com coordinates loaded on your desk."

"Great! Fast work, Tal. I appreciate your help."

"Anytime. Glad I could be of assistance."

"Computer, connect."

The face of a middle-aged man appeared on the display. In the background, Stohne could see the trappings of a large, well-furnished office. It seemed Coutier had moved up in position, not suffering banishment.

"Misyer Coutier, I am sorry to bother you. I am Ombudsman Art Stohne, investigating the death of Dom-el Kittrend, and I would appreciate a few minutes of your time."

"I'll be happy to assist in any way I can. Dom-el Kittrend's murder was a great shock to us all. I'm sure the family would like to see the case closed."

"Thank you. I would also like your permission to record this session, in the event there is some information I might need to submit to the court. That would preclude the need for you to travel here to testify. May I record?"

"I suppose so. I don't know if I can be of much help, though." Coutier shrugged.

Stohne studied the man's body language. He seemed relaxed, though reserved in a businesslike manner. He really shouldn't have expected anything else. Firstcaste men excelled at business negotiations. It took a lot to ruffle one of them.

"In particular, I'm trying to pin down exactly where Dom-el Kittrend was during the two weeks prior to his death. I assume you were still working with him at that time."

"I was still his personal assistant, that is correct."

"Did you see him on a daily basis in the weeks just prior to his death?"

"No. He had largely withdrawn from the business at that time. His son had taken over almost all of the company activities."

"Was Dom-el Kittrend on the estate every day prior to his death?"

Coutier seemed a little taken aback, then thoughtful.

"I don't think I can answer that. As I said, he didn't summon me every day."

Couldn't answer that, or wouldn't? Even if he wasn't summoned every day, surely he would have known Kittrend's general whereabouts.

"I noticed from the gate records that there was no entry showing the Dom-el leaving the estate in the weeks prior to his death, yet he was clearly off the estate at the time of his death. No one seems to think he could have been kidnapped, but do you think that would be a possibility?" Coutier laughed. "Not unless his kidnappers had some way of making him and themselves invisible. I just don't think that's at all likely."

Coutier paused. Stohne studied the face before him. He found it harder to detect nuances of body language, expression, and tone over the com, but the corners of the man's mouth tightened slightly in amusement.

"Keep in mind, Master Stohne, that it was Dom-el Kittrend who started keeping gate records. It's quite likely he ordered the gatekeeper not to record his own comings and goings. The fact that he would track his son and daughter, but not record his own travels, does not surprise me in the least. He had a rather suspicious nature."

Of course. Why hadn't that occurred to him before? Even Daks Kittrend might not have known that.

"Thank you, Misyer Coutier. You've been a tremendous help. I appreciate your time."

No matter how hard he looked, nothing supported Dahvin's account of Maxillian Kittrend living like a vagabond in the back alleys of Olde Towne. More and more, it seemed that as an off-worlder, Dahvin had simply been able to control his thoughts while under Alpha Wave. Would he have reason to construct such an elaborate story if he had triggered the laser accidentally?

CHAPTER 27

After intensive treatment at the Blaine Center, Dahvin had recovered from hypothermia with no permanent damage to his hands or feet. But he faced the actual trial with increasing anxiety.

In spite of Dr. Blaine's efforts to convince the ombudsman of his innocence, Dahvin was certain he would be convicted of murder. The Kittrend family was a powerful and influential one, and he was still an unimportant alien. How could he even be sure the judge hadn't been bribed? The only bright spot was that the crew of *EN238* would remain at Gehren to offer testimony for the trial, which meant at least he might have contact with Tess again.

The final days before the trial passed in a mind-numbing haze. He couldn't think of anything to research that would help him. He had no control over anything anyway. Even if he found out some critical piece of information, who would believe him? Or care? Blaine cared, but he would not be able to swing Stohne's attitude, or his testimony in court.

Stohne showed up at the Evaluation Center the day of the trial with C-2 Treiner in tow, not the person Dahvin wanted to see. Stohne drove the three of them in one of the local police units to the Durrand courthouse. Unlike many of the city's buildings, the courthouse appeared plain and functional in design.

It stood no more than three stories tall, built of metallic material, with evenly-spaced, square windows. In front, a stone staircase led to transparent front doors.

Stohne drove around to the rear of the building. A tunnel unfolded from the building and completely enveloped the vehicle, cutting off any avenue of escape. Stohne, Dahvin and Treiner entered the courthouse through the collapsible tunnel, which afforded more light than Dahvin had expected from its external appearance. At Stohne's insistence, Treiner didn't apply wrist or ankle restraints, but gripped him firmly by the arm, as if convinced he would escape at any moment. As far as Dahvin could see, there was no point.

They went up one flight of steps to the first floor. The stairway exited onto the center of a long hallway, as plain and functional as the exterior had appeared. A row of small storage lockers lined the wall to his left. He assumed they were used by the ombudsmen and others who spent countless hours in this building away from their own offices. Halfway down the hall to his right, massive double doors identified the courtroom in which he would be tried.

"We'll head into the courtroom in about half an hour." Stohne pointed to the doors that he'd already guessed led to his fate. "You'll need to wait here." He led Dahvin to a set of four chairs near the double doors. "I have preparations to complete before it starts, and I have to meet with the judge."

Stohne left and entered an office through a smaller door on the right side of the courtroom.

Treiner stayed. After a few minutes, he seemed to relax his grip a little. His relaxation put Dahvin on high alert. He surveyed his surroundings with a calculating eye. The hallway stretched over a hundred paces in each direction. There was one more set of heavy double doors about fifty paces to his left, then another stairway like the one they had come up. More of the original stone ran along the base of the walls with panels of antique bluewood inset into the walls as decoration.

The hallway had single doors at each end. He remembered a balcony on the side of the building. There had been no stairway to the ground, but the prospect for escape was overwhelming, even if he had to jump.

He bolted for the door on the left—and plowed straight into Moag, who came around the corner of an intersecting hallway. Without an instant's hesitation, Moag grabbed him and slammed him against the lockers lining the opposite wall. His chest struck the handle of one of the lockers. Pain shot from his chest out through his back, down into the pit of his stomach, and up into his throat, choking the breath out of him. He collapsed to the floor, and Moag and Treiner together yanked him to his feet and slammed him back against the lockers. This time, at least he missed the handles.

"Don't try anything like that again!" Treiner snarled.

Unable to breathe, Dahvin collapsed again.

"Leave him alone. Stop this at once!" Stohne charged down the hall, drawn to the hallway by the ruckus.

"He tried to escape! I've had enough of his tricks." Treiner yanked him to his feet again. This time Dahvin managed to remain standing, still unable to catch anything but short painful breaths. Treiner yanked Dahvin's arms behind him and had wrist restraints on before he could blink.

"Remove those immediately, he hasn't been found guilty yet," ordered Stohne.

Treiner glared at him.

"I said *now!* You have no authority here. You are only here to testify, not to enforce. Release him immediately!"

Treiner uttered what could best be described as a low growl, but released the restraints.

"Dahv, don't be an idiot." Stohne looked him straight in the eye. "This kind of behavior can't help you before the judge. You must trust me. You have to act sensibly. Are you all right?"

Still trying to breathe enough to keep from passing out, Dahvin shook his head no. He leaned against the wall to keep from falling, his right hand testing the damage to his sternum. It wasn't broken, but it hurt like pitfire.

Stohne pulled a small com unit from a hidden pocket in his tunic, and punched a single button.

"Are you in the courthouse, yet?"

Dahvin heard Blaine's familiar voice answer.

"Good. Meet me on the second floor as soon as you can."

It only took Blaine a matter of seconds, but they were long seconds. He watched Blaine's eyes dart from him slumped against the lockers to Stohne's tensely folded arms.

"What happened?"

"We had an incident. Dahvin tried to escape again." Stohne's annoyance was palpable. "Moag stopped him, but he slammed him up against these lockers. I don't think he's seriously hurt, but he's in some pain and is having trouble breathing."

Blaine didn't say any more, but opened a small bag he carried with him. He pulled out a small portable scanner and ran it over Dahvin's chest, then pressed a cylinder to his neck. The hypo eased the pain in his chest in a matter of moments. Blaine glared at Treiner and Moag, who glared back. Treiner threw up his hands in disgust and stomped off, with Moag close behind.

And then, seemingly out of nowhere, Tess appeared at Dahvin's shoulder. Her hair was tied back and she wore her uniform, but her eyes were compassionate.

"Hey, trying to get yourself killed, or just convicted?"

Tess looked at Dahvin's eyes. He let her read him. His mood was cold now, as cold as tempered metal—not angry, not panicky, determined. She squared her shoulders and returned the same look directly into his gaze. She would not give in, she would not let him escape, but she would stand by him.

They looked straight at each other for several seconds. Then Dahvin closed his eyes. Tess won. He surrendered.

"Walk with me," she commanded. He pulled himself away from the wall and followed Tess. They walked past Stohne, who looked after them with an air of consternation, as Dahvin obediently followed Tess down the hall.

Tess's presence gave him a semblance of calm. He wished she'd been the one they'd sent to accompany him from the Evaluation Center instead of Treiner.

"Hang in there, we'll get through this." As they reached the courtroom door, she took him by the arm, not in the threatening manner Treiner always seemed to convey, but with a reassuring touch. Her use of the pronoun "we" hadn't escaped his notice either.

When it was time for the trial to begin, Stohne asked if he felt up to proceeding. Blaine's potion had worked its magic, and he was now able to breathe normally. He just wanted the whole thing over with as quickly as possible, whichever way it would go.

The courtroom was smaller than he'd expected. The judge sat on a raised platform at the front behind a massive desk carved with stately figures in long robes. Stohne took a seat at an elongated oval table that faced the judge, and pointed to a chair on his right for Dahvin. Dr. Blaine sat to Stohne's left. The three of them sat in solid wood, ornately carved chairs, not uncomfortable, but not as soft as the flexers. In front of the table, Stohne had a stand set up with a console that looked like it might project holographic images. Behind them sat more wooden chairs for additional witnesses. Tess took a seat behind Dahvin and to his right, so he could easily glimpse her out of the corner of his eye. Treiner, Moag and a few other individuals he didn't recognize had also entered the courtroom and taken seats.

A soft bell tone sounded once. "Ombudsman Stohne, are you ready to begin?" asked the judge.

Stohne took a quick sideways glance at Dahvin. He nodded. What else could he do?

"We are ready, Your Honor."

"Present your evidence, Ombudsman."

Stohne had explained earlier that he would be the only one presenting evidence. It was his job to uncover all the facts relevant to the case and to present them to the court. The judge would expect Stohne to make a summarizing statement at the end, in which he would point out what he believed the preponderance of evidence showed, if it showed a clear direction for the verdict. When the ombudsman was convinced of a party's guilt or innocence, Stohne had said the judge rarely ruled the opposite. The suspect was considered innocent until proven guilty. On the other hand, due to Gehren's advanced forensic technology, Dahvin figured the judge tended to assume that the individual who had been arrested for a crime must be guilty.

What Stohne hadn't said was what conclusion he intended to present in this case. That spoke volumes. If Stohne had believed that he'd never fired the personal laser that killed Kittrend, or even if he believed it was accidental, the ombudsman would have told him that to ease his fears. Or at the very least, Blaine would know and would have said so. His fate was sealed. His only hope now was that the judge would decide that he did not need to be imprisoned, that he could instead be referred for "rehabilitation." But then, he'd already tried to escape twice. Either way, he would spend the rest of his life on this planet. His stomach clenched in a hard knot.

Stohne stepped up to the evidence stand between the table and the judge's platform. "On 16 Altan 2864 Maxillian Kittrend was found dead in an alley next to Maxen's Market on Northport Street in the Olde Towne district of Durrand. Coroner Keem Dorton determined the cause of death to be a shot from a low-power personal laser. The weapon was found lying next to the body at the scene. Testing conducted by the MSAPA labs on the personal laser found at the scene detected DNA traces belonging to the murder victim and an unidentified off-worlder.

"On Alliance Standard Date 2.16.5416, Gehren date 19 Janus 2867, Alliance Enforcers identified an individual on planet Mira with a DNA trace matching the imprint on the personal laser found at the scene of Dom-el Kittrend's death. That individual was fired upon by Enforcer officers and apprehended. He was later identified as Dahvin Tave, the defendant present today."

Stohne indicated Dahvin with his hand while maintaining eye contact with the judge.

"As my first exhibit, I have a photograph of the deceased's body when it was first discovered by police. The police officer found the deceased lying on his back with his hands folded over his chest. Please note the photograph shows the position of the body when it was found. The laser that was the cause of death is lying just next to him."

Stohne pressed a key on the evidence stand, and the judge looked at a display on his bench and nodded. The picture also popped up on a module on the table where Dahvin was seated. It was unnerving to see "Max" lying there, looking exactly the way he had found the old man that last day. These people knew what Kittrend looked like. The judge's face showed no hint of lack of recognition. Hard as it was for him to accept, Max and Maxillian Kittrend had to be one and the same.

"In further evidence, I submit the report prepared by the investigating police officer after Dom-el Kittrend's body was discovered."

The holo display split into two images, and an official-looking document appeared in the right pane, though in a language Dahvin couldn't read.

"Had the body fallen after death, it would not have fallen into the position in which it was found," Stohne continued. "The crime simulations developed by the Ministry of Security and Public Assistance indicate the most likely scenario is that the deceased's body was moved after the murder was committed. However, there was no evidence the body was moved after death, and an alternative explanation would be that the laser was fired while the deceased was prone. Since the simulations are based solely on the speculation of the investigating officer, those will not be offered as evidence.

"Exhibit number three is a copy of the death certificate prepared by the coroner. The coroner determined that the laser unit was fired straight up under the chin and into the deceased's brain, causing instant death."

The first two images disappeared from Dahvin's viewer and another document that he couldn't read loaded. It didn't do much good to show him exhibits he couldn't read.

"I will furthermore offer into evidence a recording of an Alpha Wave enhanced session that Dr. Marken Blaine conducted with Misyer Tave, in the course of Dr. Blaine's pre-trial evaluation of the defendant."

Stohne stopped and glanced over his shoulder at Dahvin. He could have used more advance warning. Stohne had told him the Alpha Wave recording would be used in the trial in his defense, but he hadn't expected it to come up so early in the proceeding.

"This recording is offered to the court with the approval of Misyer Tave. It will require approximately two hours to run the full recording, but gives the defendant's recollection of the events prior to the death of Dom-el Kittrend, and it is my opinion the information in this recording is both pertinent and vital to the case."

The judge raised his eyebrows slightly at Stohne.

"Very well, Master Stohne, you may proceed." Stohne pressed a key on a computer console in front of him, and a panel lit up on the wall to the right, in view of the judge and the entire courtroom.

Stohne returned to the table.

"Do I have to sit through this?"

"I'm afraid so," Stohne answered. "If asked, you will have to testify that you are the one who was recorded and that the content is true to the best of your knowledge and recollection."

"I was asleep, basically, remember?" Stohne's eyes narrowed in admonition. How could he warn Stohne that the content of the recording might throw him into a flashback. If they thought the escape looked bad, wait until he was curled up in a ball under the table.

He made it through the first quarter of the recording and began to relax somewhat. He began to suspect that the reason Blaine had that hypo at the ready earlier was because the doctor realized he'd have to be mildly sedated to make it through this portion of the testimony.

For two full hours by the timepiece in the courtroom, he suffered through listening to his own account of his last days on the Pruzzian slave ship and his short time on Gehren. Though he managed to remain in the present reality, he spent most of that time with his body tightly tensed, arms folded tightly across his chest, head down. By the time it was over, his muscles ached from exhaustion.

When the recording ended, the courtroom remained completely silent for several seconds. It seemed as if no one was breathing.

Stohne stepped back up to the evidence stand. "As you have heard, Your Honor," Stohne began, picking up as though he had just paused in his presentation, "during the Alpha Wave enhancement procedure, Misyer Tave reported that he did not recognize the personal laser as a weapon. He admits he handled the weapon, and in so doing, it is believable that the weapon could have discharged, leading to the death of Dom-el Kittrend."

Bitterness left a bad taste in Dahvin's mouth. Except that it didn't discharge. That's the one little fact that no one here seems to want to accept, that one of their precious, morally correct Gehrens actually pulled that trigger. At least Stohne let it look like an accident.

"Your Honor, I recognize that this has been a difficult portion of testimony for the court to hear, and certainly, it has been very trying for Misyer Tave. As it is currently nearing time for midfare, I would like to request that the court adjourn for one hour, and resume at 13th hour."

"The court agrees that a break at this time is in order. Court is hereby recessed, to resume at 13th hour."

Dahvin was both relieved and annoyed. Good time for a break, just after they'd all but proven him guilty of at least accidental homicide, if not murder. Give them time to mull that over while they eat.

"There is a cafeteria on the lower floor here," Stohne said, turning to Dahvin. "We'll eat there. And please, no nonsense. It wouldn't take much to make you look like a murderer."

"I can't see that I've got a lot to lose. I didn't fire that damned thing, but you sure made it look like I did."

Stohne was silent for a moment. Dahvin wished he could be as cool and constant as the ombudsman. Nothing ever seemed to push him into losing control. "Dahv, there is just no evidence to support that anyone else was involved. If the judge rules it was an accident, it's not likely to result in prison time and you will get your ship back."

That was the best he could hope for. Stohne was right. It wouldn't take much to make the judge decide on murder, especially if he'd been bribed.

"Will the Enforcer crew be eating there too?" He was reluctant to specify Tess, but he could hope. Of course, he did not want Moag and Treiner there.

"No. They have to stay apart from us because they are, essentially, testifying against you regarding the arrest." Stohne led the way to the cafeteria, but Dahvin didn't have much of an appetite.

CONNECTED

RECIEVING....

CHAPTER 28

The next hour passed much more quickly than Dahvin wished, and it seemed like they were back in the courtroom in a matter of minutes. He hadn't given Stohne any trouble. It was clear at this point that he would not escape and could only irritate the judge, the one person who stood between life in an institution and freedom.

As they filed back into the courtroom, Tess went back to the seat she had occupied earlier to Dahvin's right, and Dr. Blaine took a seat directly behind him. Once everyone had settled in, the bell tone sounded, and the judge announced that court was back in session.

Stohne moved back to the evidence stand. "Your Honor, I would like to call Dr. Marken Blaine to testify."

The doctor gripped Dahvin's shoulder as he stood up. Then he stepped around to the right and walked up to join Stohne.

"I am Dr. Marken Blaine, Master Therapist at the Blaine Mental Health and Evaluation Center."

"Doctor, will you give an honest and complete account of all facts known to you in this case?" the judge asked.

"I will."

"Dr. Blaine, on 39 Janus 2867, did you conduct the Alpha Wave enhancement procedure on Dahvin Tave?" Stohne asked, turning to face the doctor.

"I did."

"And could you describe to the court the purpose of that procedure?"

"The primary purpose was to assist Misyer Tave in accurately remembering events that had been suppressed by his conscious mind due to physical and emotional trauma he suffered at the time of those events."

Stohne nodded. "Is it common for an individual to suppress a memory when it is associated with trauma?"

Blaine frowned. "I wouldn't say it is common, but there are well-substantiated cases of that type of memory suppression in the professional psychiatric literature. There have been a number of cases in which an individual completely blocked an event from memory, as though the event never happened. In Misyer Tave's case, the physical and emotional trauma was unusually severe."

"So, in your expert opinion, it is scientifically sound to accept that Misyer Tave could have been unable to consciously recall some of the details of events that were brought forth under the Alpha Wave enhancement?"

"Absolutely."

"And, in your opinion, what trauma caused that loss of memory?"

Blaine seemed a little startled at the question. He glanced at Dahvin and cleared his throat. "The abuse he suffered aboard the Pruzzian ship, the extreme malnutrition he suffered even while here on Gehren, the pain from his injuries. All of that contributed to his trauma."

"Doctor, in your professional opinion, is Alpha Wave Enhancement an effective way to bring out true memories? Is a person likely to be able to simply make up a story or alter facts while in an Alpha Wave enhanced state?"

"No," Blaine said. "They will report what they remember, and they are able to remember events in greater and more accurate detail during Alpha Wave enhancement. Alpha Wave results have been used many times in Gehren courts to supplement other evidence. It should be noted, however, that the memory can still be colored by the individual's knowledge or understanding. For instance, if a person had never seen a tree before, they might describe what they were seeing but not be able to identify it as a tree, even if they learned later on that it was called a tree."

Stohne cocked his head to one side. "I see. But what about non-Gehren individuals. Have you ever used this procedure on off-worlders?"

"Several times," Blaine said.

"And are the results on off-worlders as dependable as the results on Gehren natives?"

Blaine sighed. "That depends on the species. In my experience, for descendants of the progenitor race with human brain architecture, such as Misyer Tave—" Blaine nodded in Dahvin's direction "—the results are reliable. I have had instances, particularly with insectoid individuals and the archeotoptrix of Indira, where their brain architecture is quite different from ours, that the Alpha Wave was not effective."

Comments the ombudsman had made in the past had shown he had a deep respect for Blaine, and Blaine felt the same toward Stohne. But just now, Dahvin could swear he'd sensed some tension between the two. He wished he could read the ombudsman better. It had seemed earlier like he was determined to convict him. Now it seemed like he was leaving room for doubt.

"So, Dr. Blaine, do you believe that the events as Misyer Tave described them under Alpha Wave were accurate according to his best memory?"

Blaine nodded vigorously. "Yes, absolutely. In the few instances where the Alpha Wave is not effective or the patient not fully responsive, there are telltale signs I have learned to identify. I did not see any of those in Misyer Tave's case. It is my opinion that he was fully engaged in the procedure."

"Thank you, doctor, those are all the questions I have for you."

Blaine believed Dahvin's account of his time on Gehren was accurate. He knew from eavesdropping on Stohne and Blaine that Stohne hadn't believed it. But Stohne had allowed Blaine's testimony with no comment. Maybe the ombudsman wasn't supposed to give his own opinion. Stohne could have chosen not to allow Blaine to testify. Was he leaving him an out? It was so hard to figure out where Stohne stood.

"Next, Your Honor, I would like to establish the conditions surrounding the arrest of Misyer Tave. I will first call to the stand Alliance Enforcer EN-2 Tess d'Tieri."

Thankfully Stohne hadn't called Moag or Treiner to testify. Either of them would have been more than willing to convict him in order to cover their own tails. Tess would have to be honest, but she wouldn't be vindictive.

Tess rose from her seat and joined Stohne at the evidence stand. Stohne touched her elbow. "Please identify yourself to the court."

Tess faced the judge. "I am EN-2 Tessiana d'Tieri from Alliance Enforcer ship *EN238.*"

"Officer d'Tieri, do you remember the events of Alliance Standard Date 2.16.5416 on the planet Mira?" Stohne asked.

"Yes."

"I would like to remind the court that ASD 2.16.5416 would be 19 Janus 2867 on the Gehren calendar. Officer d'Tieri, why was your ship at Mira?"

"We initially arrived there to purchase some parts we needed for repairs and improvements on our ship. Other systems were closer, but didn't have the parts we were looking for, so we had to travel outside the usual Alliance region to procure what we needed."

"And why were you on patrol on Mira?" Stohne asked, his voice flat and matter-of-fact.

"We weren't technically on patrol. We were just checking out the marketplace."

"Then you were not there specifically to arrest Dahvin Tave?"

"No."

"Then how did you happen to identify him?"

"Canton Treiner, our team leader, always makes genetic sweeps no matter where we are. We've stumbled onto fugitives that way several times."

"And would you please explain to the court what you mean by a genetic sweep?"

"We have a hand-held device that has a database of the DNA print of every suspect that we've been asked to track down. Our devices can read DNA for a distance of about 100 metras." Tess had a habit of talking with her hands. As she talked she formed a square the size of the instrument they had used.

"And did Canton Treiner use that device on Mira, even though you were beyond Alliance territory?"

"Yes, he did." She snuck a peek at Dahvin. "That's how he happened to identify Dahvin Tave's DNA, although we did not have an identity for him in the database, just a numbered DNA trace."

"So Dahvin Tave would have had no reason to expect to be arrested by Alliance personnel on that planet?"

Tess faltered. "I—I can't say *what* he would have expected. When I talked to him after we arrested him, on the trip back here, he didn't seem to have any idea why he was considered a suspect in any crime."

"Did your crew address Misyer Tave before firing on him, identify yourselves in any way?"

"I wasn't with Canton Treiner and the others when they first spotted him, but it would be Standard procedure to announce 'Alliance Enforcers, stand to.'"

"If your team members didn't know Misyer Tave's name, how would he have known you were addressing him, specifically?"

Tess faltered again. "I don't know, I guess."

"And in fact, did he make any attempt to elude the officers?"

"Yes, he did do that, sort of. When I first saw him, he came running around the corner of one of the stalls in the Miran market. He stopped when he saw me. Then Treiner and Moag came up behind him and Moag fired at Dahvin, I mean, Misyer Tave, and Tave raised his weapon in my direction, and I fired at him also."

"So Misyer Tave had his back turned to Officer Moag when Officer Moag fired at him, and it would be your testimony that you fired at him in self-defense?"

Tess looked at Dahvin wide-eyed. He couldn't help but feel for her, as she struggled to be honest without convicting him or herself either one. He didn't envy her position, and hoped she wouldn't be sanctioned for her actions.

"Moag did fire at Misyer Tave from the back. They had followed him from behind the booth. When Moag fired, it knocked Misyer Tave toward me, and then I fired."

"So at the time, you felt your actions were justified."

"Yes, at the time," Tess answered softly. Stohne had left her a small escape.

"Your Honor, those are all the questions I have for this witness at this time."

The judge excused Tess from the evidence stand. Tess didn't look at Dahvin as she went back to her chair.

"Your Honor, I would like Master Coroner Keem Dorton to testify."

A short stocky man with a comically bushy gray mustache stood up at the back of the courtroom and stepped up beside Stohne. At the same time, a document popped up on the display in front of Dahvin, and therefore, presumably in front of the judge as well, although again, it was in the local Gehren language.

"Your Honor, I am Keem Dorton, Master Coroner."

"Master Dorton, did you fill out this death certificate on 16 Altan 2864, based on your examination and the information provided to you by the investigating officer?" Stohne asked, showing him the same certificate he had shown to the judge.

"Yes, I did," Dorton answered.

"And was it your finding that Dom-el Kittrend was killed by a shot from a personal laser weapon?"

"By a shot from a low-intensity laser, yes."

"Did you determine whether that shot would have been fired from someone else?"

"There would be no way for me to make that determination without witnessing the act. It was the investigating officer's assumption that the cause of death was homicide."

"Your Honor, I would appreciate it if you would remind all the witnesses that there has not yet been a determination that a homicide was committed," Stohne said, turning to look at the judge.

"Accepted. Master Dorton, you and any who follow you should refrain from using prejudicial terms such as homicide, murder or murderer."

"Thank you, that's all I need from you right now," Stohne said.

Dorton returned to his seat on the back row, near where Treiner and Moag were seated.

"Your Honor, I would now like Dahvin Tave to testify."

Dahvin nearly jumped out of his skin. Stohne had told him he would probably have to testify, but he hadn't expected it so soon. Following Dorton's example, Dahvin stood up and moved over beside Stohne to introduce himself.

"I am Dahvin Tave."

"Misyer Tave, were you in the City of Durrand on 16 Altan 2864?"

"I was here on Alliance Standard Date 2.16.5416, according to my ship's logs."

"And can you tell the court where in the city you were on that date?"

"I can't tell you exactly, because I had only been here for about a tennight at that time, and I don't know the city very well. But I was living mostly in an alley that intersected Northport Street."

"Please explain," prodded Stohne. "How could you be 'living' in an alley?"

"I didn't have a building to live in. I had been a stowaway on an interplanetary cargo ship. The ship landed here and I snuck off the ship. I didn't know what planet I was on. I was afraid of being found, so I stayed in the alley, mostly."

He could only trust that Stohne would not deliberately lead him into a trap.

"And did you know Dom-el Kittrend?"

"I didn't know him by that name. I knew a man who called himself Max. He found me a day or so after I got off the cargo ship. He showed me how to find food in the garbage bins."

"So, it is your honest testimony that you met Dom-el Kittrend several days prior to his death, and that he befriended you, in a sense?" Stohne asked.

"Well, as I said, I knew a man who called himself Max." He wasn't stupid enough to make it easy for them. "He was the closest thing to a friend I'd ever had at that point."

Dahvin watched for a reaction from Stohne. As always, though, the man remained unflappable.

"And describe to the court what happened on 16 Altan."

"Well, I didn't know it was that date. I didn't know anything about Gehren, then. I have been working with Dr. Blaine at the Mental Health Evaluation Center since I was brought back here, and he has helped me remember a lot of what happened. On that particular day I came back to the alley where Max and

I were living, after hunting for some food. I had found enough that I thought I should share some with him.

"He was lying on his back. I just assumed he was asleep. He had his hands folded on his chest, and he was holding something. I was curious. He frequently salvaged stuff out of the disintegrator bins. I picked it up out of his hands. It was just a square box. I couldn't see that it did anything."

"It didn't fire a beam of light or anything like that?"

"No, it was just a plain black box, as far as I could see. But when I looked again at Max, I could see that he was dead."

"How did you know that?" Stohne asked.

"His lifelight was gone."

"Misyer Tave, that is not a term that will be familiar to the court, could you explain further?"

"The lifelight, it's the kind of light that everything that's alive has around it. When someone dies, the light slowly fades away. So I guess Max had already been dead for a while when I saw him, because there was no lifelight left around him."

"And what did you do with the black box after you looked at it?"

"I just laid it down, because I couldn't see any value in it. And, I—I looked in his pocket and found a few coins. I took them. I didn't see anything wrong with that at the time. I didn't figure he could use them."

"And then what happened?"

"I went to the shop just around the corner from the alley. I was going to get some food, to pay for it that time, because I had some coins. But when the shopkeeper saw me he chased me away. I ran about two blocks, and found the spaceport again. I ran onto another cargo ship and hid. Actually I passed out in the cargo hold. I left Gehren on that ship and didn't come back until after I was arrested by the Alliance Enforcers."

"Your Honor, I would like to ask Sharfa Maxen to testify. He owns the shop Misyer Tave just referred to in his testimony," Stohne said.

Dahvin nearly fainted. Presenting evidence that he'd stolen from the grocer would only convict him further.

A slender man, taller than Stohne, stepped up to the front of the courtroom.

His typically Gehren-gray hair had a slight yellow tint. "Your Honor, I am Sharfa Maxen, owner of Maxen's Grocery on Northport Street in Olde Towne."

"Misyer Maxen, would you tell the court what you remember about the events of 16 Altan 2864?"

"I didn't know anything about Dom-el Kittrend. I had never seen him, but I had seen Dahvin Tave, although of course I didn't know his name."

"Did he steal food from your store?"

"Yes, he did, but I wasn't angry, like he thought, and I didn't try to chase him away that day. I was worried about him. His clothes were dirty and ragged, and the back of his shirt was stained with a lot of blood. I couldn't understand how anybody could leave a child like that. He wasn't a young child, but you could tell he wasn't an adult, either.

"That particular day, when he came in, I had been watching for him, because I wanted to help him. When I spotted him, he had already gotten a handful of food and was headed to the counter. I didn't know he was going to pay, but he just had a handful of sweets, and I wanted to show him some more nutritious food. I was also going to try to find out who he was, but when he saw me start toward him, he threw some coins on the counter and ran out the door. I tried to follow him, but by the time I got to the door, he had disappeared, and I didn't know what direction he'd gone.

"You know, what really broke my heart, was that he left bloody footprints." Maxen looked down at his hands, struggling to maintain his composure. When he spoke again, his voice cracked. "I don't know how he could have run when he was so badly hurt. And he was thin. I can't believe this is the same boy." Maxen motioned toward Dahvin. "You should have seen him then, he was so thin."

Dahvin was stunned. He'd had no idea the shopkeeper, or anyone else for that matter, could have cared about the condition he was in. Yet Maxen was visibly shaken as he told his story.

"Thank you, Misyer Maxen, that is all we need for now," Stohne said. Even the ombudsman's voice seemed somewhat subdued.

It was late in the day by the time Maxen finished his testimony. The sun was low in the sky, glaring directly into the high narrow windows at the back of the courtroom. The reddish glow gave the courtroom the surreal look of some antique painting. The judge's desk glowed red, like molten lava about to erupt.

The judge glanced up toward the windows and flinched as the setting fireball struck his eyes. "I think we have gone as far as we can for today. We will resume at 10th hour tomorrow. Everyone is excused." The bell tone sounded three times.

Stohne nodded at Tess and Treiner to come and escort Dahvin back to the Evaluation Center for the night. He offered no objection when Treiner pulled Dahvin's hands behind him to apply wrist and ankle restraints.

"I don't think…." Tess started to protest.

"After the last few days, I'm not taking any chances," Stohne told her. "I'm afraid he's set himself up for this."

Dahvin nodded to Tess, signaling his acceptance of the inevitable. The three headed out the same door he'd entered from that morning, crossing the flex-tunnel to a waiting security cruiser.

—

Alone in the courtroom, Stohne reached down to pick up his tablet and noticed a message curser blinking. He touched the icon, loading the message.

> Meet me in the arboretum by the fountain at 20th hour. I have information of utmost importance to this case.

CONNECTED
RECIEVING....
CHAPTER 29

The sun had already set over the bay when Stohne reached the arboretum.

He stepped inside and looked around the manicured shrubs, trees, and flower beds. The building seemed deserted, but in the fading light, he could make out a lone figure seated on a bench near the fountain. The lights on the fountain glinted off the woman's fair hair, adorning it with tiny stars.

Long before he reached her, he was certain it was Amalya Kittrend.

Her skirt folded around her ankles, ruffled slightly by a breath of air from the ventilation system, showing off the elegant shape of her velvet boots. Stohne stopped in front of her and bowed slightly.

She patted the bench beside her. "Please have a seat. I have something of utmost importance that I must show you."

He hesitated.

"Please. It's all right."

He sat on the edge of the bench as if poised for sudden flight.

"That young man, Dahvin Tave, is not guilty of murder."

"That may well be the case. Murder requires intent to do harm, and there is no evidence that Tave intended to harm your father. The judge may well rule that it was an accident."

"No. It was not even that. Dahvin Tave did not fire the laser."

"Why would you think that?"

"Because my father killed himself—accidentally—but it was he who pulled the trigger of the laser, nonetheless."

"Doma Kittrend! How could you think such a thing?"

"Because it is true. Everything that Dahvin said in court today is true. My father was suffering from castamnesia. He was already in the advanced stages. By the end, he didn't even remember who he was. We were watching him closely, but he managed to slip away one day. We couldn't find him anywhere. Daks refused to notify the Ministry of Security, he was too afraid word of Father's illness would get out. It would have devastated the family's business dealings. Daks had worked hard to develop a rapport with Father's business partners that would allow him to take over, but it couldn't be done quickly.

"Daks feared if the business partners knew the truth, they would withdraw from some very important, but delicate, arrangements. So he hired private investigators to search for Father, and made up excuses when he failed to show for meetings. He told the partners father was grooming him to take over, which, of course, was believable."

The Doma stopped to catch her breath. Stohne tried to study her with an objective eye, but his heart pounded so hard he was afraid she would hear it. He struggled to regain composure.

"Doma Kittrend, how long was your father missing?"

"Nearly two months."

Stohne sat in stunned silence. Her revelation explained everything that Dahvin had said about his relationship with the man he called "Max." The image of the wealthy and powerful Maxillian Kittrend wandering back alleys as a vagrant, searching for food from disintegration units, which he had found so unbelievable, now made sense. Kittrend had lost his mind. But it still didn't explain why Amalya Kittrend thought her father had killed himself. He had to do his duty by her.

"But what makes you think your father did indeed kill himself? Tave's DNA is on the laser."

"The coroner originally determined that Father pulled the trigger himself, possibly even in his sleep. The coroner said he was lying flat on his back with the laser held against his chest. He said about the only way it would be in that position was if Father was holding it himself, lying down."

Again, exactly the way Dahvin had described the situation. The laser in Kittrend's hands, the man lying on his back already dead when Dahvin found him. Every word the young man had said was true.

Every word.

"Daks had the coroner falsify the death certificate, and concocted the idea of a murder to cover the truth," she continued. "He also had the coroner falsify the time of death, to list it as, I think it was around seventh hour. He actually died sometime in the early morning hours. The security officers had already told us they had found DNA from an off-worlder on the laser. They also told us they hadn't been able to find anyone who was a match, and that there was a good chance the individual had already left the planet.

She smoothed the folds of her skirt. "To Daks, it seemed the perfect out. He wouldn't have to explain what Father was doing in a deserted alley in the middle of the night. He made it appear Father had been caught on an early morning stroll. He figured the matching person would never be found and the lie would allow him to take over the business with no challenge."

And it had worked, for nearly three years. Daks Kittrend was now entrenched as the head of the Kittrend empire. Had it not been for a freak discovery by an Alliance Enforcer team, on a world that wasn't even a member of the Alliance, the lie would never have been uncovered."

One tear slid down the Doma's cheek, glistening as the moonlight caught it. She turned her head from Stohne and with a fluid, surreptitious motion, brushed it away. Firstcaste women didn't cry, not where others could see anyway. They always held their heads high. It took every ounce of control Stohne had to stop him from reaching out and embracing her.

"I am so sorry, Master Stohne," she said. "I never should have let this go so far."

"This is not your fault, it's your brother who should never have let it go so far."

"I could have influenced him more."

"Ha! Forgive my impertinence, but I'm not sure all the gods combined could influence him in any direction he didn't already plan to go."

She nodded, and Stohne thought he saw a faint hint of a smile.

"You understand my brother very well. Will you be able to get Dahvin Tave released?"

"I don't really have any proof, and I will not call you to testify against your brother. The judge would not allow such testimony. But I can stress that there is no evidence of intent to commit murder, and that the evidence suggests that your father's death was accidental."

"That is not good enough for me, at this stage. Here."

She pulled a large envelope from beneath the folds of her skirt and laid it in Stohne's lap. "This is the evidence you need. The original death certificate."

He opened the envelope she handed him and looked at the document. It bore the same date as the one he had seen before, but listed the cause of death as "accidental suicide." In addition, in the box marked "contributing causes," the document stated "castamnesia." The time of death was fifteen minutes past third hour. It was signed by Keem Dorton and had his official stamp.

"This will not only destroy your brother, it will end the coroner's career as well. Are you sure you want me to go through with this? I think the judge might be persuaded to rule it an accident based on evidence I can introduce. Tave would probably be released with no further action."

"They have had their chance to do what was right. They chose to allow an innocent youth to be tried for murder. And they would have stood by while he was convicted. You have no reason to feel sorry for them. Dahvin Tave does not deserve to have an entire planet think he caused my father's death, accidental or not."

There was so much more Stohne wanted to say, but he couldn't come up with the right words. He was sorry for the damage it would undoubtedly cause her family. Damage? Try total destruction! His heart cried out to her.

On the other hand, he felt for what Dahvin had been through. He knew how disturbing the past few weeks had been, and how terrified the young man had been by the prospect of possible imprisonment.

His own career would probably be over after this, as well. Superior Strohm had made it clear what outcome he expected. And what of Amalya Kittrend? What would her brother do when he realized she had betrayed him?

Amalya slid her hand over and covered his. "I know this will not be easy for you. But we both know it's the right thing to do."

He nodded, fighting an instinctive urge to avoid her precious touch.

"What will happen in your clan afterwards? Who will take over?"

"I will."

Stohne nearly fell off the bench. A *woman?* Head of a Firstcaste clan? In all the history of Gehren he couldn't remember a single instance in which a woman headed one of the premier clans. If such a thing had happened, it had been expunged from the history books.

"That's im—impossible. They'll never allow it."

"They won't have a choice. Ours is the most powerful clan, as you know, and there are no other heirs in direct line."

His mind reeled. Now, even more, he realized she was the new Gehren woman, capable of heading the clan and of forcing the Firstcaste men to accept her leadership. The admiration he'd felt before, based only on her beauty and grace, leaped tenfold. He shook his head and grinned.

"You are some first lady. You just might change the entire world."

"It's a start."

"I wish I could get to know you better."

"Oh, there's no telling what could change in the next few years."

He chuckled and had to take a deep slow breath. This bench was becoming a most unstable seat.

"Ah, could I ask your permission to stay in touch?"

"Why, Master Stohne, I'd be insulted if you didn't. And you wouldn't want to insult the next head of the Kittrend clan."

No, he most certainly would not. "May I escort you to your vehicle?"

"No, thank you. As you can imagine, I was not able to come alone. I have a highly trusted escort with me. And it would be best if we were not seen together at this point."

He nodded. He watched though, until he saw a figure step forth from the shadows of the arboretum trees and join her.

As he left the arboretum in the opposite direction, his mind reeled. Many questions had been answered, but the revelation had created many new ones. His predecessor in the investigation had been the first officer to arrive on the scene the morning Kittrend's body was found. Surely he would have known the difference between a man dead for several hours and a man dead for only an hour. Had he been coerced into silence? He had retired within a week after the case was placed on hold because no suspect had been found. He had died, supposedly, of an undiagnosed aneurysm, just a week after that. Stohne shuddered at his next thought. Had he been murdered to ensure his silence?

He reflected back on Strohm's emphatic instructions that the case be resolved quickly and "quietly," with no undue stress for the Kittrend family. Had his superior known of the deception from the beginning?

As he turned the corner, from straight in front of him a red-orange beam pierced the night. Stohne instinctively ducked and rolled into a nearby doorway. He smelled the stench of singed flesh before his body had a chance to signal any pain. But a moment later his right arm told him he was hit. His heart pounded and he had to consciously remind himself to breathe. In all his years of service his life had never been threatened.

He was not in a good position. He had ducked into a confined space, and his assailant had plenty of room to choose a good vantage point. Stohne crawled into the darkest shadow of the doorway and crouched down to make himself as small a target as possible. He pressed the com unit in his right ear and whispered. "Officer Stohne to Security, I am pinned down on West Central Street. Someone just tried to shoot me. I am injured and I need assistance, now!"

"You don't have to die, Master Stohne." A disembodied voice broke the still night. The sound bounced off the surrounding buildings. Stohne thought his attacker was still off to his right somewhere. But it was only a guess.

"I would have killed you already if that was my plan. All you have to do is agree to stay on course with the trial. Just present the evidence from the original investigation. Let the judge make the decision."

Stohne had left his com unit active. His attacker had an audience.

"Why should you assume I would do anything else?"

"I was hired to follow Doma Kittrend. The Dom has suspected her motives for some time. Thanks to her you've already been told more than you needed to know. The family has to be protected from the disgrace their lunatic father would have brought on them. Just goes to show why silly pampered women should be kept on a short leash."

That just proved why men with too much power needed to be knocked down a few notches.

Another flash of laser fire hissed much too close to Stohne's ear, chipping a bit of the door frame behind him and launching it into the back of his head.

"Burn the document she gave you and drop your investigation, or my next shot will be the last."

Security officers rarely required a weapon, and Stohne had never needed to carry one before. But his instincts had served him well tonight. He hadn't known who he was going to meet. In fact, Amalya Kittrend would have been his last guess. It had occurred to him it might be a trap, and he had slipped a hand laser into his jacket before he left. He needed to keep his attacker talking to get a clear bead on him. And, he needed to protect his informant.

"Amalya Kittrend did not tell me anything new. She was trying to persuade me to spare her brother. I already had the evidence I needed to put your boss away for the rest of his life."

"Dom Kittrend will never let that happen. If you don't back off, you'll never leave this street alive."

The last was just enough for Stohne to use the sound locator on his weapon. He fired back into the night. His laser pierced the dark, the hiss echoing off the buildings around him. He could hear the beam connect with a part of a building and the clatter of bits of debris hitting the street.

But he did not hear a scream, or a thump of a body falling to the ground. Perhaps his attacker was smart enough to duck after he spoke.

But at least he'd said enough. With the open com link, the shooter had unwittingly fueled the very investigation he sought to terminate.

Stohne could hear sirens a short distance off. A cruiser turned the corner onto West Central.

"Halfway down the block, I'm on your right," Stohne advised the driver. The cruiser pulled up to his position and Stohne stuck a hand out to flag him down, then crawled into the cruiser's opened doorway.

Security officers conducted a thorough search of the area over the next several hours, but of course, found nothing. Stohne was treated at the local hospital for what proved to be a superficial burn. By the time he was released, it was the middle of the night. It was too late to rouse anyone at the Blaine Evaluation Center. Besides, if he advised Dahvin of what he had learned, Dahvin might not make it to the courthouse tomorrow.

Stohne only hoped he would make it there himself.

CHAPTER 30

The radical events of the previous night had left Stohne no opportunity to let Dahvin know what he had learned. Worse, it had left him with no time to plan his presentation in court. He'd been up all night, but he couldn't get past one major obstacle. Without Amalya Kittrend's testimony, he had no way to prove that Daks Kittrend had known about the original death certificate, and Stohne couldn't bring himself to put her at risk. He didn't really believe Daks would physically harm his own sister, but she would most certainly be exiled in marriage to some abusive aristocrat for whom she had no feelings. All Daks had to do was deny knowledge of the original certificate.

The coroner's career would be ruined the minute Stohne revealed he had falsified a second death certificate. He would face fines and social sanctioning as well. But would that cause him to turn and accuse Daks Kittrend of masterminding the switch? Keem Dorton most likely had been well paid for his actions—and for his silence.

Stohne had found one additional piece of evidence to support his case—the entry and exit logs from the Kittrend estate. During the night he had reviewed every single entry, and found one that he had missed, or ignored, when he reviewed them previously. The gatekeeper did record Maxillian Kittrend leaving the estate two moons prior to his death, just about the time Amalya Kittrend had said he disappeared. There never was an entry showing his return. Why hadn't he caught that when he inspected the logs in the first place? Perhaps because the timing was so far off.

He'd worried the problem all night, but no solution had come to mind. Court would resume in a quarter of an hour. He watched for Dahvin to enter the courthouse, but didn't see him until he went into the courtroom himself. Evidently the escorting officers had brought him up by the back entry through the judge's quarters, perhaps to avoid a repeat of the scene Dahvin had caused yesterday.

Stohne sat next to Dahvin.

"Try to keep your cool, this is going to be a strange day." That was all he managed to get out before the judge called the trial back into session. Dahvin looked at him askance, but he couldn't know what was about to break loose. Stohne himself wasn't sure how it would all play out.

Stohne stepped back up to the evidence stand. "Your Honor, after court recessed yesterday, some new evidence was brought to my attention that I believe will prove that Dahvin Tave is not responsible for the death of Maxillian Kittrend."

Dahvin's mouth dropped open, but Stohne shot him a stern look. He thought he could almost hear the young man's heart pounding. Or was that his own he heard?

"The original investigation of Dom-el Maxillian Kittrend's death was predicated upon the death certificate provided to the Division of Security by Master Coroner Keem Dorton, on which the cause of death was listed as a laser burn. I believe the death certificate previously entered into evidence did not reflect Master Dorton's original determination of Dom-el Kittrend's cause of death. In fact, it has come to my attention that the death certificate provided to the Ministry of Security was not the original death certificate drawn up by Master Dorton."

There were audible murmurs behind Stohne. He shot a quick glance at Keem Dorton, who had turned three shades paler. Daks Kittrend's face, by contrast, was hot with rage. If he could have fired lasers from his burning eyes, Stohne had no doubt he would have been a dead man.

"Your Honor, may I present the evidence?"

The judge nodded, and he took both paper copies of the death certificates to his desk. The judge looked them over in silence for a long moment, and shook his head.

"Master Stohne, can you explain why you are just now presenting such critical evidence? We are already through a full day of trial."

"I apologize for the late revelation. In fact, I believe there has been deliberate duplicity at work. Not only was a death certificate falsified, I believe there has been a deliberate effort by more than one person to hide the truth."

"Master Stohne, that is an extremely serious accusation."

"Yes, Your Honor."

"All right. Proceed."

Stohne took a deep breath. The worst was yet to come. "As you see in the death certificate on your right, the coroner's original conclusion was that Dom-el Maxillian Kittrend's death was deemed either suicide or an accident, inflicted by Dom-el Kittrend himself. Please also note that the death certificate shows the postmortem examination revealed that Dom-el Kittrend was suffering from castamnesia. It's impossible to know whether Dom-el Kittrend fired the personal laser that killed him deliberately or accidentally, due to his impaired mental condition at the time of his death.

"I have vehicle logs from the Kittrend estate that show that Dom-el Kittrend left the estate on 14 Maritane 2864, but there is no corresponding log showing his return. Dom-el Kittrend had in fact been missing for some two moons prior to his death."

"Master Stohne, had that been true, all of Durrand would have been searching for him," the judge said, his voice a pitch higher with irritation.

"Under the circumstances, if it had become public that the head of the most powerful Firstcaste family on the planet was 'missing,' the effect on the family's business dealings would have been catastrophic. His disappearance was therefore kept secret while the family searched for him privately."

"Show me the evidence, Master Stohne."

"I am afraid the logs are the only proof I have of that, Your Honor."

"That only proves he went out and didn't return to the estate, or that someone was lax in their record-keeping. For all I know, he was on vacation. You'll have to do better than that!"

"Your Honor, because of Dom-el Kittrend's sudden disappearance, many of the family's business dealings and financial accounts were frozen. The family was experiencing financial difficulties as a result. Once his death was discovered, had it become known that it could have been a suicide, and that he had been mentally unstable, many of the family's pending business dealings would have collapsed. Dahvin Tave's DNA just happened to be conveniently available, and because his DNA was alien, it was easier to fabricate a murder and pin the murder on an alien."

Stohne paused to grab a quick breath. "In addition, at the time, Dahvin Tave could not be found. So the family thought they had a murder with a suspect that couldn't be found. No one was supposed to suffer from the deceit. They falsified a death certificate omitting references to castamnesia and allowed the death to be investigated as a suspected homicide, so the family could complete the outstanding contracts. What no one anticipated, or perhaps didn't sufficiently care about, was that the Alliance Enforcers would pick up on the case and eventually track down Dahvin Tave."

"Master Stohne!" The judge roared, the veins in his neck so prominent that for a moment Stohne feared one might break.

"Even I can see this is mere speculation! You will show me proof or you will immediately discontinue with this presentation!"

"Your Honor, the first death certificate...."

"I will have some proof as to which of these is valid and why there is one that is not valid."

Stohne was backed into a corner. He had seen it coming, but was bedeviled to find a way out of it. All he could do was forge ahead and hope for a miracle.

"Your Honor, I'd like to call Master Coroner Keem Dorton to testify."

He turned to look at Dorton and caught him with his hand on the door.

The coroner froze in place, as though trying to decide whether it was already too late to run.

"Master Dorton, approach the bench," ordered the judge.

Dorton turned slowly and faced the judge, then shuffled up beside Art.

"I am Master Coroner Keem Dorton." His whisper was barely audible in spite of the strained hush in the courtroom.

"Master Dorton, you have heard the statements of Ombudsman Art Stohne. Look at these two documents, and tell me which one, if either, you signed."

Dorton approached the judge's bench and took both documents, then handed one back. It came as no surprise that he had chosen the second of the two death certificates. He held the real one slightly behind his back.

"This one. This is my signature here."

"And what of that other one? Is that a forgery?" The judge reached out for the one Dorton had withheld. The coroner reluctantly handed it back.

"Y—yes, Your Honor, I believe it is."

"I have to admit, Master Coroner, the signatures look nearly identical to me. Whom do you think could have forged it so expertly?"

"I—I don't have any idea."

The judge drew a deep breath and sat back in his chair. He folded his hands and tapped his chin with his forefingers.

The courtroom was deathly silent. Dorton looked at Stohne as though he wished the ombudsman would die on the spot.

Stone resumed his questioning. "Master Dorton, I would draw your attention to the seal on this other death certificate. Is this not your official seal?"

Dorton hesitated, seeking an out. Finally he nodded.

"Does anyone else have access to your official seal?"

"Only my apprentice."

This was the first test in Stohne's mind. Would the Master Coroner be willing to sacrifice his young assistant to maintain the lie? He and Daks Kittrend had certainly been willing to sacrifice Dahvin—but that was someone they didn't know, an off-worlder. Stohne suspected Dorton had a close relationship with his apprentice.

"So is it your contention that your apprentice forged your signature and applied your seal?"

Dorton's head dropped to his chest and he heaved a deep sigh. Then he glanced at Daks Kittrend. At last he shook his head.

"No. No. He would not have done such a thing." There was another deep sigh. "I signed it."

Out of the corner of his eye Stohne saw Daks Kittrend rise from his seat.

"Dom Kittrend, I think it would be best if you remained seated, if you please," said the judge.

Kittrend sat back down, glaring at both Stohne and Dorton.

Stohne turned back to the coroner. "Master Dorton, is it now your testimony that you signed both of these death certificates?"

"Yes."

"Why did you create a second one that omitted critical information?"

"I was trying to protect the Kittrend family. There were… medical issues that needed to be kept confidential. By the time I drafted the second certificate, we already knew there was alien DNA on the laser, and that no match had been found. I never expected anyone to really be accused of anything. It was just to protect the family because of Dom-el Kittrend's… condition."

"Was Dom Daks Kittrend aware of the falsification?"

The coroner looked like a rodent cornered by a hungry predator. He looked at Daks Kittrend, then at the judge. "I—I—Your Honor, I would beg the Court to be excused from answering that question, please."

Stohne had known in his heart that the coroner was an honest man. Backed into a corner, he wouldn't sacrifice his apprentice, and he couldn't bring himself to lie. But his silence was enough.

"Thank you, Master Dorton." Stohne released his prey. "Your Honor, that's all I have to ask the coroner."

"Master Dorton, you are excused, but please remain in the courtroom," said the judge.

Now it was time to reign in the real culprit. If he didn't complete the raid, he would leave Amalya Kittrend at risk.

"Your Honor, I'd like to call Dom Daks Kittrend to testify."

Kittrend strode to the front of the courtroom like a Monarch entering his throne room, preparing to deal with disobedient subjects. He stopped a few paces short of the evidence stand.

"Your Honor, I am Daks Kittrend, and I wish to invoke my right not to testify in *this proceeding*." He hissed the last two words with all the contempt the head of the first clan of the Firstcaste could have for the lowest of nethercaste. The Judge couldn't possibly have missed it.

"By your own admission, Your Honor, this is nothing but pure speculation on the part of the ombudsman. Why, I couldn't possibly tell. But I will not have the Kittrend family debased in such a fashion!"

Kittrend's eyes met those of the judge square on. Stohne knew this judge well. He was fair and meticulous in applying the law. But eyeball to eyeball with the leader of the most powerful Firstcaste family on the planet, he was not absolutely certain who would flinch first.

"Dom Kittrend, this is my courtroom and I will decide who testifies. You will answer honestly or you will be sanctioned."

Kittrend didn't seem to catch the reality of the judge's statement at first. He raised his chin defiantly, then frowned as the realization struck that things had not quite gone his way. He opened his mouth to speak, then closed it. He stood a moment more before finally walking—no strutting, to the evidence stand.

"Thank you, Your Honor." The judge's eyes warned Stohne he'd better not have made a mistake. He snuck a peek at Dahvin out of the corner of his eye. The young man's eyes were wide, and Stohne wasn't sure he was breathing. Even Dr. Blaine, seated behind him, seemed to be holding his breath.

"Dom Kittrend, were you aware of the original death certificate, the one that identified the cause of death as accidental or suicide?"

"As I far as I know, there never was more than one legitimate death certificate, the one proving that young man is a murderer!"

"You've already heard the Master Coroner admit that he prepared two death certificates. The second one was not prepared until nearly a moon after the first. You never requested a death certificate prior to that?"

"I requested nothing. I received one death certificate."

Stohne pressed on. He couldn't give Kittrend time to think. "You never saw the original death certificate?"

"I only saw one, period."

"At any time, did you become aware that there was another death certificate, one that specified the cause of death as accidental or suicide, and which listed castamnesia as a complicating factor?"

"How dare you insult the memory of my father, a great man, by insinuating that he would kill himself, or behave in such a fashion!"

"Dom Kittrend, drop the attitude and answer the questions, please," said the judge.

Kittrend's face turned from red to purple, and the daggers from his eyes were now aimed at the judge. If Stohne couldn't make the charges stick, the judge's career would be a casualty as well.

"Dom Kittrend, at any time did you become aware of a death certificate that listed the cause of death as accidental or suicide?"

"No!"

"Your Honor, I have no further questions for Dom Kittrend at this time, but I would request that he remain in the courtroom."

"Very well, Master Stohne. Dom Kittrend you may return to your seat in the gallery, but you are *ordered* to remain in the courtroom."

"Your Honor, if I may, I would like to play a recording. This will be audio only. It is a recording of an event in which I was involved last night approximately 21st hour. It was relayed over my compiece to the Durrand Ministry of Security and Public Assistance."

"Very well," said the judge. "Since you were personally involved in this event, I will accept it as a valid entry. I presume this is pertinent to the case?"

"Yes, Your Honor."

He walked over to the table and pressed a button on his tablet. An audio replay of Stohne's standoff from the previous night played into the courtroom. It lasted only minutes, much shorter than it had seemed while he lived through it.

The exchange between Stohne and his attacker ended with the damning statements he hoped would convince the judge without Doma Kittrend's testimony. "I was hired to follow Doma Kittrend. The Dom has suspected her motives for some time. Thanks to her you've already been told more than you needed to know. The family has to be protected from the disgrace their lunatic father would have brought on them. Just goes to show why silly pampered women should be kept on a short leash."

The sound of laser fire hissed on the recording, then the attacker's voice again. "Burn the document she gave you and drop your investigation, or my next shot will be the last.... If you don't back off, you'll never leave this street alive."

Stohne stepped back up to the evidence stand. "Your Honor, while the statements made by my assailant do not prove beyond a doubt that Dom Daks Kittrend knew of, and possibly directed, the preparation of a false death certificate, I believe the evidence presented here today casts undeniable doubt over the charges leveled against Dahvin Tave. Further, Your Honor, it is my professional submission to this Court that Dahvin Tave was in no way responsible for the death of Dom-el Maxillian Kittrend, and it is my recommendation to the Court that Dahvin Tave be released from all further proceedings of law."

Stohne returned to the table and sat down next to Dahvin. He wasn't sure yet what the judge's response would be. His concern now was for Amalya Kittrend. Had he gone too far?

"You didn't tell me all that," Dahvin whispered. "Why didn't you tell me?"

"There wasn't time. I didn't get in until after first hour this morning. I hope this worked, for all our sakes."

"Misyer Tave, please stand," ordered the judge. Dahvin stood, trembling.

"Given the evidence presented by Ombudsman Stohne, this court finds that Dahvin Tave has been wrongfully accused of the crime of murder, and hereby releases Misyer Tave from any further proceedings of law. In addition, I hereby order the Kittrend Clan to pay restitution to Dahvin Tave for damages suffered as a result of his arrest due to falsification by the Clan. Amount of restitution shall be ninety thousand Alliance credits."

A gasp of protest escaped from Daks Kittrend.

He was silenced by a stern look from the judge.

"Misyer Tave, it dismays me to admit that you were sorely wronged both times you happened to land on our planet. I would like you to know that it is beyond my comprehension that a child, even an alien child, could be in the center of our capital city, starving and injured, and that no one would report his presence and see to it that he was offered assistance."

At this point the judge was looking directly at Sharfa Maxen.

"And I am further angered by the additional suffering the Kittrends' dishonesty has caused you. Therefore, I am offering you the option of two years of residential psychiatric treatment in Blaine Mental Health and Evaluation Center at the expense of the Kittrend Clan. I will not make the treatment mandatory, but I strongly recommend it. You deserve a better life than you've had."

Daks Kittrend, afraid to utter a sound, was nonetheless staring at the judge, mouth open wide in disbelief.

"Dom Daks Kittrend, it is not within my power to remove you from your position as head of your clan. But it is within my power to order you to perform one thousand hours of community service in an agency serving the poor, what you would have formerly identified as nethercaste. I hope your family and business associates will deal with you in ways I cannot."

That brought Daks Kittrend to his feet. His face was so red Stohne feared he might have a stroke on the spot. Or maybe hoped.

"Dom Kittrend, back to your seat!" The judge's face was nearly as red as Kittrend's. "Master Keem Dorton, as for you, you are hereby fined the amount of forty-five thousand gendals."

"So ordered! This courtroom is dismissed."

Daks Kittrend made it out the door first. Perhaps he had some explaining to do to his business associates. Dahvin looked at Art.

"You're free to go." Just the words he knew Dahvin had waited to hear for what must have seemed like a lifetime.

—

The judge had emphasized the offer of treatment was not mandatory, but that he "strongly recommended" it. That was not a phrase Dahvin was too comfortable with.

So, he was free—but not free.

And anything short of not absolutely free was something short of desirable.

He stood and started for the door, moving for the first time without wrist bonds or shackles. Tess waited for him, a triumphant smile lighting her face. She grabbed him as he got to the door, pulling him aside out of the crowd shuffling out the door and hugged him so hard he lost his breath.

"Knew you were innocent all along," she said at last.

"Knowing it and proving it are nothing the same. I never thought I'd get out of this one."

"Not everyone's evil."

"Maybe not, but Kittrend would have had me convicted if he'd had his way. If there hadn't been a couple of people willing to risk their necks for the truth, Stohne especially, he'd have gotten away with it."

"But there are people willing to risk the truth. Remember that. Most people I've met are honest at heart."

"You run in a different circle than I do, then."

Dr. Blaine drove Dahvin back to the Evaluation Center.

"So, tell me straight up—what rights do I *really* have and what will they do if I try to leave the planet?" he asked Blaine when they were back at the center.

"They won't do anything, Dahv. It really was an offer, not a requirement, and you're free to go whenever you want. But, honestly, you have nothing to lose. During the past two moons, I've had to focus on determining your guilt or innocence, and I haven't been able to spend as much time on helping you heal as I would like to. I've grown to care very much about you, and for your sake, I'd like to have a chance to work with you. I think I could help you go a long way in dealing with the past, maybe get you beyond the flashbacks and the nightmares. I'm actually the one who proposed to the judge that you be allowed an extended stay. Please, take a day or two to think about it before you decide. I really would like a chance to help you."

Dr. Blaine's plea seemed sincere enough, but staying anywhere for any reason still did not appeal to him. In the end, he agreed to think it over.

Over the next two days, Dahvin learned that the payment from the judgment would be enough for the down payment on a cargo ship larger than Marlon Tave's. He also learned from surfing the local media that there were plenty of openings for pilots, so the opportunity existed to boost his financial standing even further before leaving the planet. And, in truth, the prospect of being able to live without the fear of flashbacks was a major positive. He asked Blaine if he could work while undergoing treatment.

"I think that would be a great idea," Blaine said. "But I'd like you to wait a while before applying for something. I'd like to see you have at least six moons to just focus on treatment."

Blaine was probably one of the few people in the galaxy that he trusted, other than Marlon Tave. Well, okay, and Tess, and Stohne. Admittedly, the circle was growing.

"I'll try what you suggested for a moon or so. I won't guarantee I'll hold off for six moons. I'm not sure I can stay cooped up that long."

"Fair enough, we'll play it by ear. And just for the record, I don't intend for you to be "cooped up" at all. I had in mind more to let you learn to relax and have some fun."

Dahvin grinned from ear to ear. "I think I could live with that!"

CONNECTED
RECIEVING....
CHAPTER 31

The crew of *EN238* didn't have new orders yet, and that gave Dahvin a chance to make up for lost time with Tess. He spent as much time with her as he could over the next tennight. It was the first time they could see each other as equals, rather than as enforcer and prisoner.

One afternoon, near the end of the tennight, a freak low-pressure system brought unseasonably warm air flowing up from the south, and they ventured out of the city to a huge park-like area that bordered a lake. The park was large enough that they had little trouble finding a private spot on a grassy bank. Graceful birds circled overhead, sunlight glinting off white stripes on their blue wings and tails.

Tess pulled Dahvin down into the cool, blue-green grass, rolled halfway on top of him, and smothered him with kisses. He didn't have time to react. He managed to plant just a couple of kisses on her lips.

After a few minutes she rolled the rest of the way on top and sat up, perched across his hips. Then she pulled off her blouse and watched his expression as it changed from dismay to pleasure. Satisfied that he was enjoying the view, she raised up slightly, unbuttoned her skirt, and threw it in the grass. She was now sitting on him completely and utterly naked.

He held his breath. In truth, he was afraid to breathe.

Tess flicked her eyebrows at him, and wiggled her index finger, motioning to him to sit up. He raised up to face her and wrapped his arms around her waist, pulling her slightly toward him as he moved toward her. They kissed again. In one deft motion, Tess removed his shirt. He blushed. He wasn't certain, but it felt like it went all the way to his toes.

Tess slid off, and he got up to remove his pants. But Tess had hooked one finger on either side, and by the time he made it to his feet, his pants were around his ankles. He chuckled slightly.

"I see you've done this before," he chided.

"A few times, lucky for you."

He kicked off the pants and flopped back down beside Tess, grabbed her and pulled her back down beside him. He pulled her close enough to kiss her, but not so close he couldn't stroke one breast. He let his hand wander down the rest of her body and back up again.

Tess swung one leg over him, and moved his hand in between her legs. Gently, she coaxed his fingers into her favorite spots. He was a quick learner. It was a good thing they had wandered out to this isolated spot, for her moans and squeals would have aroused the entire Center.

Pressing his lower body against her, he discovered a hunger he had never felt before. Intense burning desire radiated up until it consumed him. When she neared her climax, Tess pulled him on top of her and guided him home. An instant of concerned protest rose up in his throat, but it was quickly squashed by the overwhelming desire to know her completely.

With Tess's insistent guidance, he overcame the terror in his mind associated with sex, and learned the difference between assault and making love. He moved where she directed, and his own instincts took control as he thrust deeply and rhythmically into her. Tess arched, squealed and gasped.

Where he had only known intense pain, Dahvin discovered how intense pleasure could be. He collapsed in the grass beside her, sweat glistening all over his body. He had just enough strength left to caress her breasts.

It was like awakening to a new world. All of his senses had been totally consumed in the act of making love—he had heard, felt, smelled, seen, and even tasted, only Tess. All of a sudden, he heard the birds again, smelled the air again, saw the vivid colors of the Gehren sunlit afternoon, and felt the cool damp texture of the grass again. With arms and legs still entangled, the lovers relaxed in the grass and enjoyed the warm, tingly, pleasant exhaustion of their passion.

Tess brushed back her hair, dampened by her own passionate heat.

"Wow! Creation!" she gasped.

Dahvin grinned and licked her nose. "Not so bad for a beginner, huh?"

"Not so bad, my ass! You've been holding out on me!"

"I was so afraid I would hurt you. I had no idea it would be like this."

He rolled onto one elbow, facing her, gazing into those incredible blue eyes, sometimes like fire, sometimes like ice, now burning with a contented glow.

"I wanted it to be right for you, too. I was a little afraid this might be too soon, but I have to leave tomorrow. I didn't know when I would make it back. You're okay?"

He just laughed. "Uh, yeah. What do you think?"

Tess grinned back and stroked his arm.

He gazed into her eyes. "Trouble is, now I'm not sure I can let you go. I'm going to miss you so much."

"I'll miss you, too. I promise I will vidcom you often. Subspace, you know, they'll be out of date when you get them, but I will send them. You can use the same code I gave you before. That will mark your communications to me as 'personal' and they'll be routed straight to me."

"Tess," he started, but then thought better of it. The thought of her with another man was almost more than he could bear, but he had no right to ask fidelity. Not when he couldn't know when they would see each other again.

"What? Don't hold back. Talk to me."

"Never mind, it wasn't important."

"Dahv! I love you!" Tess raised up on one elbow. "Talk to me! This wasn't just a passing fling. We made *love*. Why do you think it was so great? It isn't always. Sometimes it's just sex. It is different."

A sigh welled up from deep inside. He hadn't known. Before Tess, all he'd known was violent rape.

"Are you—involved—with anyone else on the ship?"

Tess cradled his face in her hand. "No, and I won't be. Like I said, I love *you*. I don't want anyone else. I will be back, I promise. I'll find a way."

And so would he.

Trans-space communications were a lot different than making love in the Gehren grass, and at the moment, Dahvin felt a little like his heart was being ripped out and shipped off.

But he would not give up. If anything, he knew how to hold on to a dream. A few tennights ago freedom had been the only thing important to him. Now he had Tess.

AUTHOR'S NOTE

Child slavery is *not* Science Fiction. There are images in this book and its sequel that readers may, and should, find disturbing. I wish I could say child slavery is only fiction. However, the reality is that commercial exploitation of children is a multi-billion dollar industry right here on planet Earth, and even in the United States. UNICEF estimates that two million children are subjected to prostitution in the global sex trade. Internationally, about one-third of those are boys, and in the U.S., nearly one-half are boys. Many never escape the horrors of sexual abuse and end up dead from abuse, starvation, STDs, or drugs, or end up living as adult prostitutes. If this reality troubles you, take action. Go to www.wikipedia.org and enter "organizations that combat child trafficking" in the search bar for a list of places where you can volunteer or donate.

ABOUT THE AUTHOR

Susan Eschbach grew up in Kansas City. Her writing career began in elementary school when she had a 4-H club column in a Johnson County, Kansas, monthly newspaper. Her journalistic writing continued through high school and college and came in handy for several jobs. She embarked on her first novel in 2008 at the insistence of a close friend and members of the Mid South Writers Group, convinced writing fiction would be easy because of her background in journalism. "Boy, was I ever wrong," she says. "It only took eight years to get it right."

Susan is married and the mother of two sons, one of whom is pursuing his own writing career. Their family is rounded out with a dog and five cats.